THE BROKEN AMORETTI

A Novel

SUDIPTO DAS
APARAJITA DUTTA

olive turtle

NIYOGI BOOKS

Published by
NIYOGI BOOKS
Block D, Building No. 77,
Okhla Industrial Area, Phase-I,
New Delhi-110 020, INDIA
Tel: 91-11-26816301, 26818960
Email: niyogibooks@gmail.com
Website: www.niyogibooksindia.com

Editor: Gita Rajan
Design: Shashi Bhushan Prasad/Cover: Misha Oberoi

ISBN: 978-93-86906-83-0
Publication: 2019

Printed at: Niyogi Offset Pvt. Ltd., New Delhi, India

To the people of KGP & Prembajar,
past and present

—Sudipto Das

•

To my dearest Ma and Mummum

—Aparajita Dutta

PART I

"WITH"

THE DIARY

Parush held the old diary in his hands like his own newborn baby that he might never have. Completely oblivious that I, the only other person in the room, was staring at him, he ran his fingers tenderly over the old brown pages, not to hurt them. He turned each page with utmost care, as though he was turning over his little daughter on the bed. He straightened the folded corner of a page and tried to smoothen out the wrinkles on another in a way that reminded me of how, as a little girl, I would stretch the skin of my octogenarian grandmother to see if it could be like mine. Old books rarely have crinkled pages, unless someone has crumbled them, perhaps out of despair, anger or solitude. Many pages were torn, crumbled and then unwound and fitted loosely to the diary, the wrinkles Parush was trying to gently iron out still bearing traces of some unspoken emotions and sentiments hidden along their creases.

Parush stopped at the page, which had the final draft of the poem, the same poem, written in archaic dactylic hexameter, used in classical Greek and Latin by the likes of Homer.

Parush stared at the diary for a long time. He was perhaps trying to organise the scattered thoughts running through his mind, like the shaky images of my first birthday my father would often play on his vintage VCR that could play the tape only in the fast-forward mode. As I sat quietly on the sofa, observing Parush intently, many thoughts flashed across my mind – thoughts about myself, my life, insignificant jerky images from the past and present…

***

Having grown up in IIT KGP, the sprawling campus of the Indian Institute of Technology spread over two thousand acres in the fringes of a nondescript railway colony some ninety miles away from Calcutta, my world was centred around the IIT. In a small place like Kharagpur, the IIT campus was like – at least that was what we believed – the only house in the village with a television, albeit an old black and white one, which was a symbol of pride and an object of envy for the neighbours rather than a gadget for entertainment. For all practical purposes, Kharagpur was bifurcated into two mutually exclusive regions, the campus and the outside.

After a spate of broken relationships and a failed marriage in the US, when I got a chance to return to the campus, I jumped at it. My post doctorate wasn't yet complete and my plan to settle in the US with my husband was aborted even before it had been impregnated. I spent a few weeks casually searching for jobs in India. To my surprise, the newly revamped Humanities department at IIT KGP offered me the job of teaching Lyric Mode at the Masters level – perhaps not many wanted to teach English in an engineering school. I was more than happy to accept the offer. I decided to stay at the house my grandfather had bought a few years back. The tiny neighbourhood of Prembajar, though *outside*, was still considered an extension of the campus, with many IIT professors, like my grandfather, settling there after retirement. Since his death the previous year, the house had been lying vacant. The house needed some mending, so, I managed to arrange a few months' stay at a friend's place in the campus.

My husband, rather ex-husband – I hadn't yet adjusted myself to calling him 'ex' – didn't come to see me off at the airport when I was leaving for India. Of course, he had his reasons. Why would he want to meet me, when I was the reason for his, rather 'our' broken marriage? I do not know exactly why I had called it off. Perhaps I wanted a reason to run away from him. Suddenly, the very thought of staying with him under the same roof had appeared appalling.

Once in India, I spent the days as though I were lost in a boat, in the deep ocean, the boat's sail drifting whichever way the wind blew.

Even though IIT KGP had offered me poetry to teach, I still wanted to continue with my post doctorate work on homosexuality, which for some reason had keened my interest. Having arrived at KGP at my friend's place, I was left with a room, my luggage and my laptop. I still had a few months before the semester would start – I had intentionally planned for the break. I had no access to the library and hence, it was just me and my laptop. It was during this time that I found a call for paper for a conference on '*Queer Theory: Dialogues of the Sexual Minorities,*' organised by the Department of Comparative Literature of the Jadavpur University in Calcutta. When I sent my abstract, they accepted it and soon, I landed at the Jadavpur University campus.

***

The warm weather in India gave me the liberty to wear my kaftans. The variegated wooden bangles pressed against my soft skin. I strolled around the campus, looking around aimlessly, perhaps like a tourist without a tour guide. I felt good that my skin colour, my dress and my fashion paraphernalia, which could be termed ethnic, blended so well with everything around. It's not that I would feel awkward in the US, but there was no doubt that presently I was feeling at home. Was I being carried away by an excess of a sense of provincialism? I wondered.

'Hey, do you know where is the Anita Banerjee Hall?' came a voice, directed towards me. I looked around and saw a girl, more or less my age, wearing white shorts and a sleeveless pink top. In her ebullient face, I saw something which attracted me at first sight.

'Yes,' I nodded. 'It is in the building you see in front. That is what they have written in the address. So, you are here for the conference too?'

'Ah yes! Parushni is the name.' She extended her hand.

'Oh, sweet, I am Saoli.' I shook hands with her.

Parushni had an amiable nature, and our conversation would not stop. I was happy to be with her and as fate would have it, we both had our papers later the day in the same session – *Lesbianism: Theory and Practice*. By the time we walked inside the arts building, we had already known quite a bit of each other.

Parushni changed to western formals – white ruffled shirt and black pencil skirt – before the session. I dealt with certain theories of Lesbianism and their reflection in poetry in my paper, while Parushni focused mainly on lesbianism as a practice and its reflection in popular literature.

'The two papers,' said the lady chairing the session, wrapping it up, 'are complementary to each other.' My eyes sparkled and I could see the reflection of the same in Parushni's eyes.

'We can actually work together,' she said at the canteen. 'There is a queer conference coming up in a few months, the one which is organised by Sappho For Equality. But only if you are interested,' she added.

'Of course! I am honoured,' I replied. 'Lesbians are humiliated and tabooed in our society.'

'This taboo itself is a *gruesome politics of patriarchy*...' she said firmly.

This is a fairly accepted concept in LGBTQ studies, but the force and conviction she said it with was imposing, her words revealing a certain anguish. 'A gruesome politics of patriarchy ...' her words lingered in my thoughts.

'It is too hot here,' she said, sipping her glass of coke. 'Are you planning to attend the rest of the session?'

My head shook involuntarily and gestured a 'no,' even before my mind decided to think.

'The jheel, you see, filled with lotus, is a place for lovers,' one of the students had explained during the lunch break. We were too lazy to walk, and we were too tired to stay in the closed and crowded conference room. The jheel came to our rescue.

'These youngsters really know the best places on campus,' Parushni said, taking her bite on the vanilla ice cream, as she sat legs folded, on the grass, very close to the jheel.

'Ya, true,' I affirmed, looking at my chocolate cone. 'Every campus has such a place… a waterfront or an open dale, where you would love to be idle, recite your favourite poem, written by your favourite poet…'

'So, who is your favourite poet?' Parushni asked as we made ourselves comfortable on the grass carpet.

'It changes from time to time. Now… I believe, it would be Sappho,' I answered back. 'I love her lines, *pain penetrates me, drop by drop...*'

'Oh really? I'm not much into poetry though. I just know that Sappho is from the Isle of Lesbos, which is the source of the word *lesbian*.'

'The life of Sappho was pretty interesting,' I let loose my passion for Sappho. 'A female poet in ancient Greece is not a common thing. Her poems have an enigmatic feel…'

'You remind me of my mother,' Parushni interrupted. 'She rarely spoke. But sometimes, when she would speak about poetry, she would speak like you…'

'Would speak?'

'Ya, she is no more. She read a lot of poetry, especially Rossetti.'

'Hey, I'm sorry to hear that.'

'It is okay. Doesn't matter much. Have you read Rossetti?'

Before I could reply, Parushni jumped off as a big drop of vanilla fell on her leg.

'Oh no,' she cried. 'I should really stop being so messy.'

Remembering that I had a bunch of tissues and a sanitizer in my bag, I immediately took them out and handed them over to her.

'Phew, thanks a ton,' she said, wiping away the drop from her bare leg and then slowly applied the sanitizer.

Her legs reminded me of one of those fine sculpted Greek figurines of Athena I had seen in front of my department at Princeton.

Surprisingly, the jheel, quite an ordinary water body in the campus, appeared very beautiful in the late afternoon, with the breeze kissing the virgin petals of lotus as the water celebrated their love.

'You know, you remind me of Cybele, the Greek goddess of Earth,' Parushni said, tying her bushy hair with a clutcher, revealing her floral silver earrings. 'This beige kaftan of yours matches so well with your earthy complexion. I always felt that Ramayana's Sita, who is said to be born out of the Earth, and Cybele, have some connection. I would assume both are dusky, motherly…' She stopped and stared at me. 'In my imagination… they are like you – dark complexion, wavy hair, jewellery of seeds…'

Parushni's words made me feel good and confident. For the first time in my life, perhaps, I had received a compliment for my colour.

'Parushni…' I wanted to ask her something.

'Why do you bother calling me Parushni?' she interrupted. 'Isn't it a long and winding tongue-twister? I told you, you can always call me Pushi.' We started walking.

'No, I just like it,' I replied. Yes, her name itself had some charm and I liked calling her Parushni. She asked me to stay at her house for a week, and I, having nothing to do, and nowhere to go, of course, was happy to have something like a home.

***

Parushni lived in a small single bedroom flat where it was difficult to fit me in.

'Will you mind sharing the bed with me?' she asked as I arranged my luggage.

Will you mind sharing the bed with me? These words reminded me of my ex-husband, when I had gone to see him for the first time in North Carolina. I had furtively replied, 'YES.' This time, however, it was different. 'No problem at all,' was my enthusiastic response.

Parushni settled herself on the bed. On the white bedspread, with floral prints, she lay like a creeper, who, under the light of some blue moon, would arise and wrap herself around the earthen support.

Mosquitoes were buzzing around, a few of them busy pricking us at every given opportunity. I switched on the mosquito repellent machine and fiddled with the pillow. An irritating mosquito kept bothering us, and Parushni tried to swat it. She got her chance as it sat on my leg. I felt a pinch the moment her fingers worked to remove the cause of our anxiety, and it ran through my cold nerves, creating a thrill, which I had desired for so long but never felt. I remained frozen, trying to relish every moment of that sensation, whose meaning I was still trying to figure out.

Over the next few days Parushni talked about her brother, Parush, his love for Bitasta, and Parushni's mother, a lady, who, according to her, had remained an unsolved puzzle throughout her life. I told her excitedly that Bitasta had been my senior in high school in Kharagpur and that her love affair with Parush had been a much talked about thing in IIT.

'In fact, it's such a coincidence,' I said. 'My grandfather bought the same house where Bitasta grew up in Kharagpur and I would soon be living there. I've heard so much about them. I can't believe that I met someone so close to them. Parush is now a famous name. I'm sure you would be very proud of your brother.'

'Yes,' she said, 'I am. When I was a kid I was not too fond of him. But over the years I've grown very close to him. He is now everything to me. I hope he gets out of the shit he has dragged himself into…' I knew what she was referring to – Parush was embroiled in a very high profile and nasty litigation in the US for his alleged involvement in stealing intellectual property from his former employer.

After a week's stay at Parushni's home in Calcutta I returned to my friend's place in Kharagpur, but we kept in touch. More I would talk to Parushni, more she and her thoughts would add to the chaos in my mind, a sort of chaos, which I had perhaps never felt in the past, a chaos which, my ex-husband would often complain, I lacked. 'You're cold and dead,' he would say. Was I really cold? I wondered.

One day when Parushni called me from Calcutta, she sounded very restless. 'What is it?' I asked.

'Nothing, I'm just confused and I know so are you…'

In a month my grandfather's house at Prembajar, just outside the IIT campus, was ready for me to call it my home. I have always been finicky about cleaning and started with my job at once. Thoughts reigned chaos in my mind, the incidents of my own life mocking me like the cobwebs that bewilder a poetic soul with their never-ending illusion of maze. As the particles of dust fell from the duster, they seemed to open the gateway for the more composed dust, which was hard to remove, which wouldn't come out so easily.

***

I chanced upon the diary while cleaning the house. It was tucked deep into a pile of old papers on the mezzanine floor above the bathroom – a convenient but clumsy place to dump things which should have been thrown away in the first place.

The diary, written entirely in 1979, was filled with poems in English and Bengali most of which were quite bad. Nothing irritates me more than bad poetry. When I was almost throwing the diary down on the heap of things I had decided to get rid of, I glanced upon *that* poem. It had been revised several times before the final draft was written in February.

Initially, I was not at all impressed. Being a doctorate in Comparative Literature in Classical Languages with a special focus on the evolution of poetry, I had read a wide range of poetry in multiple languages and I was very critical about anything I read. At the first read the poem just didn't do it for me. In terms of poetic achievement, it was rather simplistic. The writer appeared over ambitious, dragging characters from Greek mythology and attempting various forms of poetic garnishing like alliteration, consonance and assonance while the language was still very basic, rather weak. But then, in an hour, I was already high, the layers of hidden messages and concealed confessions unravelling slowly like the intoxication of an old scotch. Somewhere I could relate to the writer, who was no doubt unacquainted to me, but perhaps, not unknown any longer. Perhaps, I could realise myself better through each of the lines of the poem. Perhaps I could hear my own voice, which I never knew was mine.

I also felt the urge to get in touch with Parush and Bitasta, whose references in the poem, though indirect, were strong enough for me to get interested in knowing everything about them. Over the past few months I had heard a lot about them from Parushni, but still I felt there was a lot more to know, that they were still shrouded with obscurities.

'Ma never wanted my brother to get married to Bitasta, come what may,' Parushni's words were banging on my head like a hammer. 'Why would Parushni's mother not want Parush to marry the girl he loved?' I wondered.

Something inside me kept on saying that there was more than the apparent negation of Parush and Bitasta's love, that there was something which must have prevented Parush's mother from giving social recognition to their love. Somewhere deep inside my mind, I was almost sure that I knew why it had been a taboo to her – the diary seemed to have divulged it all to me in a very cryptic manner. Knowing everything about Parush and Bitasta and their mothers would only reinforce my thoughts.

And somewhere, I felt connected to Parush's mother, to her feelings, her frustrations, her hopelessness and her apparent stern stand against Parush and Bitasta's relationship. Somewhere, it all pointed to the hopelessness in my life too. I was really confused at that point of my life. The thoughts of a hopeless future denigrated my cowered heart, like the mounds of dust which had built a deep patch around the shelves.

I climbed down from the mezzanine floor and started cleaning the shelves. The dark patches required the duster to be moved in certain ways, at certain angles. I felt as though each patch of dust were something of a lock, which needed the right key, which would pierce through that perfect hole and open the door for me.

***

A sudden noise disrupted my thoughts. I realised Parush had kept the diary on the table. He walked towards the open window, staring out, holding the grills tightly, shivering a bit. I brought a shawl for him. He wrapped it around carelessly.

RIKSHI & KALYANI

By the time I arranged the dinner on the table it was quite late. I watched Parush drawing circles on the steel plate, the small mound of rice soaked in dal still lying at the side, almost untouched. He hadn't eaten much. He got up after some time, apologising for wasting so much food. He opened the door and went to the front yard. He walked towards the dwarf compound wall surrounding the house and sat on it. I brought him the shawl once more and helped him wrap it properly – outside it was quite cold.

Parush would have sat on the wall, silently, for quite long. I didn't have a measure of the time that might have elapsed. I was leaning against the wall, by his side, the door of my house open in front of me. I could see the diary lying on the table in the living room. It had been the only thing which had kept me busy all these days. I could still feel the excitement of discovering it sometime back, while cleaning my house...

***

I would have fallen asleep, being tired of cleaning the house. When I got up it was evening. I took a bath and then took a stroll along the pebbled pathways of Prembajar. I rediscovered that here the nights always fell so suddenly. In these few months that I had been in Kharagpur, I had been rediscovering so many things, which would amaze me when I was a kid. I remembered how I would sit with my father in the lawn, in front of our sprawling bungalow in the campus, waiting for the moment when the evening would suddenly turn into night. I never identified that moment and my father would always claim he did.

I didn't want to cook anything. I walked into the campus and ate dinner at Sahara, a place we would often go to in our childhood. Back home, I took the diary and read the poem again and again. What attracted my attention were the small lines under selected letters and the slashes breaking each verse into several parts in its earlier revision versions.

Ravishing / looks, and the / raven hair / locks, she is / ravenous / Rikshi,
Artemis / nymph, the prime / mistress of / wild, bare Ar/cadia / pristine,

Ravishing looks, and the raven hair locks, she is ravenous Rikshi. A very crude attempt, I felt, at creating alliteration with the sound 'rav'.

Artemis and Arcadia in the second line were names from Greek mythology – Artemis characterised as a virgin huntress and the goddess of wilderness and virginity, and Arcadia a place of unspoiled beauty. I was amazed at how the writer had even attempted using classical Greek mythology in English poetry, something which had been a snobbish obsession even for many great English poets.

While trying to figure out the relevance of the underlines and slashes it occurred to me that the latter could be nothing but what we would often use in our prosody classes to scan a verse for its meter. To identify the feet, I recalled, we would break a line into smaller segments with the slashes. I noticed that each line in the poem was broken exactly into seven segments or feet. This meant each line was a hexameter. I was excited with this observation. By then I already knew what the underlines could mean – the stresses on the syllables, as they are to be pronounced. To my surprise I observed that each of the first six feet in every line, bounded by the slashes, had exactly three syllables, like rav-ish-ing, rav-en-ous or rav-en-hair, of which only the first one was stressed, as indicated by the small line under it.

'Each foot is a dactyl,' I muttered to myself in disbelief, 'and the meter of the poem, dactylic hexameter, the Homeric meter of the heroic epics.' How many people, acclaimed poets included, had ever tried this meter in English?

I read and re-read the poem, many times. The more I could peel the layers of obscurities off the cryptic verses, the more I had a weird feeling. I couldn't fathom if whatever I had understood was my blemished imagination or the bare unspeakable truth poured out of someone's heart in some dangerous moment of weakness. Was this poem the outcome of a desperate urge to divulge to the world something which had been suppressed forever, something which shouldn't even be whispered to a wall?

I was sure that even Parush and Bitasta didn't know anything about it. They might not even be aware of the existence of this poem, which talked about them too, though in a very arcane and occult way. I stared for a long time at the two lines which I felt referred to none other than them.

Knotty Pa/rush flowed / with her Kal/yani's al/lure and all / kallos.
Surged it out / from her vi/tasti, as / Arca the / damsel of / Rikshi.

What would be their reaction, I thought, when they would realise the implications of this poem?

Given the fact that Bitasta's mother had spent a major part of her life, till she lived, in this house, there was no doubt that the word *vitasti* in the second line referred to Bitasta. In fact, Bitasta is the Bengali spelling for the Sanskrit word Vitasta. And who else could be Parush?

***

Any affair of an IITian guy with a campusite girl was always much talked about. It would be a major topic of gossip in the otherwise dull campus. But very few affairs survived beyond the IIT. Neither did the affair between Bitasta and Parush survive long. Their mothers, both daughters of IIT professors and once best friends, allegedly didn't agree to their relationship due to some unknown reasons and they broke off within a year of Parush leaving the IIT. 'I would have done anything to marry him,' my friends would say about Parush, when we were growing up in the campus with staple doses of campus gossip. Knowing Bitasta – she had been few years senior to me at St. Agnes – I was sure she too would've done everything possible.

Parush's meteoric rise in the corporate world, replete with thrilling shots of passion, sacrifice, betrayal and controversies, had been an interesting case study for the business magazines and a risqué topic for the tabloids. As the young and dashing COO of GameIT, he was credited with revolutionising the mobile gaming experience, something like Google's revolutionising the internet and Facebook's social networking. He had been in the limelight since the late nineties, when he was still in his early twenties.

Then suddenly Parush became the fallen guy for allegedly passing insider information about GameIT through his once girlfriend Bitasta, who immediately became the voyeuristic vamp in the racy story of illicit love and extraordinary greed. The media, weary of excessively thrashing Wall Street for the recent subprime crisis, got a new lease of life with one of the greatest corporate scandals of its time. Someone wrote in *The Wall Street Journal* that the only option for Parush to save himself from this ignominy would be to commit suicide or vanish into a hidden cave in the Himalayas. In reality, Parush didn't go to the Himalayas, but tracking him down would have been indeed a Himalayan task for anyone else.

By the time I got the diary and wanted to meet Parush, he had already gone incommunicado. Even Parushni, his sister, didn't know for some time where her brother could be. 'I *have* to meet him,' I said. 'Without him I may not be able to decipher the poem fully. You wouldn't ever understand your mother. And…' I suddenly lost words to speak.

'What?' she asked.

'And… it's about me. It's about you too…' I stressed on "you". 'It's about *both of us* getting the right directions in our lives. Please find him out…'

'Okay.' She didn't ask anything further. That was one of the best things about her. She was never inquisitive or intrusive.

Few days later she called me. 'Dada is in India,' she said excitedly. 'He will come and meet you in person at Prembajar. He doesn't want you to come and see him where he is staying now. Hope you understand…'

I eagerly waited for Parush to come to my place, the place where Bitasta and her mother had grown up, the place which had been Parush's refuge for love and peace for a few years, the place where, I knew, Parush would surely like to come back again and again.

***

'Should we go inside?' I heard a voice. I looked up and found Parush standing in front of me. The mist had become quite heavy. Parush's words hurled a dollop of foggy smoke towards me.

'Ya,' I said, 'it's very cold. Let us go.'

The open door had brought all the chill inside the room too. I shut the door, brought the heater and switched it on. Parush took the diary in his hand and opened the page he had been staring at some time back – it had the poem.

'*Kalyani's allure and all kallos*,' he uttered, staring at me. 'What do you call it? Alliteration?'

'No,' I said, 'it's called consonance. The *al* sounds in "Kalyani", "allure", "all" and "kallos" don't appear at the beginning of the words. By the way, are you sure that it was written by Bitasta's mother? Do you still remember her handwriting?'

'Yes, I do. I can see her voice distinctly in these lines though I don't understand the meaning. Artemis and Callisto and their Indian counterparts Rikshi and Kalyani – it has to be Kakima, I mean Bits, Bitasta's mother.'

'*You can see the voice of the author?*' I tried to be light. 'That sounds so much like Gulzar. Do you like Gulzar?'

Parush stretched his lips a bit, indicating that he was trying to smile. He didn't look like anything I had seen of him so many times on TV and in newspapers. He took his stare off me and looked at the floor. 'Kakima was a great fan of Gulzar,' he said to himself. His forlorn looks hurt me. 'He can't be what the world is saying about him now,' I said to myself.

'You mentioned about Rikshi and Kalyani?'

He looked up at me again…

***

Ho Ajia, my dear sisters, today I'll tell you the story of two beautiful girls who live in a huge, dense, primeval forest, ajgar arna bir. Rikshi, one of the girls, is the goddess of the jungles and the mistress of the animals. The other girl Kalyani is the most beautiful of the hunting partners of Rikshi. Hit pirit menakkoa, they love each other so much that they are always an inseparable pair. Kalyani is not like the typical girl who spends her time in spinning the soft fibres of wool or arranging her hair in different styles. Wearing her tunic pinned together with few brooches made of polished stones, her tresses carelessly caught back by a white ribbon, and carrying in her hand a light javelin, she moves around from one bir to another, hunting wild animals, with Rikshi always by her side. In front of the sal and sonajhuri trees they vow to remain virgins forever. They believe that they have already entered into a nuptial relationship with nature.

One day, after a long and tiring hunt, Kalyani is lost in dayak dayal mundu, the dense forest she is not familiar with that much. She frantically searches everywhere for Rikshi, but can't find her. Worried and exhausted, she falls asleep by the side of a river. The Lord of the Sky has been watching her for a long time from a distance. He is highly fascinated by her beauty. But he knows very well that she would have no interest in him. He disguises himself as Rikshi and comes near her. He takes her in his arms, crosses the river and reaches a beautiful green meadow. Fended by tall trees, the place is like an open eye in the safe havens of the eyelashes, very much like this place of ours. He lays her on the soft grass and sits beside her. He stares at Kalyani, her body beautifully arched like a mermaid sleeping on the sea of grass, the end of her tied plait tossing like a bunch of areca trees stroked by wind, her slender bare legs crossed beyond the end of the tunic, her curvaceous breasts moving up and down with the resonance of the life within her, her dark and polished skin, seen through the splits between the brooches, shining in the rays of the fallen sun. She opens her eyes and sees Rikshi by her side. She embraces the Lord of the Sky, not realising his real identity, and again falls asleep. The Lord of the Sky feels a strong desire to implant his seed within her and see it germinate into a new life.

By the time Rikshi finds her, the Lord has gone. Kalyani doesn't realise that she hasn't been with Rikshi all the time. She also doesn't realise what the Lord of the Sky has done with her while she has been asleep.

Few months later when Rikshi and Kalyani are bathing in a river, Rikshi identifies the swell in Kalyani's stomach and becomes furious.

In a few days, Kalyani gives birth to a beautiful baby boy. To punish Kalyani for breaking her vow, she transforms her into a daru bana, a big black bear, while the baby is brought up by Kalyani's father.

Few years pass by and the little baby grows up into a naughty boy. He runs around in the jungle with the other kids, hunting animals, very much like his mother. Not knowing anything about his bear mother, one day he sets out to hunt Kalyani. The Lord of the Sky appears at the right moment and saves Kalyani from being killed by her own son. He transforms her into a star and hurls her into the sky. Later he transforms her son into temret bana, a small bear, and hurls him too into the sky. The Big Bear and the Small Bear have ever since stayed in the sky close to each other as two constellations in the northern sky.

***

'That's almost the myth of Artemis and Callisto with Indian names set against, perhaps, a Santal backdrop,' I exclaimed. 'And Bitasta's mother would tell such stories to the tribal women?'

'Yes, that's correct. Even I was surprised when, for the first time, we walked for half an hour through the Hijli forest adjoining Prembajar and reached the sudden open space surrounded by tall eucalyptus and sonajhuri trees. The place was a natural amphitheatre and almost like an oasis in the middle of the jungle.'

I didn't interrupt Parush. He was opening up, slowly.

'I saw Kakima, Bitasta's mother,' he continued, 'seated at the centre, a group of young Santal girls reciting Kalidasa's *Meghaduta* with her and someone playing the *tumdak* to the rhythm of the poem's complex Mandakranta meter – dum-dum-dum-dum, di-di-di-di-di-dum, dum-di-dum-dum-di-dum-dum. It's amazing that Kakima would tell stories from classical Greek and Sanskrit literature to tribal girls who were barely literate.'

'Do you remember any other story she would tell?'

'Not in particular. She liked the Callisto myth very much. Callisto was one of her favourite Greek characters. She felt that the myth of Callisto represents all the motifs commonly used to depict women across the ages. She is first shown as a virgin girl, wild and boisterous, a huntress who runs around in the jungle. Then she transitions into a woman and mother. She has sex and gives birth to a boy. Then there's a phase of extreme sadness and solitude when her motherhood is wrenched from her. She is turned into a bear and exiled in the jungle. The final element in her story combines both death and apotheosis. She is nearly killed by her son when Zeus rescues her at the last moment and enshrines her in the sky as Ursa Major, the Great Bear constellation.'

'That's an interesting angle to the Callisto myth. I'm wondering how you could still remember so much.'

I felt Parush was getting comfortable talking to me. He stretched back on the sofa, joining his hands behind his head, and stared at the roof for some time. I waited patiently until he spoke again.

'Saoli, when did I forget anything? Perhaps those are the only memories I want to remember forever. I want to forget everything else, all that I struggled to attain in life, and all that I don't feel like struggling any more to retain.'

He paused and shut his eyes. I really felt bad for him. In a single stroke, he was ruthlessly pulled down from a pedestal where he had been placed so ceremoniously. The same media which had once called him the Big Bong was now hounding him like mad dogs.

'Parush,' I said, 'all the evidence is against you. Still I believe you should say something in your defence. Why are you so silent?'

'My world had shrunk to a few people long back. I know *they* don't believe I did it all and I don't care for anyone else. I want to live on my own terms. Defence is for losers, for those who come second. I'm not used to defending myself.'

The way he spoke in such an intrepid manner was quite astounding, given the condition he was in presently. The discussion was digressing from the direction I had planned for. Still, I wanted Parush to open up in the way he felt on his own, for I could not quiz him directly about the questions I had in mind.

I wanted to know why Bitasta's mother was so fascinated with Callisto.

'Mind going out now?' Parush asked me suddenly. 'I know it's a little late.'

'No, I don't mind. Where do you want to go?'

'Let's go towards the Santal village in the middle of the Hijli forest. It would be quite cold though.'

I knew where he wanted to go. It would be easy, I felt, getting back to the discussion I wanted. December in KGP was chill indeed. I put on a warm pullover and a scarf to cover my head. That was when I realised that Parush didn't have suitable warm clothing. He might have totally forgotten about it before leaving Calcutta hurriedly late this evening. 'Why don't you take one of my jackets?' I offered.

'Anything will do.'

We left the main road leading to the Air Force Station at Salua and took an unpaved pathway entering the jungle. The trees swayed with the chill winter wind. Parush walked fast with me struggling to keep pace with him. 'Don't you find the Callisto myth a little unusual?' I asked after some time.

'Most Greek myths are unusual. We have Oedipus who desires his mother sexually. Then there are lots of cases of incest – Kakima told me that Zeus' consort Hera happens to be his sister. Callisto's partner Artemis is Zeus' daughter – so Zeus has impregnated his daughter's friend. The relationship between Artemis and Callisto has a strong lesbian undercurrent. But then, considering it's Greek mythology, it shouldn't be unusual.'

'There's a lot of male same sex love in Greek mythology. But comparatively, a lesbian theme is rarely found.'

We didn't talk for quite some time till we reached that open space. I had grown up here but still I hadn't known that a place like this could exist so close to the campus. It appeared to be the site where there could have been a shallow pond sometime in the past. The almost round periphery was flanked by tall trees. The place where Bitasta's mother would have sat was still there in the centre – a small low stage created with a few stones. Parush knelt on the carpet of dried fallen leaves in front of it. Bending forward, he rested his head on it. I stayed back at a little distance, from where his contour was visible through the mist, which was gradually growing heavy. A few moments later I felt as if his contour was shaking. I knew he was crying. I was baffled, not knowing what I should do. I proceeded slowly towards him and sat on the raised platform. The cold stones made my legs numb for some time, but I adjusted to it soon. I raised Parush and made him sit beside me.

'Parush, tell me everything,' I said, after a while, when he had composed himself.

'What do you want to know? Is there anything still not known? The whole world knows even this that my father had an affair with his friend's wife whom he married within months of my mother's death. Just the other day I read the news that I've slept with a mother and daughter pair – the mother is a cousin of mine, who tended to my dying mother in her last days when neither I nor my father were around, and the daughter is the one who has sheltered me now and is among the very few who still trusts me. What else do you want to know?'

'I know all that and many more you haven't yet got the chance to read. I don't want to know the stories. Anyone can make up stories. I want to know the characters that make your stories. I want to see their flesh and blood and not their skins in digital photos. Only then would I be so sure about something which has been driving me crazy over the past few days.'

'Well, let me see. Where I should start...' he said, looking straight towards the low hanging late night moon that had just popped up in the sky above the clouds of mist.

'It was the day after the Babri Masjid fell... that's eighteen years back, when we were in our first year in IIT... We were at the NCC camp, something which was compulsory for all to attend in the first year of engineering...'

As he spoke, he pulled me by my hand and started walking through the forest...

KALAIKUNDA

'Popeye ki ma ki... sala,' Parush heard Arav say from behind. Had his sister not been obsessed, like a maniac, with comics and cartoons even at an age of fourteen, Parush wouldn't have comprehended the quip.

Just a few seconds back Wing Commander Naqvi, the Commanding Officer in charge of the 3 Bengal Technical Air Squadron and 1 Bengal EME Coy NCC, and perhaps the most hated living being in the NCC camp, had announced in an emergency assembly that only rice and spinach curry would be served for lunch and dinner the following day. He mentioned casually, as though it was a normal thing, that curfew had been declared at most places in the country, but he didn't say why. The camp was supposed to get its new provisions the next day, but due to the curfew that wouldn't be possible. Presently the kitchen had only enough rice and spinach for the five hundred people in the camp. Getting the stock either from the nearby Kalaikunda Air Force Station or the IIT campus was not a possibility.

Parush couldn't but smile. Since the past few months, he had started liking these Hindi expletives which certainly had to do with some secret things belonging to anyone's mother and sister. An open-ended statement like 'Popeye's mother's' might not mean anything anywhere else. But in Hindi that very open-endedness is harnessed for its unending possibilities, one of which certainly must be, though not trivial why, among the best cuss words. And, as always, mother is indeed universal – 'Naqvi's mother's' and 'Popeye's mother's' are the same thing.

'Meh,' someone uttered the sound, which had become the audio signature of the camp. The signature was soon passed from one person to another, very much like a basketball, resulting in a peculiar sound wave, which made Naqvi wild. 'Stop it,' he shouted, and the wave propagated with an amplified amplitude. That had lately become a common *game* in the camp.

Once the assembly was over Parush walked slowly towards his tent. 'Then what happened?' someone asked Dicks, Sameer Dikshit, who was already at the centre of a big gathering barely fitting into the small tent.

Dicks had been on night duty, keeping a watch on the southern boundary of the camp ground adjoining the railway track, when he heard people talking excitedly in the kitchen. Approaching closer he realised what they were talking about. He slid a ten rupee note into the hands of one of them, took his bicycle and rode fast along the railway track towards Khemasuli station. He called his father at Ayodhya from the only STD booth, which was closing for the day. He came running to the camp and entered the tent like a warrior returning from a battle with the news of victory.

'Finally, at 4:30 in the evening the karsevaks razed the third and the final dome,' he announced to his sleepy tent-mates. 'Wake up, assholes,' he shouted, perplexed that no one was realising the significance of something that was going to mark the beginning of a new epoch in Indian history. 'Finally, we've reclaimed our lost glory. We've completely demolished the Babri Masjid, which was built wrongfully at Ram's birthplace.'

'What?' exclaimed Parush, not being able to grasp properly what he had just heard. 'Ghazni had destroyed the Somnath temple seventeen times,' continued Dicks, 'and each time we rebuilt it. Now we'll rebuild the Ram temple which Babar had destroyed four hundred and fifty years back. The world should know that Hindus too can protect their Mecca and Bethlehem.'

'How did it all happen?' someone asked.

'More than a lakh karsevaks had arrived in Ayodhya, by the end of November, for today's karseva. The VHP had planned to begin the prayers at 11:30 in the morning on the terrace of the Ram Katha Kunj. But long before that, at around 10:00, some karsevaks managed to get very close to the disputed and heavily guarded masjid. When the RSS volunteers and the police tried to stop them from getting closer still, the crowd hurled stones at the police. In the chaos one intrepid karsevak managed to jump the railing of the masjid and climb on top of one of its domes. This was the signal for a mass surge…'

'Karsevak ki ma ki,' someone interrupted, 'cut it short Dicks. It's not a lab report.'

Dicks didn't seem to have taken the advice seriously. He continued with his minute to minute description of the events about which his father had heard second hand from his neighbour, whose second cousin had been there at the site. 'Outnumbered by the huge frenzied mob, the police fled the spot. By noon the karsevaks were all over the domes. Though Advani, Rajmata Scindia and many other senior leaders of the temple movement appealed to the karsevaks to come down, they didn't listen. They anchored grappling hooks to the domes, while many thousand others battered the bases with hammers and axes. At 2:00 pm the first dome collapsed. The second one fell at 3:30.'

'Advani?' asked Parush, 'that chariot guy who lost the election to Rajesh Khanna last year? Didn't he organise that cross country chariot ride to mobilise people for the demolition of the mosque?'

'Grow up Porus,' someone rebuked from the darkness. 'Be a responsible citizen. There's a world beyond your music and books. It's for people like you that the pseudo secularists get a free run in India.'

'Advani didn't lose to Rajesh Khanna idiot,' someone else clarified. 'He won with a slim margin. And FYI, the entire temple movement was not meant to demolish the mosque, but to build a temple at Ram's birthplace.'

'But there was the mosque at that very place,' Parush tried to argue.

'Forget that asshole,' shouted Dicks from his strategic epicentre.

By that time Arav had woken up. 'So, Dixie,' he said, rubbing his eyes, 'you're happy that the motherfuckers have finally demolished the mosque?'

'Aye,' Dicks thundered and advanced towards Arav menacingly, pushing his august audience. 'Whom do you call motherfuckers? The karsevaks?'

'Who else?' answered Arav.

'Mind your language asshole, my father is also a karsevak. He couldn't attend today's karseva because he had a sprain in his hand. How dare you call my father motherfucker?'

Arav was unperturbed. He stretched his arms, pulled the fingers of his hands one by one, and slowly deliberately cracked his knuckles, all the while people trying hard to hold back Dicks. Arav suddenly started laughing. Knowing him well, Parush got the indication of what could happen next. 'So, Dixie,' Arav said, 'your father fucked someone else's mother?'

Even Dicks couldn't help but join the uproar of laughter in the tent. 'Cool it man. Relax,' Arav patted the calmer Dicks. 'Sorry for the interruption guys. By the way Dixie, whose mother has told you that there was a temple earlier?'

'There are lots of historical texts from the Mughal period which imply that the place had been always considered as Ram's birthplace and that there was a temple too,' Dicks started explaining. 'Abul Fazl's *Ain-i-Akbari*, written in late sixteenth century says that Awadh was the abode of Shri Ram Chandra...

'Alamgir's daughter wrote sometime in the seventeenth or eighteenth century that the place was demolished on the strength of Islam and that a mosque was constructed there...

'Mirza Jan wrote in 1856 in *Hadiqa-i-Shahada*...

'The interior of the mosque was replete with Hindu motifs...'

While Dicks was trying to convince everyone about the authenticity of the existence of an older temple at the site of the mosque and, unbelievingly, a tent-full of people were listening to the historical discourses with rapt attention in the middle of a cold night on the outskirts of the Kalaikunda Air Force Station, Parush felt a little out of place. He realised that something, which had been so insignificant and irrelevant to him, was a binding force for many. He could tell from the faces of many of his batchmates presently huddled in his tent that they were extremely happy. Any other night they would have all crashed immediately after dinner. But now they were all awake and seriously listening to, of all people, the commie Dicks, whose name in the list of occupants for Parush's tent had been a major concern for the rest. It was something, Parush felt amazing. Or was it amazing that he himself was so disinterested in something which could eventually change the course of Indian history? Was he, as someone had pointed out, really living in a utopian world of books and music, totally disengaged from the reality?

'The first clash at Babri mosque was recorded in 1855 during the rule of Nawab Wajid Ali Shah...

'A bloody clash happened in 1934 after which the doors of the mosque were shut till 1950. Hindus continued to offer prayers outside the mosque...'

Dicks had to stop as someone barged into the tent and asked everyone to assemble immediately at the ground. 'Naqvi has to make some urgent announcements,' he said.

Back to the tent after Naqvi's emergency meeting, Dicks continued with his lecture. 'Secularism has come to mean allergy to Hinduism. All our holy places like Benares, Mathura and Rishikesh have become industrial slums...'

Parush lay on his bed and drowned himself in Ru's fantasies, something he had been doing ever since that day many years ago, when Ru had suddenly transitioned him from a kid to a boy and then to an adult. Her thoughts lifted him up from the tent and placed him in the clouds from where Ayodhya and Kalaikunda were undistinguishable dots. Riding on a chariot, not the one Advani had ridden during his cross-country show, he hopped from one dot to another, mobilising people to build a new castle for Ru at the place where her old castle had been destroyed many years ago. A million people from a million villages across the world brought a million red bricks and gathered around Ru.

'Every brick is baked specially for you in special kilns,' Parush said. 'Ru, we'll build a castle which can't be destroyed again by anyone in the world. Are you not happy, Ru?'

'I don't need the castle,' said a melancholic Ru, holding Parush's hands. 'Just stay with me. Don't go so far that I can't call you. Don't keep me in a castle. Keep me in your heart…'

***

'It's curfew everywhere,' the head cook said, immersing buckets of water soaked rice in a huge vessel atop a large clay stove burning dangerously on big chunks of wood. 'Not a single shop is open in the nearby Khemasuli, Dharenda and Nimpura villages.' While refilling another bucket with soaked rice, he turned towards the old and fragile bearded person sitting at the corner of the makeshift kitchen, cutting spinach. 'Don't worry,' he assured, 'nothing will happen to you. We'll protect all the Muslims in our village.'

Parush, permanently on kitchen duty, was settling down at his temporary abode, a naturally elevated platform padded with multiple folds of a worn and torn tent-cloth cleaved from a discarded tent. Trying to identify a relatively smoother contour of the heap of wood pieces to rest his back against, he stared at the person cutting spinach, unperturbed, expressionless and too diligent at his work. 'What happened?' he asked him. He didn't answer. Seeing him quiet the head cook responded. 'Dadabhai,' he addressed Parush as an affectionate elder brother in a homely and endearing lingo, 'you know, all illiterate people in the village – of all places, they fired crackers in front of his house, all by mistake. He is very scared.'

The celebrations, Parush realised, had spread quite far, cutting across language and literacy levels. Stretching his legs forward he opened his book.

'Naqvi sir is calling you,' he heard someone saying. He raised his eyes from the book and found the dark short guy who they believed replaced Naqvi's shit tank during the night when everyone would be asleep. Naqvi was the only one in the camp to have a closed latrine fitted with a detachable tank underneath. Everyone else had to use the DTLs, Deep Trench Lavatories, dug little away from the tents alongside the railway tracks, providing an unusual visual of a genuflecting battalion of cadets to the morning trains.

'Why?' Parush asked, not quite understanding why Naqvi would suddenly look for him.

'You have visitors – a sir and a madam. They are waiting in Naqvi sir's tent.'

'Visitor for me?' Parush was surprised. 'Who could come now? And that too, during curfew?'

'I don't know sir. Someone from the base has brought them.'

Parush was not excited at all. He was stuck at a crucial juncture in the book and he didn't want any distraction.

He got up and walked fast towards Naqvi's tent.

THE WABASH CANNON BALL

'Oh, so you're the one?' Naqvi greeted Parush. 'What disease did you mention?'

'*Xeroderma pigmentosum*,' Parush replied. 'I'm not supposed to be exposed much to UV rays.'

'What?' someone asked from behind Naqvi. That was when Parush saw the sir and the madam, the prospective visitors. The sir was someone past his middle age but not old yet, someone as old or young as his father. The madam was a young girl of incomprehensible age, as are most girls for many years of their young life. She was quite tall, as tall as Parush, and toned enough to be nagged by her mother to eat properly. She was staring at Parush with looks which could be of suspicion, or even shock. Nevertheless, with eyebrows little frowned and the oblong face a little tilted to the left, she had a smile, which couldn't be anything but naughty. For a few moments all the parties in front of Naqvi's tent were silent, rather confused as to who should initiate a conversation. The sir broke the ice.

'Parush, I'm Shaunak Roy. It's not for you to remember me. I saw you last when you were a kid. Your father and I were batchmates in KGP. Presently we stay in Prembajar, just outside the campus…'

'Oh, I've heard so much about you,' Parush interrupted. 'Baba has asked me so many times to meet you. Sorry I didn't get a chance to go to your place.'

'Yes, you should be, my boy,' he patted Parush's shoulder. 'You can ignore us, but how could you ignore my beautiful daughter for so long?'

'You should be court-marshalled,' Naqvi quipped quite uncharacteristically in his characteristic shrill voice. Parush saw Naqvi smile for the first time and realised why he rarely smiled – a well-wisher might have advised him not to, given how funny his round face became when its muscles contracted to give expression to his humour.

'Hi, I'm Bitasta,' the beautiful daughter extended her hand to Parush. 'And yes, you should be court-marshalled for declining our invitation not once, but twice.'

Parush shook hands with her. 'I'm really sorry for that,' he apologised, cursing himself for really being so discourteous. It was not that he couldn't have gone to their house. But knowing that their daughter was the same age as his sister, he really wanted to avoid an encounter with another girl staying in a pink world stuffed with teddies and cartoons. But he hadn't known that they had an elder daughter too.

Suddenly it occurred to him that he didn't know yet why they had come here. Was everything fine at Calcutta? Should he ask them directly?

'Wondering why we're here?' Bitasta asked, resolving his predicament. 'With curfews everywhere, your father was worried about you and called Baba. That's why we're here to see if someone's kid is fine.' She stressed on the "kid", retaining that naughty smile on her face.

'Absolutely fine,' Naqvi butted in. 'We've taken sufficient care to ensure the safety and security of our cadets. No other place can be safer than this. My lieutenants are keeping a constant eye within the camp so that no rumour could be spread by anyone. I'm constantly in touch with the AOC, Kalaikunda Air Force Station, and...'

'Mr Naqvi,' Bitasta interrupted, 'would it be possible for me to see around the place?'

Even Parush was petrified with the idea of Bitasta taking a round of the camp. Not that he was bothered how awkward she might feel being the only female at the focal point of a thousand thirsty eyes, he was bothered more about what could happen to him once he would be back to the camp. Naqvi would also have felt the same. 'Well, there's nothing much here,' he said, making Parush feel he was not as dumb as they usually thought him to be. 'Let me ask my driver to take you to the Air Force Station. Parush, go with her. Meet Group Captain Mehra. He will show you the place. Don't miss the old B-29 aircraft of the XX Bomber Command.'

While waiting for the driver to come with the jeep, Parush could hear people shouting his name: **'PO RUS, PO RUS, PO RUS.'**

Bitasta started laughing.

'What?' asked a confused Parush.

'You seem to be quite popular,' she quipped.

The jeep arrived and they left the camp – and more importantly the 'Porus' chorus – behind. Parush was relieved. Bitasta tightened her headscarf against the wind and pulled out a pair of big goggles. She looked quite different with those.

'How's the reaction at the camp after yesterday's incident?' she initiated a conversation.

'Many people were happy and justified the whole thing.'

'And what about you? What was your reaction?'

Parush didn't have a readymade answer for that. Perhaps he didn't have any reaction, like he never had when the kids fought while playing in the field adjoining their house in Rupsa.

'Don't worry Porus,' Bitasta assured him, pronouncing 'Porus' with stress and an expression in her eyes, 'you can tell me the truth.'

'I think, to have a reaction you have to be connected to it. I never took any interest in the whole thing. But at face value, the entire episode looks stupid. What was the point in demolishing the old building?'

'So, you condemn the incident, and so did the press and so did many people, despite a million others celebrating it. Both sides have their reasons to either condemn or rejoice. But the reaction in the media and in the West is very stereotypical and hypocritical. We've got so many calls from Nova Scotia, the place where we used to stay in Canada. I don't know why they are making such a big deal out of it.'

'Isn't it a big deal?'

'It is, if it's a big deal elsewhere too. But in this case, it's being made a big deal just because it's India. The West expects only India to have the conscience in such cases. A similar thing in the West would have been downplayed. Just tell me this, have you heard of the Polish city of Warsaw?'

'I've only heard of Polish jokes.'

'Quite expected. It's the capital of Poland. When the Russians occupied Warsaw in the seventeenth century they built an Eastern Orthodox Christian Cathedral in the principal square in what had been the capital of the once independent Roman Catholic Christian country. When Poland became independent in 1918 they pulled down the cathedral.'

'My God!' Parush interrupted. 'How do you know all these? Did you prepare before coming here?'

'Don't interrupt. I had recently prepared for a debate at school. Let me complete. When the Mughals ruled India, Babar built the Babri Masjid in Ayodhya and Aurangzeb built mosques in Benares and Mathura, all important places in the previously Hindu country. Now if the Hindus pull down one in Ayodhya, how is it different from what happened in Warsaw? But still you haven't heard of it and even after hundred years Ayodhya will be a symbol of intolerance.

'That's my problem. Yesterday's incident was bad, and similar incidents anywhere else are equally bad. But in the history books Ayodhya will always get undue attention…'

While Bitasta was speaking, Parush had been observing her more than listening. She was facing him, turned sideways on the back seat of the open jeep, as was he. Somewhere she had removed the goggles, her long beautiful eyes speaking more than her words. She was occasionally tapping on his knees, stressing on certain points.

Parush wondered why he was so detached from reality, from everything that surrounded him, from everything that made sense to everyone else. For the first time in his life he felt embarrassed that he didn't have any opinion of his own about most things. He spent hours with people who had complicated problems, faced complex situations and solved myriad mysteries. But none of those were real. They were in the books, in his imagination, in his thoughts. By sheer luck he had never had any major crisis in his life. He didn't even know how he would react if a real crisis ever hit him.

The jeep stopped in front of the Officer's Club. While the driver went to look for Group Captain Mehra, Parush and Bitasta waited outside the club. Suddenly, Bitasta pulled Parush by his hand. 'Come inside, want to show you something.'

Bitasta crossed the lobby, turned left, took the staircase and came to the first floor. Parush followed her. She strode along a corridor in long steps, several officers turning to look at her as she passed by. Parush followed her to the last room – it was a library.

'I had been here in September,' she said, 'for the forty-eighth anniversary of the club. Few days before that, a Squadron Leader had retrieved an old diary from a heap of declassified papers which were being sent for disposal.'

She went ahead to a bookshelf spilling with journals and picked up an old file from the top shelf. 'See, this was written in 1944 by some Captain Joseph Paxton of the 1st Air Transport Squadron,' she said, opening the file in front of Parush. 'This diary was the main attraction of the function. Someone mentioned that the 1st ATS was a sort of a private airline for the XX Bomber Command of the US Air Force which operated from Kalaikunda during the Second World War.'

She flipped through the old typed pages until she reached 23rd September 1944. 'See this,' she forwarded the file to me. 'This was the song sung at the inauguration of the club on 23rd September 1944:

We crossed the Great Atlantic where the little fishes play
And fought the fierce mosquitoes of the Gold Coast for a day,
Then on across the skyway of a barren, dusty land
Ray led his twenty raiders through the beetles and the sand.'

Parush had no idea why she was so excited about this song. 'I'm sorry, is there anything special about this song?' he asked hesitantly.

'The diary says it's a parody of the American folk song "*The Wabash Cannon Ball*", which goes like this:

From the great Atlantic Ocean to the wide Pacific shore
From the queen of flowing mountains to the south belt
by the shore
She's mighty tall and handsome and known quite well by all
She's the combination called the Wabash Cannonball

She sung four lines of the song, an old rock-n-roll type, like many of the Jim Reeves and Pat Boon songs Parush's father had gramophone records of. 'It's been one of my favourites since I was a kid. I first heard the song at a Purdue University football match. The All American Marching Band played the tune before the match started and I just loved it.'

She kept the file back on the rack and they started walking towards the entrance of the club. 'Later Baba got me the song, an all-time popular number recorded by Roy Acuff. As a kid I was fascinated by this song about a mythical train whose whistle could be heard from all the stations in America and which was so fast that it just took off and went into space. Much later I learnt that it was a fantasy of the hobos, many of whom had died constructing the railway lines in the US in the late nineteenth century.'

They had already arrived at the lobby. It occurred to Parush that he was remarkably less informed about the folk culture and society of other countries. He knew his Keats and Tennyson well but, unlike Bitasta, couldn't connect well with the ethos of the hobos. For that matter, he thought, how much did he really know about things closer? He was suddenly exposed to this whole other world and whole other influences. It was like pulling him out of his own cocoon of dreamy fantasies, mostly insulated from happenings even in the near surroundings, and throwing him into a whirlpool of a frothy brew of realities and fancies.

Parush again felt embarrassed that suddenly he had nothing to say. He looked for an analogy which could be more personal, more domestic.

'Have you seen these two movies of Satyajit Ray,' Parush asked suddenly, "*Goopi Gayne Bagha Bayne*" and "*Hirak Rajar Deshe*"? Perhaps he expected Bitasta wouldn't have seen these movies.

'Of course, I've seen them,' Bitasta said.

'Really?' Parush was more shocked than surprised.

'We had a lot of Ray's movies at home. Baba would collect them from everywhere. Ma had once organised a show of *The Adventures of Goopi Bagha* in her school. As kids we all loved the singing duo Goopi and Bagha.'

'What did you like about them?'

'Poor guys, they were banished from their village. Then they got three boons from the Ghost King and their lives changed. They travelled across the world. They captivated a tiger with their singing prowess. They fought against the treacherous king in *Hirak Rajar Deshe*, The Land of The Diamond King...'

Bitasta stopped suddenly and stared at Parush, with surprise in her eyes. 'Why do you suddenly ask about it?'

Parush himself didn't know why exactly he had asked. Was it that he was excited to discover two seemingly ordinary people at home too, who, perhaps unknowingly, did extraordinary things, much bigger than their own small worlds of hardships and fantasies? Weren't they, Parush might have thought, very much like the hobos and this anonymous fighter, who had written the parody of the hobos' song?

Parush was presently surprised at how he had always nurtured a thought in his mind that the moment he would get connected to the reality, outside the comfort and convenience of his own small world, he might lose the bliss of dreams and fantasies. Wouldn't the bigger world outside, he pondered, be worth venturing into? He could still, he felt, have his dreams, his poems, his books.

From the great Atlantic Ocean to the wide Pacific shore/ From the queen of flowing mountains to the southbelt by the shore– The Wabash Cannon Ball lingered in his mind.

***

That night, only Arav noticed something unusual. It was not Dicks, but Parush, who occupied the epicentre in their tent, debating about the hypocrisy of the western media.

Next morning Parush didn't go for the kitchen duty for which he had concocted a story for Naqvi. 'What about the UV rays?' Naqvi asked.

'I'm bored there,' Parush said. 'I'll be back to the kitchen if I have a problem.'

***

'Who was she?' Arav asked Parush during lunch.

THE PRELUDE

A queer, frightening sound froze my nerves and I jumped in fear, shrieking at the pitch of my voice. Parush acted quickly, grabbing me by his hands. The apparent cold that had settled in his heart revealed itself in his hands.

'Chill,' he said calmly, as though nothing had happened.

'What… what was that?' I asked in a shivering voice.

'Just a wild cat,' Parush answered with confidence.

'How are you so sure it is just one wild cat?' I protested. 'It can be a fox too!'

'Saoli, I know every sound of this forest.'

'Err … how?'

'I came here with Bits, I mean Bitasta, so many times…'

'Aha…' I tried to be frivolous, to be normal, feeling little embarrassed that perhaps I had overreacted. 'Let us talk about Bitasta. So, you were head over heels in love with her after seeing her at the NCC camp?' I had already composed myself, but I didn't release his hands, which gave me a sense of security and warmth in this cold and desolate corner of the world. I had barely acclimatised myself to the forest, engulfed in a dull moonlight sieved though the dense mist.

'Well, it has been so many years,' Parush said in a very cold tone. 'I think… no, no… I'm quite sure. I didn't fall in love with her at first sight. But I didn't ignore her either. She was different...'

'Oh and?' I asked.

'Yes, it was hard for me to believe that she was perhaps my sister's age. I mean, she appeared so much more mature than my sister. I can't believe Pushi talking like that at that age. But …' he paused, perhaps to recall something. 'Some of her ways still seemed to be like the girls of Pushi's age.'

'Why so?' my inquisitive soul could not stop asking.

'Whenever Bits wanted to be naughty, which would anyway be the case most of the times, she would frown and make her eyebrows look like wonderful arches… She too would giggle... She too would make faces… She was naturally beautiful and… Pushi was like a Barbie doll, always neat and preen, wearing typical pink dresses...'

'Bitasta was beautiful. Even so was Parushni,' I interrupted – I preferred calling his sister by her given name, Parushni, rather than the shortened Pushi. 'Don't you think just because you were blindly in love, you are extolling Bitasta?' Something inside me could not tolerate it. For some reason, I felt Parush was exaggerating Bitasta.

'Of course not,' Parush defended, perhaps with a little smile on his face, a smile which had eluded him since evening. 'Pushi is still my fancy doll, something I've started adoring as I grew older. She is a wonderful, precious, invaluable thing in my life. When I met Bits for the first time, I was not very fond of her. The more I knew Bits, the more I realised she was so different from my sister; rather she was different from all the girls of her age… Instead of the high heels, which Pushi and most of her friends would wear with shirts with low neckline and shorts, she would wear sneakers … She was not like one of those wannabe fashion queens, neither was she a tomboy… Sometimes she would jump in the mud to catch a butterfly and while eating puchka, she wouldn't mind dropping the crumbs on her clothes and ruining them, to eat quickly and beat me in the race… She was not one of those snobbish, convent-educated tyansh Calcutta girls like Pushi… you know… the typical snobs who would find fault in everything Indian and would try to act like western girls.'

'You are calling Parushni *tyansh*?' I was a little offended – the Bengali colloquial slang "tyansh" is generally used derogatorily.

'Of course,' Parush replied. 'I still remember how Pushi would manicure her nails for hours and cut the cake delicately in such a way that the strawberry cream would not get mixed with the chocolate icing… Bits would never do that…'

Though I couldn't acquiesce, still I listened to Parush without disturbing him. From what he said, Bitasta seemed to be an enigma that would allure you with her scarlet hue but the moment you touch her, everything would turn to jolly yellow.

It was clear to me that, after he had Bitasta in his life, he barely had any time to notice his growing sister.

I felt it useless to pique Parush about Parushni's childhood. No matter what I would ask, he would just give me a silhouette of Parushni's life, while when it came to Bitasta, he even remembered the minutest of things. I could feel the softness in Parush's eyes, as he spoke of Bitasta's silk tie, hanging loosely from her long neck, the visible collar bones falling upon her well buttoned shirt. 'Saoli,' he asserted, 'there was something in the way Bits carried herself, she dressed and she accessorised, that made her look much older than a typical fourteen-year-old. It's close to two decades since I've seen her last. But still, a few images – like when I would stare at her for some time, the way she would stare back at me mischievously, leaning against the wall, tilting her head a bit to the left, and shaking her bare shoulders she would gesture at me "What?" – I feel I've seen her just a few days back…'

I could visualise Parsuhni, struggling with her growing adolescence, locked up in her own world, while someone, of her own age, was enjoying a wide exposure. The situation reminded me of a verse of Sappho.

Set are the Pleiades, the Moon is down
And the midnight dark on high.
The hours, the hours, drift by,
And here I lie,
Alone.

I felt the lines were written for her.

***

'So, what happened after the NCC camp?' I asked, as we walked through the forest.

'I went to their house … at Prembajar …' he paused and stared at me, 'your house … just after the camp, before going to Calcutta for the short winter break…'

ARCADIA

Parush remembered that day, so vividly, when he had gone to Prembajar for the first time, immediately after the NCC Camp. He was not used to what Bits would refer to as PDA, Public Display of Affection. He didn't remember any instance when his mother would have hugged or kissed him. For that matter, he didn't even remember how many times his mother would have even touched him. He had once seen a sepia coloured photo of his mother, holding him in her arms and posing in front of the Taj Mahal, his father's hand over his mother's shoulder. That was perhaps the only proof that there had been once something physical between his parents. He didn't completely discount the possibility of being adopted by his parents even though the facial resemblances between him and his sister made that possibility a statistical wonder.

Parush would stare at the wall full of photos of his friends, kissing their parents. He wondered why there was not a single photo like that on any of their walls. They never had to request anyone to take a group photo of their family, posing in front of the Eifel Tower or the Sphinx or the Grand Canyon. They didn't have any album, perhaps because they didn't have any memorable moments of togetherness to preserve.

That day, when Parush had been to Bitasta's house for the first time, her mother hugged him tight and kissed his forehead and cheeks. Initially, Parush felt very uncomfortable, not quite knowing how to react in such a rare instance of physical proximity. His biggest problem was that he didn't know what to do with his hands, which were not even conditioned to a reflex action which would be apt in the present situation. But then, Parush realised, human beings are the most adaptive living creatures on earth. His hands rose slowly and wrapped Bitasta's mother from behind and his head drowned deep into the depth of her flowing hair. Those few moments felt like eternal bliss suddenly snapped off its perpetuity.

Parush realised why the smiles on his friends' faces in *those* photos on their walls had always appeared so different to him. He smiled, one of *those* different ones, when Bitasta's mother spoke the words, 'bhalo theko', stay well, harbouring his face between her tender palms, like sheltering the fickle flames of a lamp from the gushing wind. Her round face, full of grace, was everything that his mother wasn't. She looked like a mother, or at least the idea of a mother that Parush carried in his mind.

The only other woman whose fragrance he had ever breathed and whose bodily movements of life he had ever felt with his own body was Ru.

'What should I call you by?' he asked Bitasta's mother.

'Call me Panchali,' she said, stroking his hair.

'No way,' Parush protested. 'Kakima is better.'

'Call me anything,' she said, indicating Parush to sit on one of the sofas.

All the while Bitasta had been a mute spectator. 'I'm feeling so shy,' she said to her mother, leaning against the wall, her head slightly tilted towards the left, her lower lip softly bitten by a few teeth.

Parush saw the expression of mischief in Panchali's face. '*Oh sweetheart, you're feeling so shy*?' she asked in an unusual tone. '*May I know? May I know why?*'

'*The PDAs are flying so high!*'

'*O darling, Come on, let them fly.*'

'*Oh mother, I should say, lucky guy.*'

The mother and daughter giggled.

'Porus,' Bitasta said, sitting on the sofa beside him, 'it all started with this poem of Keats: *Then he found...*'

'*That the ground*,' supplemented Panchali immediately, she and her daughter supplying the alternate lines in a seamless natural conversation:

'*Was as hard*'
'*That a yard*'
'*Was as long*,'
'*That a song*'
'*Was as merry*,'
'*That a cherry*'
'*Was as red –*'

While Bitasta and Panchali played the rhyme game with each other, Parush sat like an umpire of a badminton match, shuttling his stare from one to the other.

'Take him to your room,' Panchali said to Bitasta, at the end of the badminton match. 'I'll make some snacks.'

On the door of Bitasta's room was written "Arcadia" alongside a cartoon of a girl with a bow and arrow in her hand, aiming at a bear. Parush stopped to stare at the cartoon with amazement. 'Doesn't the face of the girl look like you?' he asked.

'Ya, that's me, Arca, and Arcadia is my abode.'

'Who made the cartoon?'

'Why? Isn't it good?'

'It's quite good. I could recognise you.'

'It's me Porus,' Bitasta pulled the collar of her shirt and said, hurling herself into the revolving chair, which started moving fast till she jerked it stop just before it was about to crash against the bookshelves behind. 'My art teacher in Nova Scotia gifted this cartoon to me when we were leaving Canada. It's inspired by one of Ma's favourite paintings by some German painter.'

She indicated Parush to sit on the bed, pulling the chair close to him. One wall of the room was packed with shelves jammed with books stretching till the ceiling. A writing desk lay at the corner. Adjoining it was a TV atop a trolley in front of a closed window, half covered with curtains hung from a string. The bed lay in the centre of the room flushed against the wall facing the bookshelves. Empty spaces in the walls were austere and almost bare, barring a Bengali calendar and a photo of a small girl – doubtless it was Bitasta – with red ribbons and pink frock, jumping on black grapes. 'Is this your room?' Parush asked.

'Of course not. I snatched it from Ma.'

'And which one is your sister's room?'

'Sister? What're you talking about? I don't have any sister.'

Parush was surprised. 'But I was told that Panchali Kakima and Shaunak Kaku have a daughter as old as my sister.'

Bitasta was suspicious. She stared at Parush with frowned eyebrows, her face tilted to the left, a typical pose Parush would soon become so fond of.

'Are you indirectly asking my age?' she asked. 'I'm the only daughter of my parents and I too was told that I'm the same age as your sister.'

'You're fourteen?' Parush exclaimed in shock.

'I'm fifteen. I lost a year in relocating from Canada to India. Any problem?'

'Do you like pink?'

'Yes.'

'Do you like cartoons?'

'Yes.'

'Do you like teddies?'

'Yes, but why do you ask all these?'

Parush scanned the room with bewilderment, the expression of which showed up well in his eyes and face. 'Even your room looks different. Where are the pinks and teddies and cartoons? Well, there's one on the door, but that's not what I mean. Pushi, my sister, and her friends are the only elements – all identical I would say – in my sample space for fourteen-year-old girls. Aru, my fourteen-year-old niece, is an unknown element in the sample space. Keeping her aside, I've formulated a law about fourteen-year-old girls and…' he took a breath, 'my law is failing for the first time in your case.'

'Should I take that as a compliment?'

'I think so. I felt you're much older. I'm shocked that…' He couldn't complete. Bitasta snatched the words from him. 'That I'm not so old?' she asked, pushing her chair so close that her bare knees touched his legs. 'I'm anyway a year older than your sister, *not much older though*. By the way, Mr Porus, how do you treat a not-so-old girl?'

Parush mined for the right words. 'Under normal circumstances,' he said, choosing each word very carefully, 'I would treat them quite badly. But I've decided to make an exception, just to prove the law.'

***

'I would organise a lot of functions in Acadia University,' Panchali said during the dinner, 'to celebrate three hundred years of *Grand-Pré*. The entire Canadian province of Nova Scotia was once part of a French Colony called Acadia. The name Acadia comes from Arcadia, a very beautiful place mentioned in Greek mythologies. In one of the functions, I did a play on the Greek mythologies around Arcadia. I tweaked the stories a bit for a kid's production. She played the role of Arca, a naughty boy of Arcadia whose mother has been converted into a bear. Arca is not aware of this. In the climax he is about to kill his bear mother….'

'How old was she then?' Parush asked, once Panchali took a pause.

'I was five,' answered Bitasta. 'I looked so sweet that everyone started calling me Arca. Eventually, it became my nickname.'

'And Kakima?' Parush asked. 'Which role did you play?'

'What else?' replied Bitasta, 'her favourite Callisto, of course.'

'Callisto? Who's that?'

'Oh no,' Bitasta sighed, 'she'll again get started with the wackiest of the stories. Let me tell in short. Callisto is Arca's mother. Arca's father is Zeus, who has another wife Hera. Hera is jealous of Callisto and converts her into a bear. And the interesting thing is that Callisto is a lesbian – her partner is Artemis. I really don't know why Ma is so obsessed with her. I find her quite weird. Anyway, let's talk about something else. Porus, tell me this. How many HDCs did you finally find at the Officer's Club party in Kalaikunda?'

'What's HDC?'

'Hot Defence Chick!'

Parush was embarrassed, not because Bitasta had asked it so bluntly, but because such a thing would be unthinkable in the presence of his mother. For that matter, he wondered if he could ever use the word 'lesbian' in front of his mother the way Bitasta had done just now, so comfortably. He also wondered how two girls – his sister and Bitasta – almost of the same age could be so different. Pushi, his sister, he felt, was still a kid, while Bitasta was already a woman, not much different from Ru, though separated by a generation – Ru's daughter Aru was Bitasta's age.

Seeing Parush go insipid, Bitasta started laughing. 'Okay,' she said, 'if you're not comfortable talking about girls in front of Ma, we'll talk about it later.' They came to the living room after dinner.

Parush hadn't seen the drawing book lying on the centre table earlier. He took it up and flipped through the pages. 'Amazing pencil work,' he commended. 'All yours?'

'Ya,' she took the book from Parush and opened a page from the middle. 'This one is my favourite.'

Parush leaned towards her and looked at the page. He was awestruck at what he saw. It was a wonderful pencil sketch of a beautiful young girl, naked, her eyes shut, her hands stretched beyond her head, her long hair laid casually like the tail of a mermaid, and a fragile face of a young man resting peacefully on one of her breasts. Below the drawing was written:

Pillow'd upon my fair love's ripening breast,
To feel for ever its soft fall and swell,
Awake forever in a sweet unrest,
Still, still to hear her tender taken breath.

He couldn't but keep gaping at the page. Bitasta started laughing. 'I'm happy to see you staring at it like that,' she said. 'It gives me confidence that it looks real.'

'It's wonderful, Bitasta. And the caption is just so apt.'

'It's the last poem written by Keats. He was dying and he remembered Fanny Brawne, his girlfriend and inspiration. I love these lines. It's so passionate... so romantic... And it's just so terrible when you try to imagine what that twenty-six-year-old dying guy would have felt while writing these lines...'

Parush could feel her heavy breath.

***

A few months later when Parush knocked the door at Bitasta's house at Prembajar, their live-in maid, who was almost a family and whom Bitasta called by the name 'Pishu', opened the door. She looked serious and embarrassed too. It didn't take more than a few moments for Parush to figure out what was amiss. He could hear the intense arguments from Bitasta's room:

Bitasta: *I hate lesbians. I think they are yuck, pervert, abnormal and psycho. How dare she think I'm a lesbian like her?*

Panchali: *You shouldn't talk like that. She is also a human being like you… like me. She too deserves dignity.*

Bitasta: *What's the problem with you Ma? Why are you taking her side?*

Panchali: *Arca, you're growing up. Remember, what you speak tells about your education, your thoughts, your upbringing…*

Bitasta: *I give a damn. What the fuck…*

Parush heard a slap. 'Stop it,' shouted Panchali. He didn't want to stay any longer. 'I'll come some other day,' he said, hesitantly. 'Please don't tell them that I came.'

By the time he reached RK Hall, his hostel at the other end of the campus, there was already a message for him. 'Parush Babu,' shouted the person who ran the store in front of the phone. 'Someone had called from Prembajar.'

Parush dialled Bitasta's number. 'Come to our place, immediately. Have dinner here,' she said and put the phone down without waiting for any response or reaction from Parush.

HIJLI BIR

Bitasta's house was behind the Prembajar market, at a corner which seemed to have suddenly filtered out all the noise of the adjoining market. With the lights of the market warded off by a row of eucalyptus trees and colourful bushes lining the unlit and unpaved road lying idle most of the times, the quiet hamlet gradually and very naturally merged into the Hijli forest. Lying on the small grassy front yard of their house and staring at the clear starry sky, a languid late evening could be as silent and calm as a night in the jungle, the languishing melody of the crickets lingering listlessly all around.

Parush rode as fast as possible, but still took ten minutes to cross the entire campus. Passing by the empty shops in the market readying to close for the day, he slowed down on the red gravel which made up the road leading to Bitasta's house. From a distance he could see the house and then the silhouette of Bitasta sitting on the stairs at the main entrance of their house, the door shut behind her. Reaching the fragile iron-gate affixed loosely to the dwarfish boundary wall he got off his bike, opened the gate, entered the lawn, and closed the gate behind him, Bitasta not moving a bit from her position all this while. He sat beside her, not saying anything. 'Why did you run away like a thief?' she asked, without looking at him.

That was not how he had expected the conversation to begin. He was prepared to face an uncomfortable situation, but this question made him more uneasy than he had readied himself for. 'I didn't run away. I just felt I might have appeared at an inappropriate moment.'

'Doesn't your mom slap you?'

'No, never,' came the prompt answer from Parush. 'No PDA – Public Display of Anger.'

'Lucky guy.'

'Really?' asked Parush. He had always waited for that moment when his mother would finally scold him, beat him. But any sort of PDA, be it affection or anger, was not the tradition at home. He would aspire for something, which his friends despised. He wanted to tell Bitasta that the slap had made him jealous.

'That was the first time ever,' she said after some time, during which she hadn't removed her stare from Parush's sad face. 'I was more amazed than shocked. Had I not seen Ma hug and kiss you the first time you came to our house, I wouldn't have known she too could express affection in that way. I was jealous. She rarely hugs or kisses me, though we're quite close. She loves you. Every time you come, she's so happy. I never miss the sparks in her eyes, the excitement within her. When you come, it can't be an inappropriate moment.' She paused, but didn't take her stare off Parush. 'You shouldn't have left like that. Ma felt very bad. And…'

'And what?'

'I felt bad too. I would have told you anyway.'

Parush wondered if he should say sorry. In reality, he felt good, rather very good, that he had become an important part of their lives. The air was fragrant with the smell of a fifteen-year-old, who too loved pink, teddies and cartoons and reminded him of Ru, though he couldn't well explain the connection. 'Where's Kakima?' he asked.

'She's gone out.'

'Where?'

'She didn't tell, but I know where she has gone.'

'Where?'

'Hijli Bir, the forest nearby. Let's have dinner, I'll take you there. You'll like the place.' She leaned on the door behind. 'Want to know what happened?'

'Yes, tell me.' Parush too leaned against the closed door, stretching his legs along the stairs. He turned towards Bitasta, who had her stare affixed to his bike.

'There's a new girl in our class ... Liza,' she started. 'She stays in the hostel. I heard the other girls say she's a lesbian. Everyone avoids her, though I never found anything unusual about her. She sings very well and the two of us were selected to lead the choir. I would stay back most days after school for practice. One day I noticed few girls whispering something in the class. I somehow got a feeling they might be talking about me. Then they started avoiding me too. Today the principal called me and asked if whatever she's hearing is true.'

'What do you mean?' Parush sat straight.

'Apparently they are claiming that Liza has told them something about me.'

'What's that?'

'I don't know. But that's enough for them to think I'm a lesbian too, like Liza.'

'What did you say to the principal?'

'I was shocked when she hinted at what she had heard. I just couldn't say anything for some time. I felt like killing that fucking bitch. How dare she spread such filthy rumours about me?'

'Why would she do that?'

'Why not? Now she's not alone.'

'But have you talked to her? How do you know that she has spread the rumours?'

'Who else could?'

'Anyone. You have been spending time with her every day after the school. It doesn't take much creativity to exploit the situation and come up with something juicy. Why do you blame that poor girl? She might be feeling even more horrible.'

'Now I know why Ma loves you so much. She too has told me the same thing. But I was so pissed off that I just started blurting out anything. And somehow, I always found the idea of lesbianism very repulsive. How can a girl love another girl in that way? But Ma went on taking Liza's side. I've been anyway quite jealous of you and now there's one more…' She stopped suddenly, realising she had revealed something which she didn't want to.

'It's okay Bitasta,' Parush tried to comfort her. 'It's an honour to make you jealous in this way. I envy you so much. Ma rarely talks to me. She's in her own world with her books. I feel suffocated at home. I started breathing here. You don't have to be jealous of me.'

'I heard your mom is extremely beautiful.'

'Who told you?'

'Ma.'

'Yes, she is perhaps the most beautiful lady I've seen in my life. But she's like a wonderful portrait, always silent and expressionless. She always looks sad. I don't know why she is so melancholic. She looks barren, from within. I heard she dated my father and then married him. But, seeing them now, that looks like a remote possibility to me. Ru tells me she's like the extremely beautiful but barren landscape of Ladakh.'

'Who's Ru?'

'Rusha. She's a distant cousin, twelve years older than me. She's a single mother. She stays beside us in Rupsa with her daughter. She's the only one I can talk to at home.'

'Is her daughter the fourteen-year-old niece you had once talked about?'

'Wow, what a memory,' Parush exclaimed.

'When did Ru become a mom?'

'When she was seventeen. Before that she had aborted twice, first time when she was your age. Hers is an interesting life. She didn't disclose the identity of Aru's father. When she was twenty-two she lost her parents in a car accident. Baba was in the US at that time. He brought her to India. Her parents had left enough money for her and she got even more in insurance after their death. Now, she freelances as an editor for several publishers in the US. Without her, our household would have disintegrated a long time ago.'

'Why's she still single?'

'I wanted to marry her when I was ten. I think she's waiting for me to grow up!' Parush started laughing. Bitasta stared at him with an eyeful of amazement. She came so close that her breath felt warm on Parush's face. 'Don't grow up,' she whispered into the sparse air fluttering between their faces.

***

'Ma is supportive of almost everything which would be condemned heavily by anyone in India or even in the West,' Bitasta said, as she led Parush through a narrow trail winding its way into the forest. 'She is exceptionally sympathetic to lesbians. She doesn't find any problem with teen sex, infidelity, two timing or for that matter, anything. If you do something from your heart, it's absolutely fine – that's her argument. Two years ago, just before we were leaving Nova Scotia, one girl in our neighbourhood got pregnant. She was thirteen, a year older than me. She was into drugs too. Ma didn't allow her parents to scold her or even discuss anything about the issue. She would go on long walks with her, leaving me alone at home in the evening, keeping aside our packing and other errands. I felt so jealous. Most times, I just feel jealous. I don't understand her well even now. But lately I've started appreciating her viewpoint. Do everything from your heart, she says, and don't think much about the world, about right or wrong.'

It was spring, just a few days before Dol, the festival of colour. The gibbous moon sprinkled through the mesh of leaves and branches of the tall sonajhuri, sal and eucalyptus trees, the gentle wind pleasantly playing through them, hissing around, caressing the two young people, who might not mind getting lost in the bir.

'I would often fight with her about her views on lesbianism,' Bitasta continued. 'But it never reached this point. She angrily left the house, leaving me fuming. Very soon I realised I had over-reacted. I felt bad.' She stopped and looked back at Parush, trailing her noisily on the narrow path padded with dried fallen leaves. 'And I felt worse when I got to know you had come. Say sorry!'

'Sorry,' Parush said like a robot.

'That's good. Once Ma had been gone, I saw an edition of AJP on my desk.'

'What's AJP?' asked Parush.

'It's the *American Journal of Psychology* published by the University of Illinois. Ma did her doctorate from UIUC on the evolution of prosody in classical languages like Greek and Sanskrit...'

'Evolution of what?' interrupted Parush.

'Will tell you later. Don't distract me. I'm going to tell you something really wacky. Ma's often requested to write articles for various journals, mainly published by UIUC. I heard her talking to someone over the phone recently about writing another article for AJP after ten years. Apparently, she had written a very controversial article for AJP in 1983. It was about the handling of lesbians and lesbianism in ancient epics and mythology. Given her love for lesbians I was not surprised that she had once written an article like that. This morning she had asked me to get some books and journals from an upper shelf. The edition of AJP should have been one of them. Knowing you wouldn't come soon I was browsing through it when I got the article. It was titled "*Draupadi Syndrome: Camouflaging Lesbianism Through Obscurities.*"'

'What?' Parush stopped walking. Bitasta pulled him by his hand. He walked by her side, wrapping her arm.

'It was a small article of a few pages and I read and reread it many times. She starts with Callisto, her favourite. Looks like, lesbianism is very rare in Greek mythology. Though there are indications that Callisto and Artemis are lovers, yet both are shown to have male partners, Zeus for Callisto and Endymion for Artemis, perhaps to camouflage the lesbian aspect. But then, Ma believes, the poets throw in some subtle obscurities which make the relationship with the male partners fishy, perhaps with the hope that some intelligent reader would see through the camouflage and realise the true identities.'

They heard a sound on the dried leaves behind them. Parush got scared. Bitasta held his arm tighter. Parush felt assured, not thinking how Bitasta could really save them, should they come across some danger.

'Zeus is shown to have sex with Callisto disguised as Artemis. On the other hand, Artemis, in a different avatar as the moon Goddess Selene, fantasises a sleeping Endymion. Under natural circumstance why would a man have sex with a woman disguised as a woman? And why would a woman fantasise about a sleeping man? Ma feels these are obscurities intentionally inserted by the poets.'

'Endymion?' asked Parush. 'Isn't it a poem by Keats?'

'Yes, it's one of his best ones – a very long one though, which starts with his signature line: *A thing of beauty is a joy forever*.'

They could hear faint sounds of drums. 'We're close by,' she said. 'Those are the sounds of tumdak, the Santal drums....' She stopped walking and listened to the sounds with more attention.

'*Dum-dum-dum-dum, di-di-di-di-di-dum, dum-di-dum-dum-di-dum-dum*... That's Mandakranta. Ma is reciting Kalidasa today.' She pulled Parush. 'Come, there's a surprise for you.'

They started walking towards the sounds of tumdak.

'At one place Artemis is surnamed Calliste, indicating that Artemis and Callisto may be the same person. This may be another level of intentional obscurity, which, Ma thinks, may indicate that the two girls are united in love, that they have become one in love. Now let's come to Draupadi. Very controversially, Ma says that Draupadi may be five girls united in love. Here too, the lesbian aspect has been camouflaged by bringing in male partners.'

'That's quite ridiculous. And where are the obscurities here?'

'There are many. I don't remember all of them. But there's one I remember, a very popular one. It's said that Arjun wins Draupadi at the swayamvar and the five brothers bring her proudly to their mother Kunti. "Mother," they say, "see what we've brought." At this point, it's ridiculously claimed that Kunti thinks her sons have brought the daily provisions. She asks the five brothers to *divide it equally* among them – that's the justification given for Draupadi's marriage to all the five brothers. Ma feels, a writer like Vyasa couldn't have written this crap without a purpose. It's said elsewhere that Kunti herself divides the daily provisions and that the provisions are never divided equally – Bhim gets half and the remaining half is for the rest of the family. So, this very incident of Kunti asking the Pandavas to *share it equally* is bullshit. Vyasa, Ma feels, has used this as an intentional obscurity to arouse suspicion in the mind of an intelligent reader.'

'But what's the point in camouflaging and then again leaving a pointer?'

'That's because the sensitive poets might not have wanted their strong female lesbian characters to face the wrath of the common people. But at the same time, they hoped that a good reader would surely find out their true identities and respect the characters the way they are. Draupadi, Callisto and Artemis are all very strong characters and the poets, true to their sensitivities, took extra care to preserve their dignity.'

'But isn't it cruel or insensitive to force male partners on lesbians, even though it's a camouflage?'

'Porus, I'm impressed,' Bitasta said coquettishly, pressing his hands.

They could see lights at a distance. The base sounds of the drum became louder. Parush could identify Panchali's voice. The jungle suddenly ended and, like a suddenly opened fist, burst ajar into an open space. Parush saw Panchali seated on a raised platform, her back towards them, reciting something, and a group of Santal girls repeating the same along with the beats of the tumdak.

'*Teero-panta, stanita-subhagam*,' Bitasta recited with her mother, '*pasyasi-swadu-yasmat / sabhru-bhangam, mukham-iva-payo, vetravatyash-chalormi*.'

'What does it mean?'

'There, Vetravati's stream ambrosial laves / A gentle bank, with mildly murmuring waves; / And there, her rippling brow and polished face / Invite thy smiles, and sue for thy embrace...'

Suddenly she turned towards Parush, embraced him and started crying, drowning her face into his shoulders. 'Ma, I'm sorry... I really don't understand you, Ma ... I'm sorry... Ma, I love you, I really love you...'

PDAs, Parush realised again, made him uncomfortable.

Parush didn't notice when Panchali had appeared behind them.

RUPSA

When Srinjay, Parush's father, had brought Rusha from the US, Parush was just ten. He wanted to keep her and her four-year-old daughter Arushi in his own house in Rupsa, a small neighbourhood in suburban Calcutta. But Rusha wanted to stay alone. Sairandhri, Parush's mother, who neither showed any fondness nor animosity towards any of Srinjay's relatives, surprisingly developed an instant liking for Rusha. She came up with a solution, something that she rarely did in any family affair. Srinjay bought a plot beside theirs and constructed a house for Rusha. The live-in maid who had been with Srinjay's household for long, was deployed to take care of Rusha's household.

Rusha very soon overcame the initial suspicion and indifference with which her new neighbourhood would look at her, given her single mother status and outrageous background already known to all in bits and pieces. The same elders, who would initially talk about her in the post-lunch all-women gossip sessions with sarcasm and acrimony, gradually became sympathetic to her. Rusha tried hard to adapt to the alien land she never had seen before. She struggled to follow the *bangal* accent of her neighbours who spoke in various dialects of East Bengal. Within a few months she too could speak a form of comprehensible Bangla. So much was she in the good books of the neighbourhood elders that it was totally overlooked that she had started having male guests, mostly foreigners from Alliance Francaise she had got associated with, some of whom would stay quite late, or even overnight.

Young girls in Rupsa looked at her as their role model, independent, strong, but friendly and homely too.

The one who was most happy with her arrival was Parush.

Parush would often babysit the toddler Arushi, who was the same age as his own sister. The two girls fought violently with each other and Parush tried to keep them apart, while Rusha corrected manuscripts. She wore dresses – denim shorts that exposed her legs, small tops that showed her belly and the small ring on her belly button, spaghettis and halter tops that showed her deep neckline – which he had only seen in movies. He would look at her long bare legs with amazement. He would stare at her face for many moments, unnoticed, watching her scribbling on a bunch of papers, biting the end of the pencil and thinking, chewing her nails, stretching back on her chair and relaxing with her hands behind her head. 'What are you staring at?' she asked Parush one day.

'I want to marry you when I grow up,' he answered. 'You're so beautiful Ru.'

'It'll be my pleasure if you still love me like this after ten years,' she said. Parush didn't understand what she meant. 'Come here,' she called him, 'I want to give you a tight hug for such a sweet compliment.'

Parush would run to her house after returning from school. He no longer had to spend the afternoons lonely at home, babysitting his little sister or flipping the pages of the books he would get from the school library, their maid dozing off in some corner of their big house.

One afternoon he found the door of Ru's room closed. He peeped through the key-hole of the door and instantly stiffened, like a statue. Ru was lying on the bed, frantically scratching the bed-sheet with her nails, her clothes scattered on the floor and a boy's head inserted between her half folded, wide open legs. She appeared to be moaning in pain, but something within him told him she was not in agony. Something within him told him he shouldn't look at the unblemished bare body of Ru. But still, he didn't move a bit, remaining stuck to the key-hole. The boy got up and jumped on her and she tightly crossed her legs over him. While he rocked violently she groaned and moaned till Parush no longer could keep his eyes on the key-hole. He felt uneasy. He ran away from Ru's house. He went to his room and lay on the bed. But he couldn't lie for long. He was feeling more uneasy. He felt a peculiar sensation in his legs, a sensation he hadn't felt earlier. To his pleasure he realised the sensation was not actually in his legs. He stared at his pants which seemed to be wet. But he hadn't peed. What was happening to him? He was panting. He felt tired. He ran to the bathroom.

That night he fell sick. Ru came to see him. She sat beside him, putting her hand on his forehead. He couldn't look at her.

The next day, when he felt better, he went to Ru's house. He climbed the stairs silently and appeared in front of her bedroom, which was also the place she worked. The door was open. He entered the room. He could hear the water gushing out of the shower from the attached bathroom, which strangely didn't have any door – Ru had told that was how it was in the US. He stood still in front of the bed. The shower stopped. He felt the similar sensation he had felt the previous day. He didn't move. Slowly Ru appeared in the room. Still, he didn't move. Ru was shocked to see him standing in front of her, perplexed, his face down, breathing heavily. In a fast reflex action, she snatched the towel lying on the bed and wrapped it around her body. He stayed where he stood. 'Sweety,' she said gently, water dripping from her body, 'you can enter Ru's room anytime without asking. But for anyone else, please knock before entering.'

Ru went to the dresser and returned shortly in her typical attire – shorts and a tee. She found Parush sitting on the bed, crying.

'What happened, my dear?' she asked affectionately, wrapping him in her arms.

'Ru, yesterday I saw everything through the key-hole,' Parush managed to say and broke down. 'Am I a bad boy Ru?'

It didn't take longer than a moment for Ru to realise what had happened. She left Parush and sat on her working chair, covering her face with her hands. She didn't speak for some time. When she turned she found Parush standing in front of her. 'Ru, I saw it again in the night, in my dream,' he said, rubbing his eyes.

She stared at him for some time. 'Go to the bathroom,' she said, getting up from the chair, 'and clean yourself. I'll get a new set of clothes for you.'

***

Over a weekend Parush had come to Calcutta, to see Ru. Waiting in the living room for her to complete her phone call, Parush had been thinking of her, the woman who, very unusually had made him feel like a man when he had still been a kid. Over the years she became a very special person, someone who couldn't be described by any conventional or commonly understandable relationship. She was a part of everything – his dreams and fantasies, his secrets and expressions, his excitement and ecstasy, his feelings and sentiments, his satisfaction and frustration, his home and life. It was perhaps only to see Ru from time to time that he would come to Calcutta from KGP, almost every week.

Parush glanced at the new stock of La Terra and Sutter Home at the small bar tucked in the corner of the living room.

Ah! She looked so sophisticated and elegant while drinking wine – glimpses of Ru whizzed through Parush's thoughts. She had the elegance he had rarely seen in anyone else. He ruminated on how fabulous she looked in her Vero Moda, Guess or Pierre

Hardy dresses… and her diamond earrings … and her exclusive accessories, kinds of which were still not available in India. Ever since he had outgrown the age of total incomprehension, he had realised how different Ru was from everyone, in every aspect.

Sitting alone in Ru's living room, Parush played around with a collage of scattered images, in his mind – her low neck slim dresses, gowns, her shorts, tees … her loose straight hair… her slender hands and legs…

'Is Baba having an affair with Stuti Auntie?' Parush asked, when Ru ended the call.

'Why do you ask that?' Ru came and sat beside him.

'Yesterday I reached home a little late. As usual, Ma had fallen asleep. A little unusually, Baba was waiting for me. After dinner we were chatting in the living room. The phone rang at around midnight. I lifted the receiver as it was closer to me. Baba had almost jumped to take the call. There was a brief silence after my "Hello", when I heard Stuti Auntie's voice. After asking me some stupid questions she asked if Baba was around. I went upstairs to my room. The lights in the living room were on for more than an hour.'

'Can't a married woman talk to a married man in the night?' Ru asked, straight-faced.

'I've noticed a few other things too.'

'Sweety, your father is one of the most wonderful men I've seen in my life. Any woman would fall for him. So did your mother long, really long ago, if I believe whatever I've heard. But you know your mother is just an exquisite mural, a sexy piece of art. She is a mystery woman to me. Even I feel allured by her beauty, her charm. I'm sure your father would have fallen head over heels the first time he saw her. She would've been even more beautiful some thirty years ago. I see people just gaping at her wherever she goes. Even I feel jealous when I'm with her. From outside she's just the perfect woman a man can desire. She's the heady mix of glamour and glory. When she talks, people can't but listen to her. I can spend hours just listening to her talking about anything ranging from classical literature, her own subject, to contemporary politics like Babri Masjid and Mandal Commission. Her views are crisp and arguments razor sharp. But then you also know she hasn't slept with your father for ages. It's not that she doesn't care for you, but still, don't you wish she were like the other mothers? So why can't your father think of other women?'

That was exactly what Ru was for. It was not that Parush couldn't fathom what Ru had just said. But hearing from her, sort of legitimised the thoughts. That way, he felt better.

'Why is my family like this, Ru?' he asked.

'Because,' Ru replied, 'you too are like that.'

'What do you mean?'

'Has it ever occurred to you how weird it could be for me to know your thoughts … your sentiments … your fantasies … about me? But still I've accepted you the way you are, the way you behave naturally, without any inhibition, without any prejudice. Don't judge things on face value. See from within. See with your heart…'

***

'Ma,' Parush called out from outside the room which had been closed all the times he had passed by since the previous night. Finally, he decided to knock in the afternoon.

'Come in,' Sairandhri said from inside.

Parush pushed open the door and entered his mother's room, a room that was one of the lesser frequented ones in the house. He looked around the room. He remembered Panchali's room in Prembajar currently occupied by Bitasta. Even the smell of this room, he felt, was different. All the windows were shut. Sairandhri was reading a book at her desk under an old-fashioned table lamp.

'Can I open the window?' asked Parush.

'Yes, go ahead,' Sairandhri said, closing the book she was reading.

Parush sat on the bed, facing her. He wondered how his mother looked so beautiful anytime of the day.

He had rarely paid attention to anything in this room. Perhaps for the first time he noticed books at her desk. He got up and took the two books of poems written by Elizabeth Barrett Browning and Christina Rossetti in his hand. 'I think I've seen these two books somewhere else,' he said.

'You would have seen them at Kalyani, I mean Panchali's place,' Sairandhri said promptly and immediately added, 'I haven't met them for such a long time. I confused Panchali with Kalyani, another friend of ours.'

Yes, Parush recalled, that was absolutely correct. Among the heap of books and journals he had seen at Panchali's desk the first time he had been to their house, were these two books. Parush hadn't heard before the names of any of these poets. 'Ya,' Bitasta had said, 'they are not among the most popular English poets of the nineteenth century. Both are among Ma's favourites…'

'Rabindranath had translated quite a few poems written by his contemporaries in England and America,' continued Sairandhri. 'We came to know of Mrs Browning, Augusta Webster and Rossetti in that connection. They became our favourites.' She paused, as though to remember something, closing her eyes and leaning back on the chair. '*Golden head by golden head*,' she started reciting, '*Like two pigeons in one nest / Folded in each other's wings, / They lay down in their curtained bed: / Like two blossoms on one stem, / Like two flakes of new-fall'n snow, / Like two wands of ivory / Tipped with gold for awful kings…*'

She opened her eyes and looked at an amazed Parush. 'I still remember searching for a whole day for two copies of these two books in the lanes and by-lanes of College Street.'

It was perhaps the first time Parush heard his mother recollect something with fondness. He had started to believe that perhaps she didn't have any memory worth remembering. He knew that she and Panchali had been closest friends. They had grown up together in KGP. They had studied together at Shantiniketan. They had even dated his and Bitasta's fathers together during their occasional visits to KGP. But she, or even his father, rarely talked about those days. Given their current state of affairs, Parush was not surprised at that. But at that moment, he was pleasantly surprised.

'Why are you suddenly out of touch?' he asked.

Sairandhri didn't respond immediately. She got up from the chair, walked towards the open window and leaned against it. 'How are they?' she asked. 'I heard you go to their place pretty often.'

'Not very often,' he said. 'I've been a few times. Kakima is a wonderful woman.'

'And how's Bitasta? She and Pushi were born at the same time.'

'She's at least a hundred times more mature than Pushi,' he said with a vengeance. 'I just can't understand how two girls of the same age can be so different. I wish Pushi would grow up faster.'

'I have never seen her. They moved to America and then... We lost touch...' The sadness in her face made her look even more beautiful. He felt like running towards her and hugging her like a child.

'Why don't you come to KGP sometime?' he asked.

***

'Get a fag,' Bitasta asked, once she and Parush had settled on the raised chairs of Scoop overlooking the Ganga at Outram Ghat.

Early Sunday morning Parush had got a call from her. 'Ma and I have come to Calcutta last night,' she informed. 'Didu, my grandmother, is not keeping well.'

'How long would you be in Calcutta?' asked Parush.

'Don't know, may be a few days. I'm getting bored here.'

Parush tried to figure out if she was giving any hint. 'Want to meet?'

'What else do you think I've called for?' She never minced words. A few hours later he picked her up from New Alipore.

'Fag?' Parush asked in surprise, adjusting the height of the chair. 'You smoke?'

'Don't irritate me,' she shrugged. 'I'm having my cycle.'

'You're having cycle?' Parush said so loud that the couples at the nearby tables looked at them, the girls concealing their smiles and the guys feeling ashamed on his behalf. He was perforated by the piercing glare of Bitasta's eyes. Between the slit of her lips he could see her teeth, holding back the anger she tried to control with her closed fists.

He got up. 'I'll get it,' he said and ran out of Scoop. He almost collided against a street vendor selling cigarettes and other stuff on a hand pulled trolley. 'Give one packet,' he said, pointing towards the rows of cigarettes. 'Kaunsa?' asked the vendor. That was when he realised he didn't know which brand Bitasta preferred. He ran towards Scoop.

Bitasta was still glaring at him. 'Which brand?' Parush asked.

'Baba takes Dunhill; so do I.'

Parush ran back to the vendor and asked for Dunhill. The vendor started laughing. Parush was irritated. 'What's your problem?' he asked.

'If that's how you want to impress a girl, take her to better places. I only have these,' the vendor said, pointing towards the packs of Charminar and Gold Flake.

'Where do I get Dunhill?' Parush asked him, ignoring his remark.

'There's someone in front of Akash Vani. He may have it.'

Parush stopped a taxi, knowing very well that no one would agree to go such a short distance. He lied that he wanted to go to Howrah Station. 'Go via Akash Vani,' he said while the driver pushed on the accelerator. He found the vendor in front of Akash Vani and asked the driver to stop. After buying one pack of Dunhill and exhausting a good part of his weekly cash reserve he asked the driver to take him back to Scoop. 'I've forgotten my bag there,' he said convincingly. The unsuspecting driver drove him back to the place where the amused cigarette seller was still waiting, perhaps for Parush to return. He threw a twenty rupee note to the perplexed driver and ran to Bitasta with the catch of the day.

Very casually Bitasta lit the cigarette from a half burnt one a guy sitting beside them was holding in his hand, causing his girl companion to stare at her with suspicion. 'You really don't know girls have menstrual cycles?' she whispered, coming back to her seat.

'Oh no,' Parush exclaimed, and then immediately brought his voice down. 'I knew you call it periods. I'm really sorry. I didn't know…'

'Dumbo,' she interrupted, blowing smoke on his face. 'What do you know?'

That was a very philosophical question, Parush felt. He somehow knew that silence would be one of the more acceptable responses to such questions.

'You don't smoke?' she asked.

'No.'

'You don't smoke. I haven't heard you ever say "fuck" or even "shit". What kind of a guy are you? Do you have girlfriends?'

'Girlfriends? Plural?' Parush started laughing.

'Expected. Girls prefer masculine guys. You're too feminine.'

'You don't like me?'

'Oh, when did I say that?' she blew smoke again on his face. 'Don't irritate me.'

The guy Bitasta had lighted her fag from was leaving. 'All the best dude,' he whispered to Parush while passing by them.

Parush inhaled the smoke.

MANDAKRANTA

Parush had bunked the entire second half that day and gone to Prembajar just after lunch. His family – his parents and sister Pushi – would be arriving from Calcutta sometime in the evening, along with Bitasta's father.

***

'*O thou sweet lotus-smelling little flirt, my plump little darling, call it a Mandakranta.*' Panchali was talking about *Shruta Bodha*, a treatise of Sanskrit prosody written by Kalidasa. 'That's how he teaches a beautiful young girl. And then, to enliven the dull subject, he makes love to her while explaining the meters. I believe love was like a poem to Kalidasa and lovemaking the prosody, the meter of the poem.'

'Ma, someone here may be already fantasising about his English teacher,' Bitasta commented. Parush seriously repented for the titbit he had shared with her about their English teacher whose classes went housefull, even on Friday evenings. Bitasta cherished his embarrassment. 'Don't blush Porus. You should go for private classes like this babe of Kalidasa.'

Parush's discomfort was visible in his face. Panchali came to his rescue. 'Arca, why do you have to always tease him?' she mock-rebuked Bitasta.

'Ma,' Bitasta complained, 'why do you always take his side? This is unfair.'

Parush looked at Panchali, who was staring at him. Panchali, he felt, might not be as strikingly beautiful as his mother. Her round face with not-so-long eyes and not-so-sharp nose were in stark contrast to his mother's well chiselled features etched out artistically, as though, on a glittering rock. But all her plumpness created the effect of a mellifluous music whose notes were blended with each other, making the identification of each discreet note impossible. What would Ru say about her? If his mother was, in her words, like the landscape of Ladakh, teeming with the sharp contours of barren mountains, wouldn't Panchali augur the grace of a lush green meadow?

Meadows, he realised, mesmerised him more.

Panchali pulled Bitasta's ear. 'Like most classical poets,' she continued, 'Kalidasa uses prosody as the background score for his poetries. Like a raga, a meter too signifies emotions, colours, day and night, winter and summer...'

Parush wondered if he kept visiting Prembajar to meet Bitasta or to see Panchali. What was that which attracted him so much to Panchali? Was it the fact that she had hugged and kissed him like his mother never did, or was it something else? For a moment he could visualise himself in Ru's room, seated on her bed, beguiled, like that girl of *Shruta Bodha*, listening with rapt attention to her.

'Homer uses dactylic hexameter in his epics as the background score for his heroic tales, to create an everlasting myth out of his grand characters and magnificent events. The meter is best suited for such grand odes. And Kalidasa uses Mandakranta for his *Meghaduta*, *The Cloud Messenger*, to create the perfect ambience for a languid and stretched love-making with a long and leisurely foreplay.'

Daktulos, she explained, means finger in Greek. With its three bones, one longer, followed by two shorter, it's the origin of dactyl, a metrical foot which sounds like "**dum** di di", the first syllable "**dum**" being stressed or longer and the following two shorter.

'The dum and di are like the bols of tabla, the notes or symbols used to denote a beat,' she said. 'You can also think of "dum" and "di" as the whole and half notes in a staff notation. "**Twin**kle **twin**kle **lit**tle **star**" sounds like **dum** di **dum** di **dum** di **dum**, and so does "**Jack** and **Jill** went **up** the **hill**". A rhythm like this suits a nursery rhyme. But a rhythm, which goes like **dum** di di – **dum** di di – **dum** di di – **dum** di di – **dum** di di – **dum dum**, creates the aura of an august and grandiose setting. That's the perfect ambience for a heroic narration.'

She closed her eyes and joined her palms in the posture of a namaskar. 'Listen to these verses from Odyssey: ***An**dra moi – **en**nepe, – **Mou**sa, pol–**u**tropon, – **hos** mala – **pol**la / **Planch**the ep–**ei Troi**–es hier–**on** ptoli–**eth**ron ep–**er**se.* Tell me, Muse, of the man versatile and resourceful, who wandered many a sea-mile, after he ransacked Troy's holy city.'

She opened her eyes and stared at Parush. 'You have to feel it. You must get into it. It's just like music. Unless each note, each sound, doesn't resonate within you, you don't get high; you don't feel intoxicated. This rhythm arouses a sense of respect, grandeur and valour. It may not be a mere coincidence that Rabindranath too used dactyls for our national anthem. ***Bha**rata – **bha**gya vi–**dha**ta, **dra**vida – **ut**kala – **van**ga*: the same dactylic feet. The meter of *Jana-Gana-Mana* may be a variation of dactylic heptameter.'

It suddenly occurred to Parush that despite being two totally different personalities, Panchali and his mother had a surprisingly similar way of reciting a poem. That day, when he had heard his mother recite a poem for the first time, she had the same passion, the same posture and the same looks. He had been wondering for some time what exactly might have brought them so close that his mother could tell him so confidently that Panchali would still have those two books of poems on her desk, despite not being in touch for close to twenty years.

'Kakima,' he said, 'I wonder why you and Ma haven't been in touch for so long.'

'Tell me Ma,' suddenly Bitasta sprang up, 'did you two fight over a common guy and then fall out? Or...' she paused, and seemed to have got a really naughty idea. 'is it that you originally loved Porus' father and his mother Baba, and then both of you started cheating on them with the other one and finally landed up marrying each other's boyfriends?'

There was a sudden silence, punctured by Bitasta's loud laughter.

'Parush,' asked Panchali, 'can you please beat her on my behalf? I've given up on her.'

'Thanks Kakima, for the privilege,' Parush got up. Bitasta too got up from beside her mother and walked towards him. She stood in front of him, her back towards her mother. 'Want to beat me?' she almost whispered, arching her eyebrows and coming uncomfortably close. Before he could react, she made a gesture of a kiss with her lips and winked at him. 'Beat me,' she said loudly, audible enough for her mother to hear, who for sure hadn't seen or heard anything else. She allowed a few more moments to lapse and then got back to her seat.

'Ma, he dares to get physical,' she said. Slapping her mildly on her head Panchali got up to oversee the arrangements in the kitchen – Parush's family, his parents and sister, and Shaunak, Bitasta's father, would be arriving soon.

***

'Come here,' Bitasta signalled with her index finger once Panchali had gone. Parush got up and sat beside her on the sofa which still had Panchali's warmth. 'Are you still confused how a frowning countenance could be seductive?' she asked, referring to a light discussion they had had the last time he had been here. They were discussing about a verse from *Meghaduta* where *sa-bhru-bhangam-mukham*, a frowning countenance with arching brows, is meant to be seductive. Frowning eyebrows, he had argued, means irritation or anger, but no way kinky or suggestive.

Suddenly, Bitasta pulled his shirt by her right hand and dragged him very close to her. With her left hand she opened the first button of her shirt. While she went on to open another button she took a deep breath, opened her mouth, frowned and released the breath on his face with a deep hushed sound. She winked at him again and whispered slowly, moving her lips and tongue more than necessary, 'Dumbo, do you still think a frowning countenance is not seductive?'

They heard a car stopping in front of the house. 'They've come,' Parush said, trying to extricate himself from this awkward moment.

'It'll take at least a few minutes for them to get out of the car, take the luggage out, walk to the door and press the bell. I'm not going to leave you so easily Porus. Tell me what else do you think is more seductive?'

Bitasta was wrong in her estimation. The bell rang sooner than she had expected.

***

Shaunak and Srinjay, Bitasta's and Parush's fathers, had always been in touch since their graduation from IIT KGP in 1968. They had initially worked together with *Hellmuth, Obata and Kassabaum* in the early seventies for a few years. Since then they worked in various architecture consultancy firms in the US and India. Lately Shaunak had returned to HOK, shuttling between KGP and the

US, and Srinjay had been with Venkataraman Associates, working out of Calcutta. Since the past few years they had been nurturing the idea of setting up their own firm in India.

With an eminent economist at the helm of financial affairs in India and the nascent signs of liberalisation already visible in various forms, they saw very good prospects in India, in the nineties. 'I'm sure there will be a huge demand for world class malls, office spaces and housing in the coming years,' Srinjay had told Shaunak the previous year when they had met for the *AIA Convention* at Boston. At the same convention they bumped into Tuhin, their KGP batch-mate, whom Shaunak hadn't met since 1968. He too was excited with the concept of IPC, *Indus Planning and Consultancy*, the name they had already chosen for their venture, whenever it started. 'Indus Valley was great in urban planning and we're also going to do the same,' Srinjay said to Tuhin. 'IPC will stand for international standards. We'll use a lot of elements from traditional Indian architecture...'

A week ago, Srinjay had got a call from Shaunak. 'I'm returning to India next week,' he had said. 'From the airport I'll directly come over to your place. I've something important to discuss with you about IPC. Then we all are going to Prembajar.'

Bitasta and Parush had been very excited about this, which would be a sort of reunion of old friends, especially their mothers, Panchali and Sairandhri. They had made an elaborate plan for the weekend. Bitasta had never had such an occasion in Prembajar, she had told Parush, where there would be so many people at their house.

'I've heard so much about your mother,' she had said a day before. 'I just can't wait to see her in person...'

Parush had expected some dramatic moments when his mother would finally meet Bitasta's mother after so long. But the union was very sober, rather too restrained to be true. He could understand his mother's reaction, or rather the lack of it. But what was surprising was Panchali's behaviour, the way she met his mother, as though they hadn't been out of touch ever.

As expected, Parush could feel the uncomfortable vibes between Bitasta and his sister. Pushi announced she wouldn't share the bed with Bitasta. 'I can't sleep with you,' she said. 'That's fine,' replied Bitasta, 'I'll sleep with your brother then.'

In a chorus both Parush and Pushi asked, 'What?'

'Relax,' Bitasta smiled, 'you sleep alone here. We'll make some other arrangements.'

***

Relishing the lavish dinner spread, Srinjay threw the idea. 'Guys,' he said, 'we're meeting here, at this place, after twenty years. It's time to celebrate. Let's do the same thing we did last time. Let's go to…'

'Bhonsraghat,' Sairandhri, Parush's mother, snatched the word from her husband, her eyes sparkling. 'Yes, let's go to Bhonsraghat. That's a wonderful place on the banks of Subarnarekha.' She turned towards Panchali. 'Kalyani,' she asked her excitedly, 'isn't Bhonsraghat very much like Sonajhuri on Kopai, the place we would visit so often from Shantiniketan?'

Panchali looked uncomfortable. 'Sairi,' she said hesitantly, addressing Parush's mother as Sairi, something which Parush hadn't heard anyone calling his mother by, 'how did you forget my name?'

Sairandhri too seemed uncomfortable. 'Sorry Panchali,' she apologised, 'I'm really sorry.'

'Who's Kalyani?' asked Srinjay.

'She was one of our classmates in Shantiniketan,' Panchali replied immediately, 'I… I used to give her proxy … and … and people jokingly called me Kalyani.'

Parush stared at Bitasta. She too would have realised the cover-up. He recalled Sairandhri had referred to Panchali as Kalyani yet another time, in front of him, when she had mentioned casually that Panchali might also have the two books of poems written by Elizabeth Barrett Browning and Christina Rossetti on her desk. Who was Kalyani?

***

After dinner everyone packed into two cars – Srinjay's Tata Sierra which he had driven from Calcutta and Shaunak's Maruti 1000. Parush drove the Maruti, Bitasta sitting in the front seat and his sister Pushi behind.

Bitasta tried to initiate futile conversations with Pushi during the forty-five-minute journey to Bhonsraghat, a major part of which was on the straight road via Salua Air Force Base through dark stretches of forests.

'You're in Modern High, right?' Bitasta started.

'Ya,' replied Pushi with exceptional brevity.

The short answer stopped that line of communication. But Bitasta persisted some more.

'Does your brother flirt with your friends?' she asked after some time.

'No. He hates them and so do they.'

'Why?'

'I don't know.'

'What type of girls does your brother like?'

'He doesn't like girls.'

Bitasta took no time to realise the insurmountable gap between the siblings. She didn't continue with her effort.

***

They stopped their cars on the dry river bed close to the bank. Initially, all of them sat together. But when Shaunak and Srinjay started talking about IPC the others got bored. 'Why don't you stay here and talk for some more time?' offered Bitasta. 'We'll take a walk by the water.'

'Is it safe?' asked Pushi.

'Absolutely,' assured Shaunak.

'I'll stay here,' said Pushi. Bitasta and Parush walked with their mothers towards the water. The half-moon provided just the right degree of lighting required. The tall eucalyptus and sonajhuri trees lining the banks appeared like dark boundary walls and the sandy river-bed more barren than it might be in reality. The sparkling water, without any ripple or wave, lay listlessly over the bed, without any urgency to flow. They sat on the hull of an upturned boat.

'Kopai is so much like Subarnarekha,' Panchali spoke first.

'Do you remember,' asked Sairandhri, 'we had identified a particular place on the bank of Kopai which, we believed, resembles Kalidasa's description of the Gambhira River in *Meghaduta*?'

'What description?' Bitasta asked before her mother could respond.

'***Tasya-kimchit***,' Sairandhri started reciting, '*kara-dhritam-iva,* ***prapta****-vanira-****shakham*** */* ***hritva-nilam****, salila-vasanam,* ***mukta-rodho****-nitambam*. It's Mandakranta, a very seductive meter. It goes like this: **dum-dum-dum-dum**, di-di-di-di-di-**dum**, **dum** di **dum-dum** di **dum-dum**. But when it goes on and on, and Kalidasa weaves eroticism around it, it's more than just seduction...'

Parush was no longer amazed that his mother was talking like Panchali. That day, when she had recited a poem for the first time in front of him, he had realised that his mother had another façade, hidden from them, which only Panchali could make her reveal.

As Sairandhri talked, Parush felt as though his mother was oblivious of the presence of anyone else, other than Panchali. 'The banks of the river are like her nitamba, buttocks, and the water the garment which covers them. When the water recedes, exposing the banks, it's like a lover pulling the garment off his girl, revealing her bare back. The trees whose branches droop into the water are like her arms with which she tries to hold her blue water-garment. But finally, she fails. She gives in…

'O friend, if thou art gliding down to her, thy departure will be difficult; for who that has known their taste, would be able to leave a girl whose garment has slipped off her thighs…

'Her girdle-band of a row of birds tinkles, and gracefully gliding, flows away, leaving her whirlpool navel exposed to view. She can't talk, for the first word of love in a woman is confusion in presence of a lover…'

As Sairandhri recited the verses from *Meghaduta*, Parush visualised himself as the cloud messenger, flying over rivers transformed into wonderful girls, more alluring than the student of Kalidasa whom he would teach Sanskrit meters. But who was the girl, whose skirt he saw slipping off her waist, slowly, like the slow advances of mandakranta, whose girdle he saw gliding down her thighs, whose navel he could presently see, unconcealed, unadorned, unblemished, untouched, moving up and down, slowly, as slow as the slow advances of mandakranta?

'Her cool breeze, carrying far the love-cooing of the cranes in the early morning and impregnated by the fragrance of the blooming lotus, removes the love-making lassitude of the women, like their flattering husbands…'

Why was Parush not able to see her face? He knew, for sure, she was not Ru. Her oblong face was tilted to the left. She was pulling him by his shirt. '*You want to beat me*?' she whispered into his ears.

Sounds of heavy breaths, like a wild wind hissing through a drenched and exhausted forest, interrupted Parush's fantasy. He stared at Bitasta. She was staring at him too, her face tilted to the left.

The heavy breaths were of his mother, sitting just beside him.

Panchali's eyes sparkled. Was she crying?

The next day she was unusually quiet, as Parush had always seen Sairandhri to be.

ILLU

The Durga Pujo was perhaps the only time of the year Parush really enjoyed himself at Rupsa. Lately the Durga Pujo in their para, the name by which any small neighbourhood like Rupsa is colloquially known, had attained a grand status. An over-creative, hyper-enthusiastic and unbelievably passionate but mysteriously jobless *dada*, a unique species available in every para in Calcutta, had become the self-proclaimed captain of virtually all events in Rupsa. A few years back he had done something really crazy. He converted a small pujo in a nondescript suburb of Calcutta into a '*theme-er pujo*', which literally means a *pujo* with a *theme*, but actually conveys a much greater idea in the context of Durga Pujo, the most lavish carnival of Calcutta. It means that the pandal, the enclosure in which the idols are kept during the auspicious period of their worship, and its entire decoration would be done in one of the wackiest ways unfathomable even in the common man's wildest dreams. The very aberrance of the entire concept of a '*theme-er pujo*' guaranteed instant popularity.

In the first year Rupsa had used paper cups, the ones used by the street-side vendors to dispense the smallest amounts of ice-creams, for creating the exterior and interior façade of the pandal and almost everything noticeable. The next year Rupsa witnessed autos-full of metal caps of Thumps-Up bottles being unloaded in front of the scaffolding of the pandal few days before the pujo. This year it was a simple diya, the small earthen lamp, which constituted the fundamental element of the theme for Rupsa's silver jubilee Durga Pujo. Parush, atop an elevated rostrum, making continuous announcements for lost parents and found kids, saw Bitasta behind a few thousand-people winding towards the main entrance of the pandal at a speed which would make a snail laugh.

Bitasta was literally struggling with her sari, revealing and divulging totally unexpected and unintended things comprising the paraphernalia of a girl's pujo-fashion. 'Rita Bose,' Parush was announcing, 'your little son is with us at the office. Please come here immediately and collect him. Nayana Sen, your daughter is waiting for you at our office... Bitasta, you've lost something. Please come and collect it from our office. Bitasta, Bitasta, can you hear me? Please come here...'

'So, she's the one who has dethroned me,' Ru whispered into Parush's ears, when Bitasta waved her hands finally. 'What a smart girl and what a stupid thing she has lost. I'll announce. You go ahead.' Parush handed over the microphone to Ru and started climbing down the rostrum. 'Bitasta,' Ru announced, 'we're sending your stuff to you. Please take care and don't lose it again...'

'Doesn't it look like our Illu, without the light?' asked Bitasta, staring at the façade of the huge diya shaped pandal made of diyas. 'That's what you call a theme? You guys have been doing it for forty years and still you find this intriguing?'

That was when it occurred to Parush that the grandest of the inter-hostel events in KGP, the Illumination competition, popularly known as Illu, would perhaps make for the most majestic *theme*. Seen from a distance, thousands of lit diyas attached to huge bamboo structures appeared like flickering pixels on a dark screen, creating wonderful pictures, some simple, some expressionist, all lasting just for a few minutes till the diyas had enough oil to burn the wick.

'That's Ru, right?' Bitasta asked, pointing towards the rostrum.

'Ya,' replied Parush.

'Fuck,' Bitasta exclaimed, 'she's so hot!' Few heads turned towards her, like reflex actions. Parush dragged her fast towards the rostrum.

***

The IIT opened after the DPs, the Durga Pujo holidays. Parush was at Bitasta's house a few days later, immediately after she had returned to Prembajar – she too had been to Calcutta during the Durga Pujo.

'Why do you think RK can't win Illu this time too?' Bitasta asked, referring to the Radha Krishnan Hall of Residence, the hostel where Parush stayed.

'Pushpen, our main artist, has fractured his right arm and can't do anything,' Parush replied. 'Moreover it's really tough to beat Nehru – they are the best.'

Bitasta thought for some time. She went inside and brought the cordless phone and dialled a number. 'Sister,' she said over the phone, 'I'll give one more painting tomorrow. Please don't send the magazine to the press now.'

'Why didn't you tell me earlier?' she asked Parush, after hanging up. 'You could have told me before the DPs. Anyway, if you listen to me, RK can win this time.'

'What do you mean?'

'I'll tell you what Nehru is doing this time. You do the same.'

'Nehru and RK putting up the same stuff? Everyone will say we stole from them. Given that Nehru has won it the last three times no one will ever think they could steal from us.'

'And what if they finally do something else, much worse than what they've planned to do now?'

'Why will they suddenly change their plan and do something worse?'

'Well, they wouldn't change the plan or do something worse by choice. They wouldn't have any other choice.'

'I don't understand. And how do you know what they are doing?'

'Because it was me who gave them the idea this time...'

'How's that possible?' Parush interrupted. 'How can you get involved in campus events? You're not a campusite.'

'Most of my friends are campusites – their parents are professors in IIT. Though I don't stay in the campus, thanks to my friends, I'm virtually a campusite for all practical purposes. My best friend Meher's latest victim is Rohit, the GSec SocCult of Nehru Hall. Few weeks before the DPs I met him at her place. Somehow the topic of Illu came up and I asked what they were planning this time. As expected, they too had planned something that anyone else would do this time – something on communal harmony in the backdrop of the demolition of Babri Masjid. I just threw a weird idea which had come to my mind and few days later Meher called me to tell me that Rohit would treat us – their core team had jumped at the idea. Just before the pujo holidays Meher and I ripped him off at the Woldies.'

'You didn't tell me anything about it?' Parush looked upset.

'Tell you what? That a guy treated me or I helped Nehru, RK's arch enemy?'

'Why should I bother about who treats you or whom you meet?' Parush said quite sternly, his voice a little loud.

Bitasta looked at him. She seemed to enjoy seeing Parush getting irritated. 'Okay, you don't care. But do you care if I tell you what they are going to do this time?'

'That's cheating. What's the point in winning by deceit?'

Now Bitasta was irritated. 'What do you mean? Winning is winning. And every win is at the cost of the loser, in some way or the other. You got into IIT because your IQ is perhaps better than the others who didn't get through. It's like a few lakh people aspiring to climb the Everest and only a few thousand having the proper mountaineering gear. Is it a fair game? What the hell are you talking about? And you're not going to win just by stealing the idea from them. We've to manipulate many other things, make a fool of many people and only then you can win.'

'I don't believe in manipulating and winning. I can't believe you can stoop down so low just for...'

'For what Porus?' she shouted, shutting Parush off. 'Tell me, for what? It's for you Porus, not for me.'

'Why for me? I didn't treat you anyway.'

Bitasta started fuming. 'Fuck you. Just go to hell.' She rushed into her own room, leaving Parush alone. Their live-in maid came running from inside the kitchen. Parush sat on the sofa for some more time and then left the house. While riding fast on the red pebbles he skidded from his bike. He got up and started pedalling faster, blood trickling from the fresh cuts. In the haste he had forgotten his jacket at Bitasta's house and the chill winter wind cutting through him made him shiver. He tried to pedal even faster. He fell again, trying to manoeuvre his bike at a turn. He got up, more blood oozing from new cuts. When he reached his hostel, he looked like an injured knight returning from a lost battle. Evading prying eyes he ran to his room and crashed on his bed, drenching the green bedsheet with the dark blood, like an angry evening storm suddenly filling a green meadow with the darkness of a night.

***

Parush woke up suddenly with the noise of loud bangs on his door. He got up from his bed and walked towards the door feeling as though he was carrying a loaded trunk on his head.

He was shocked to see Bitasta standing at his door with his best friend Arav.

'I'll be back in a few minutes,' Arav said. He waited till Bitasta entered the room and then closed the door from outside. It was the first time Bitasta had come to his room. She didn't even look around the room. She sat on the untidy bed, opened her bag and took out a bottle of Dettol and some cotton balls.

'Come here,' she ordered. Parush stood in front of her. Without saying anything she folded the sleeves of his shirt and cleaned each cut with Dettol. He wondered why he didn't feel any burning sensation. Perhaps, Bitasta had an anaesthetic effect. Once she was done with the cuts of his elbows and wrists, she kneeled on the floor and folded his pants till the knees and cleaned the cuts on his legs. She removed the green bed-sheet from the bed, exposing the dirty mattress made of coconut coils. 'Do you have another bed-sheet or a bed-cover?' she asked.

'In the cupboard,' Parush said.

'Can I open your cupboard?'

'Yes… Bitasta, I'm sorry.'

'You better be,' she said very casually and opened the cupboard. He suddenly felt embarrassed that his untidy undies were there in the cupboard. But before he could react, she had already found the only bed-sheet he had. She laid it evenly on the bed. Parush wondered why he could never lay the bed-cover so neatly. 'Sit,' she said, herself sitting at the corner.

He heard Arav's voice outside. 'Can we come in?'

'Yes,' replied Bitasta.

'You asshole,' Arav greeted Parush in the mildest form known to him, courtesy the only girl in the room, 'thank God you had told her about me. Otherwise we wouldn't have had any chance at Illu this year too.' Arin and Arko, two juniors, entered the room behind him. He shut the door.

Parush understood what would have happened in the past few hours. Their maid would have waited for one hour till Bitasta came out from her room. Hearing that he had skidded badly in front of their house, Bitasta would have thought for a while and then left immediately on her bike. Reaching RK Hall, she would have asked for Arav, the name she had heard often from him.

***

The core team of Illu swung into action in RK. For the first time, one of the chatais, the bamboo structures which would soon metamorphose into large canvases, would be forty feet high. The small drawing Bitasta had given was divided into ten sections, each mapping into one chatai twenty feet by twenty feet.

One late night, shutting all the doors and windows of the common room and pulling all the curtains down, each section of the drawing was projected on the widest wall through a projector. Only the core team, comprising six students from various years, was allowed into the room. The size of the projection on the wall was adjusted to twenty feet by twenty feet, matching exactly the size of a chatai. Each chatai was placed against the wall, the corresponding section of the drawing projecting on it. Arin and Arko, under the guidance of RK's ace artist Pushpen converted the smooth curves of the projection into slices of mathematically definable and delineable contours, which were then marked on the chatais with a paint brush.

All the contours on all the chatais, put together and upheld in the right order, would make for a super blow up of the small drawing on a piece of paper only when all the diyas, placed closely enough along the contours, would be lit together, and the entire thing would be viewed from a distance. Till that time, no one would have the slightest inkling what it could be – that was the only way to prevent this precious intellectual property from leaking to other halls.

***

Few days later, still quite some time from the D-Day – Diwali Day – when Illu would take place, Bitasta asked her friend Meher to call Rohit, the GSec SocCult, General Secretary, Socio-Cultural of Nehru Hall.

'Bits,' asked Meher, 'tell me one thing. Why are you helping him so much?'

'I think I'm flipping for your guy,' Bitasta replied, with a naughty smile on her face.

'No way,' refuted Meher. 'You're at least ten times as fussy as me when it comes to guys. I just needed someone who would have the balls to screw a professor's daughter and make me feel like a woman whenever I wanted. He's just awesome in that aspect. Tell me, what's going on?'

'Be with me. You'll find out baby.'

They met at Meher's place. 'Rohit,' Bitasta said, 'there's a big problem. I had given the drawing to our school magazine least hoping that it would fall into the hands of someone from RK. I just got to know that they are doing exactly the same thing. Our principal told me today that someone from RK had called her up to take her permission to use my drawing for Illu, the same drawing you guys are also using.'

'Shit,' Rohit sighed, 'what should we do now?'

'You still have ten days. Change it totally. If both are same you both will be disqualified. The judges will assume that either of you have cheated.'

'But we haven't cheated and we've been winning for three years. How can the judges disqualify us?'

'Well, I go every year with the judges. I know what they would think. If RK is disqualified that's not a big deal, because anyway they never win. If you are, that's a big deal, given you've a good chance to win this year too. So, change it – you still have the time. I'm giving you three ideas, each one will be great.'

'What are the ideas?'

'Idea one: Use Fatehpur Sikri as the canvas for creating a collage of the diversities of India with the tag line – The different Sparks of India.

'Idea two: Showcase Srirangapatna, perhaps the only capital of a Muslim ruler named after a Hindu God.

'Idea three: Make an expressionist painting metamorphosing India's map into a woman being burnt alive, with the area around Delhi under fire.'

***

RK's budget for this year's ambitious Illu overshot by 100% and their GSec SocCult had to call for an emergency General Body Meeting of the hall council. The sheer size of the scaffolding of the prime mover on the mess top and the meticulous planning involving the whole hall virtually working round the clock in batches kept no room for any suspicion that this year RK really had a chance. Parush's main challenge was to balance the entire network of chairs and tables, placed one atop the other and supported delicately by a crude mechanism of pressure points and counter weights. This apparently unstable network would hold the hundred people supporting each other through a collective feedback loop, reaching up to a height of forty feet, attaching the diyas to the chatais, filling them with oil, inserting the wicks and finally lighting each of them in a matter of a minute before coming down safely and dismantling it into invisibility even faster, just in time for the judges to witness the few minutes of glowing glory – the culmination of thousands of man hours of sweat and toil amidst the impeding threats of serious backlog and the fast advancing end semester exams.

Much later did Parush realise, when he read the book *Illuminati* written by a fellow KGPian, that the Illu is an '*evolved version of a calculated solution to a challenging engineering problem*', something that had guided and inspired him at various stages of his life and work.

***

Getting ready to receive the entourage of judges, Parush was still not very sure if whatever had happened over the past few weeks was correct. After all, it would be a win through deceit, whatever Bitasta might say.

When the chairs and tables were removed, people gaped with awe at the huge cinemascope screen. It looked like a giant poster of the blockbuster movie *Sholay*, something which everyone had seen on the covers of cassettes and magazines. The authenticity of the reproduction and its massive scale stunned everyone. At the centre, the huge canvas of twenty by hundred feet jutted out by another twenty feet, holding the bold letters of "Sholay" in English and Devanagari in the same font as seen in the posters. The ruthlessness of Gabbar's smile, the firmness in the eyes of Thakur, the void in the looks of the outwardly staring Jai and the romantic gazes of Viru and Basanti – all seemed to have frozen into a single shot of the movie playing on a huge screen hung from the pitch-dark sky.

In the right side of the screen were the words: '*The Sparks that weld the many Indias…*'

Parush saw Bitasta and Meher behind Prof. Mugdha Banerjee, who was leading the team of judges accompanied by a large group of enthusiastic campusites and their friends. Bitasta winked at him and touched her index finger to her lips in a silent gesture of a kiss which, unnoticed by everyone, flew towards him.

'In his *Ode on a Grecian Urn*,' Parush started his narration, written by Bitasta and her mother, 'Keats uses *ekphrasis* to describe a Greek urn. He mixes imagination with reality to make his readers see the vase in front of them. Here too we attempt using *ekphrasis* to describe a picture, a poster of the blockbuster movie *Sholay*, with a mix of imagination and reality. What you see in front of you is just a simple representation of that...'

'As far as I know,' interrupted Prof. Banerjee, '*ekphrasis* is a rhetorical device used in literature to describe a visual form of art. How exactly is that relevant here?'

Parush was not comfortable talking about something he didn't know. But Bitasta had insisted it would make a big difference with the judges. He looked helplessly at Bitasta.

'Do you mean,' Bitasta asked very seriously, staring at the glowing pixels ahead, 'your narration is the rhetoric, or rather the *ekphrasis*, with which you're going to describe an abstract picture?'

Parush didn't quite comprehend anything, but still nodded his head fervently. 'Yes, yes, exactly,' he said excitedly, realising he was sweating.

'That's quite interesting,' said Prof. Banerjee.

He led the entourage off the pathway from the main gate to the left, into the lawn, so that they could get a frontal view of the giant illuminated structure on the mess-top. He stared shortly at Bitasta. She winked again, showing a thumbs-up.

'Communal harmony,' he continued, 'is a very relevant topic today, especially when the very foundation of India seems to be shaken by the demolition of the Babri Masjid. We, very humbly, would like to say that despite some hooliganism, some acts of terrorism or vandalism, the fabric of our country is still a collage of many Indias, welded together into a single identity. And what more than a poster of *Sholay* can speak about it? Barring the Utkal, *Sholay*, which means sparks, connects Punjab, Sindhu, Gujarata, Maratha, Dravida and Vanga, thus encompassing almost the entire contour of India as depicted in our National Anthem.'

The entourage sat on the chairs placed strategically on the lawn. Parush allowed them to settle down. Bitasta didn't sit. She stood behind, staring directly into Parush's eyes.

'Dharmendra,' Parush resumed, 'who plays Viru, is a Punjabi; Ramesh Sippy, the director-producer is a Sindhi; Sanjeev Kumar, the Thakur, is a Gujarati; the movie is made in Bombay, the capital of Maratha land; Hema Malini, a Tamil Brahmin who plays Basanti, is from the Dravida; the music composer RD Burman and Jaya Bhaduri, Jai's love interest, are Bengali and finally the movie is made in Hindi, the national language of our country…'

The euphoria and the hysteria just after the departure of the judges spoke of something that no one in RK had imagined – this time, perhaps, they did have a fair chance at winning.

'Hi, I'm Bitasta Roy,' Bitasta introduced herself to Parush before leaving. 'It was a nice narration. Wish you all the best.'

Parush stood still, stunned. He watched Bitasta leaving with the entourage of the judges to the next hall.

***

Approaching LLR, the next hall to be judged, Meher pinched Bitasta. 'They have also done Fatehpur, isn't it?' she asked.

'Ya, I knew it,' Bitasta whispered.

Someone came forward and greeted the entourage. He smiled at Bitasta. It didn't elude Meher's eyes. 'You know him?' she asked.

'Ya, I do,' she whispered, very casually. 'By the way, he's the GSec SocCult of LLR…'

Meher pulled Bitasta back. 'Bits,' she talked loudly now, being away from the crowd, 'you just rock baby. From the time you found RK had picked your drawing from the school magazine, you've been sabotaging Nehru to improve RK's chance. First you convinced Nehru to scrap the idea of *Sholay* and do something from scratch. Then you made sure that they do something which wouldn't be unique. But, why did you give three options to Rohit? You already knew what LLR was doing. You could have convinced him to do the same. You know by now he can't say no to you. What if he had chosen something else?'

'Sweetheart, I was sure he would choose Fatehpur.'

Meher looked at Bitasta suspiciously. 'So,' she asked, 'tell me, who's the lucky RK guy for whom you're doing all this?'

Bitasta took a long breath. 'Will let you know sweety,' she said, hugging her best friend. 'And, just for your information,' she whispered into Meher's ears, 'RK didn't pick it up from the magazine...'

'What?' Meher shrieked.

'We've fallen behind. Come on ...' she pulled her friend by the hand and started walking fast to catch up with the judges.

***

When the entourage came to Nehru, Bitasta whispered into Mugdha's ears, 'Mugdha Auntie, don't you think they have spied on both RK and LLR?'

'Why do you say so, my dear?' asked Mugdha.

'They took the idea of Fatehpur from LLR and they took the tag line "*Different Sparks of India*" from RK. The usage of the word "*spark*" in the context of harmony is very unique. Each spark in the fire doesn't have its own identity. It's the fire you see in entirety, not the individual sparks. I really doubt Nehru came up with exactly the same interpretation independently.'

'Yes, you may be correct.'

Meher stared at Bitasta with eyes wide open. Rohit greeted them and began the narration. When he fumbled quoting the Persian inscription engraved on the Buland Darwaja, the grand entrance of the Fatehpur Sikri, Meher recalled what Bitasta had said while preparing him.

'Quote it in original Persian. That will have the right impact.'

'If I forget?'

'Try it out first. If you forget, shift to the English translation. Don't fumble.'

Meher realised Bitasta had known Rohit would fumble.

'*Isa, son of Mary said, "The world is a Bridge, pass over it, but build no houses upon it"*,' Rohit shifted to English uncomfortably.

Once Rohit's narration was over and they were proceeding towards Azad, Bitasta looked back. 'Meher,' she pulled her friend, 'your guy is amazing, even outside your bed. Just look at the perfection of the Buland Darwaja and the Panch Mahal. Compared to LLR, this one is far better. And, they did all this in just ten days!'

'But then,' Meher sighed, embracing her, and dragging her face close to hers, 'they had to lose.'

'No,' Bitasta said firmly, '*RK had to win*.'

***

Late that night Arav, Parush and Bitasta were sitting on the pebbles by the railway tracks beside Chhedi's, IIT's epicentre of all late-night activities, amidst the strumming of guitars, the fragrance of grass, the smell of the *tinkus*, the egg-burgers in their indigenous avatar unavailable anywhere else, and the hushed noise of human voices.

Parush was exhausted after the VP, the Victory Procession around the campus. Arav had carried him all along on his shoulders, not letting him get down even for a moment. With the bursting of crackers and beating of dhak the frenzy of the RKites reached a crescendo when they reached Nehru. Some dejected Nehruites threw a bucket of unused oil on Parush's head. A fight erupted and turned ugly in no time with people plucking the diyas out of the chatais and throwing them on others. People from the neighbouring Azad and Patel halls rushed to control the situation. Parush was badly injured. His eyes burned with the oil which had seeped inside. At around one in the night he called Bitasta. A few minutes later Panchali dropped her at Chhedi's. 'Congrats,' she said to Parush. 'Call me when you guys are done. I'll pick her up.' Just before leaving she called Parush back. 'Don't allow her to smoke here,' she threw the words before speeding away. Bitasta looked perplexed. 'How the hell does she know that I smoke?'

Arav lay down on the pebbles, staring at the sky. Parush leaned on Bitasta's shoulders and she gently played her fingers through his hair. Suddenly all his cuts and bruises seemed to have healed miraculously.

Parush was the unanimous hero of this year's Illu.

Parush had always loved to dream, but now he realised that he had also learned how to enliven his dreams. He felt proud, and confident too, that it was perhaps only for him that RK had dared to even think of an Illu so grand in scale. Bitasta had no doubt manipulated many things in their favour, but her biggest contribution was perhaps the sparks she had ignited within him. *Sholay*, he muttered to himself.

Arav, perhaps, didn't fail to notice Parush's slow transition into someone he hadn't been just a year back. He stared at Parush for a long time.

'What?' Parush asked him.

'Nothing,' he smiled and turned towards Bitasta. 'Bits, what if you hadn't met Rohit by chance and given the idea?'

'Who told you I met him by chance?' Bitasta replied calmly, without raising her face.

Arav jumped up. 'What do you mean?'

***

Not much later, Parush himself would orchestrate another win, perhaps the biggest in his life, in the same way Bitasta had done now. He would just repeat each of the steps she had taken now. But then, he wouldn't even get to thank Bitasta.

And what he would then think of a win through a series of deceits would be something that only time would tell.

THE LONGEST NIGHT

'*The shore of the Ganga,*' Sairandhri read out from Shesher *Kabita*, Tagore's Farewell Song. '*From the lowest level of the paved bathing area rises an ancient banyan tree, laden with aerial roots... To the south is the moss-encrusted paved bathing ghat, the stone cracked in many places, eroded in patches. At that ghat is tethered our slim, elegant boat, painted green and white. On its blue flag, inscribed in white lettering, is the name of the boat...Through the garden flows a narrow channel, bearing the pulse beat of the Ganga...*'

It was Bitasta's seventeenth birthday. Shaunak, Bitasta's father, had organised an exotic night-out at his farmhouse at Achipore at a picturesque bend on the Ganga not only to celebrate Bitasta's birthday, but also to commemorate the registration of IPC, *Indus Planning and Consultancy*. All the three founders, the three classmates from IIT KGP – Shaunak, Srinjay and Tuhin – were present with their families, as was Ru. Srinjay, Parush's father, had wanted Ru to look after the branding and liaisoning for IPC. As a condition for that he had to reluctantly accept an investment from her, thus making her one of the stakeholders of IPC.

Everyone had reached Achipore by afternoon. After lunch they assembled in the lawn, which rolled into the river. Everyone had asked Sairandhri to read out from *Shesher Kabita*.

It again occurred to Parush that there was an uncanny connection between his mother and Panchali. He recalled Bits had recently mentioned that Panchali felt this place in Achipore resembled a description from *Shesher Kabita*…

***

Just before the winter holidays, Parush had been to Prembajar to meet Bitasta and Panchali. Exhausted after the third semester exams, he lay on the sofa, resting his head on Bitasta's lap. Plying her fingers tenderly through his hair she didn't speak for a long time. Parush felt something was unusual. He opened his eyes and stared at her. 'How come someone is so silent today?' he asked.

'Can I ask, or rather request something?' she said, hesitantly.

'Come on Bits, these words don't suit you. What happened?'

'Can you cancel your Gangtok trip?'

She knew of the entire itinerary. She also knew how excited he and his gang of RKites were about this forthcoming trip to celebrate their recent victory in Illu.

Parush got up. 'What's up Bits? Tell me,' he asked, turning Bitasta's face towards him.

'OK,' she shrugged off the unusual embellishment of shyness and said firmly, in her usual tone, 'this is a little embarrassing for me, but still you're just so shameless and discourteous that I can't help it. I know you've totally forgotten that my seventeenth birthday falls on 22nd December, when you'll be busy chasing some fat nosed babes in the hills.'

Parush immediately started thinking of some not-so-dirty ways to dodge his friends.

Later, after the dinner, while he and Bitasta were taking a stroll in the dark alleys of Prembajar and listening to the sounds of their own footsteps on the red gravel, Bitasta spoke about their farmhouse at Achipore, an old Chinese settlement, some thirty kilometres away from Calcutta, overlooking a beautiful bend on the Ganga, long abandoned by the Chinese. 'Baba is planning to throw a party at our farmhouse on the night of 21st December. I haven't been there for ages. It's so beautiful – the old house with the creaking doors, the walls with unusual graffiti created by the cracks, a high ceiling that towers up into darkness, the lawn which slopes gently into the water, the old banyan tree almost drooping into the river, the slippery stairs of the ghat, the narrow canal with a ramshackle wooden bridge which passes through the lawn, everything. Ma tells me the place matches with the description of a dream-house mentioned in *Shesher Kabita*. In the novel, the hero Amit finally abandons the idea of staying in that house. But I would like to stay in our farmhouse … with my guy … on each of my birthdays…'

They sat on the round platform at the base of a large banyan tree on the fringe of Prembajar, bordering the Hijli forest.

'The night of 21st December is the longest night of the year and I wish my guy would stretch it even longer. He would wish me "Happy Birthday" at midnight and then make love to me for the rest of the long night, in the most amazing ways, making the night, a night of longing, a night of yearning. In the morning I'll stand by the river. *Her cool breeze, carrying far the love-cooing of the cranes in the early morning and impregnated by the fragrance of the blooming lotus, removes the love-making lassitude of the women…*'

***

Hearing his mother read out from *Shesher Kabita* at the farmhouse in Achipore, Parush realised Panchali too would have read out the same lines to Bitasta many a time, with the same passion. Could that too be called an *ekphrasis*, a narration so well read out that one could fantasise on that?

Parush looked for Bitasta, sitting at a disadvantageous point, not in direct line of sight, in a distorted circle formed carelessly by everyone in the lawn. The late afternoon sun was gliding gradually towards the horizon, across the river, taking along with it the comfortable warmth of the day. The breeze blowing from the river was no longer as pleasurable as it had been even some time back.

***

Bitasta met Raka, Tuhin and Aleya's daughter, for the first time. She looked at Parsuh with amazement when Raka slammed on him, throwing her arms around his neck, and whispered into his ears loud enough for her to hear, 'I'm no longer a kid that you'll ignore me anymore.' Raka barely allowed even a mosquito to come close to Parush. 'What a flirt,' Bitasta said, when she left him alone for some time. 'If you guys want to make out, you can use any of the rooms.'

When the sun sank into the horizon on the other side of the Ganga everyone assembled in the lawn around the bonfire. Shaunak had arranged for a perfect evening. By the time everyone settled down on the lawn, the barbeque and bar had already been setup by their side. The heat of the burning wood gradually created a realm of comfort and warmth around them, making the chill air blowing from the river bearable and then enjoyable. The lights on the other side of the bend of the river faded gradually behind a mist, which enveloped the river, the half-moon in the sky, and the brick kilns close by, making the place of the bonfire an isolated cocoon.

Raka sat beside Parush, holding his hands tight. His sister Pushi never took the ear-phones of her new walkman off her ears, perhaps listening to her present favourite Madonna. In her tight jacket, short skirt and tall boots, all made of black leather, and her black stockings she looked like a Barbie doll that had undergone a serious wardrobe change, replacing everything pink with black.

Parush couldn't remember when he had seen Aru, Ru's daughter, the last time in any social function like this. After a very long time he observed Aru closely. She too had grown up from a kid to a lady, something which had remained unnoticed by Parush all these days. She, along with Ru, was replenishing everyone's plates. Parush felt bad that he had never tried to understand this girl raised by a single mother. Didn't she want to know about her father? How did Ru handle such situations? Didn't her silence, her indifference, say something? Had Parush ever tried to cross the barrier she herself had created around her and reach out to her, understand her? Now that he suddenly realised that she too had grown up, and would be sixteen soon, like his own sister Pushi, like Raka, he felt a sense of guilt within him. Why had he always ignored her? Was it because whenever he went to Ru's house, he always wanted to meet only Ru and Aru's existence was just like that of the many delicate and costly pieces of furniture and paintings he never bothered to notice?

Bitasta sat opposite him, beyond the fire. In a simple red embroidered cotton sari, an attire very unlikely of her, and with almost no accessory, her hair left loose, floating around her face carelessly, she still looked resplendent in the gleaming flare of the bonfire. She removed her jacket and kept it beside her. Seated with her legs folded by her side, she never took her glance off Parush. When Aru came to refill her plate, Aru's eyes followed Bitasta's gaze and stopped on Parush.

Parush got up, released his hands from Raka's grasp with some effort, and took the tray from Aru's hand. Aru didn't say anything.

Sairandhri and Panchali were seated side by side. When Sairandhri resumed reading from *Shesher Kabita* – the concluding sections – Parush went back and sat beside Raka. Lately, he had realised that his mother was not always a frozen glacier that held back all its water from flowing into a murmuring stream. When she read out something or recited a poem, the solidified snow would melt for a moment.

'*Blow gently across the terrace, O southerly breeze, For in an instant, My eyes will meet my beloved's…*'

She shut the book and closed her eyes.

Perhaps it was only Parush who noticed a sparkle in Panchali's eyes, something which might have eluded even Bitasta's sight. Why did she always have tears in her eyes whenever Sairandhri recited a poem?

Everyone clapped. 'Panchali,' Srinjay said, 'now it's your turn. We want Kalidasa.'

Panchali looked at the sky for a few moments and then started reciting from *Ritusamhara*, explaining each verse in Bengali. '*Lovesick will enjoy the clear late nights of these summer days on delightful and well-fragranced rooftops, savouring strong drinks that are commoved by the suspires of their ladyloves, while the passion-intensifier, melodious instrumental and vocal music, is cross-fading…*'

Perhaps only Ru noticed that Sairandhri suddenly stopped drinking the red wine. Holding the glass close to her lips she looked at the round ripples on the surface of the wine created by her breath. After some time, she kept the glass down, by her side.

***

Bitasta asked Parush to be by her side when she would cut the cake. 'I never knew this state of affairs between you and Raka,' she whispered as they arranged the table. 'Believe me,' Parush defended, 'it's nothing like that. And she does it more so knowing that I get uncomfortable.'

'You really get uncomfortable?' she asked, winking at him. 'Do you have the balls to resist such a voluptuous and gorgeous female?'

'Bits, please,' Parush pleaded.

'She's damn sexy, I should admit. But the show stopper in your entourage is undoubtedly Ru. Aru has good potential. And your sis too can drive guys crazy if she ever removes her earphones.'

Everyone gathered around the table when it was midnight. 'At the stroke of the midnight hour,' said Shaunak dramatically, 'when the world sleeps, my little queen will awaken to a new life and new freedom.' Bitasta cut the cake in the clichéd ritual which always seemed to be fresh. She fed the first piece to her father. 'Sweetheart, I would like you to remain seventeen throughout your life,' he hugged her. When Parush got the second piece Raka shouted, '*decorate* her.'

'No, no way,' Bitasta protested first, but then turned towards Parush, closed her eyes and put forward her face. Parush removed a handful of cream from the surface of the cake and started applying it gently on her face. Raka and Ru dug out more and fudged her face.

***

Parush noticed Aru was standing away from everyone, facing the river. He walked towards her and stood by her side. She appeared to get a big jolt of electric shock. She moved away a bit. 'Aru,' he reached out to her, 'are you angry with me?'

'No,' she said with a promptness that surprised Parush. 'No,' she repeated, 'why should I be angry with you? You barely talk to me. How can you piss me off?'

Parush understood the sarcasm. 'Aru, I'm really sorry. You too never talk to me.'

'When do I get to talk to you?'

Bitasta appeared from behind with a piece of cake for Aru and fed her.

'Time to get into the waters,' announced Shaunak. 'We've to walk a bit towards the jetty. The launch is ready.'

While everyone collected their warm clothing to get into the launch, Panchali wanted to stay back by the bonfire. 'You all go ahead. Let me and Sairi stay here.' Neither Shaunak nor Srinjay pleaded with them to come along. Parush wanted Panchali to come, and as for his mother, he was used to her absence on any such occasion. Aleya, Raka's mother, wanted to stay back too with them. 'Didi,' Panchali said, 'it's fine. I may not be comfortable in the cold. Sairi and I have barely talked in so many years. Let us spend some time together.'

When the launch pushed away from the shore Parush could still see the silhouette of Panchali and Sairandhri against the orange flames of the bonfire. He knew they were not talking. Soon they were hidden behind the brick kilns lining the shore.

Everyone aboard spent the next few hours singing, dancing and drinking in the enclosed hull of the launch Shaunak had managed to get through his connections at the Haldia Port.

Shaunak took the guitar and sang Jim Reeves: *Railroad, steamboat, river and canal, yonder comes a sucker and he's got my girl, And she's gone gone gone and she's gone gone gone, I'll bid her my last farewell…*

Bitasta and Srinjay joined the chorus – *she's gone gone gone, and she's gone gone gone.*

Apart from the old gramophone plates which only Parush listened to at times, he didn't have any reason to believe that his father too could love music. People rarely talked in their house. But outside, in his own circle, which surely didn't include his mother, Srinjay would be a totally different person. Perhaps only in parties like these, would he get a glimpse of the real disposition of his father – what he saw at home was surely not real.

'There's an interesting story behind this song,' Shaunak said. 'Few of us were big Jim Reeves fans. He had died a few years back in the mid-sixties and sometime in our third year we decided to do a few of his songs in a TMS show. At that time Srinjay was already mad for Sairi. She was there at the show along with Panchali. But exactly when we were doing this number, someone called Sairi and she left. The timing was just perfect – we were singing, *yonder comes a sucker and he's got my girl and she's gone gone gone...*' Everyone broke into laughter. But Parush sighed, which didn't go unnoticed – Bitasta stared at him. Had his mother been different then?

When Shaunak, Srinjay and Tuhin started talking about IPC and Pushi and Aru were asleep at a corner, huddled under a blanket, Bitasta and Aleya kept the others entertained with more songs, jokes and anecdotes. Parush had always envied Raka. Aleya auntie, a very busy doctor by profession, was a typical mother Parush never had. Hers, he always felt, was a *family*, unlike theirs.

***

While it was still dark the launch returned to Achipore as Aleya had to reach her hospital on time in the morning. Bitasta, Parush, Ru and her daughter Aru stayed back in the launch for a sunrise cruise on the river. Raka gave a big hug to Parush before disembarking. Bitasta gawked at Parush, silently showing a reaction which could mean anything from a sigh to a taunt.

Once they had left the shore, Bitasta and Parush climbed up to the open upper deck, shivering in the cold wind cutting through them as the launch zoomed through the early morning mist. Bitasta removed her jacket and hugged him from behind.

'Thanks for ditching your friends, just for me,' she hissed into his ears. 'And thank yourself for being alive, for I would have killed you otherwise. Anyway, Raka was a far better choice than those flat nosed chicks, isn't it?'

Before Parush could say anything Bitasta pulled him by his hand. 'Come,' she dragged him downstairs. He too had heard it. They hesitated to enter the hull where Aru was shouting at her mother.

'Why don't you leave me alone, mom? Don't I do everything you ask me to do? It's always your life, your preference, your guys, your affairs, your pleasure. What about me, mom? Do you think I don't know about each of the guys you sleep with? But I don't know my father. The only guy I ever knew my whole life, the only guy who comes in my dreams, who awakens me from my sleep, whose thoughts make me feel good, whom I miss every moment I live, loves you, mom. The sparks in his eyes, which I wish were for me, are actually for you, mom. And you know that, don't you? I can't fight any more, mom. I can't fight any more. Please leave me alone. I don't want to see any sunrise. You all do whatever you like. Just leave me alone…'

Her shouts became wails, while Parush clenched Bitasta's arms, stunned and shocked. 'Come up,' Bitasta pulled him back.

Ru was already behind them, standing on the stairs.

Parush wished the night had ended. But the night didn't seem to end at all. The mist seemed even heavier.

That was indeed a very long night, the longest in a year.

MAHALAYA

After that night out at the farmhouse in Achipore, Parush met Bitasta the very next day at the Scoop. As if he were sitting in a confessional in a crowded church, unperturbed by the presence of anyone else around, he poured out everything, even those which he had never thought he could reveal to anyone. He felt relieved after emptying himself entirely in front of Bitasta. He felt as if he were a child, whose nakedness doesn't evoke any surprise or embarrassment. Bitasta dragged his hands close to hers. 'Do you have any feeling of guilt for your feelings for Ru?' she asked.

'No, I didn't have, till yesterday, till I heard Aru talk like that.'

Bitasta played with Parush's fingers for some time, staring at the grey water of the Ganga flowing lethargically on a winter morning, just a few days short of Christmas. Parush had been a little surprised when he had seen her waiting at the bus-stop in front of the Mint, just a short distance from their house in New Alipore, wearing a brown oversized hooded parka jacket and a matching pair of knee high brown boots. That was a total contrast to the sari on her birthday. Upon reaching Scoop, she removed the jacket and hung it around the back rest of the tall stool, lighting a cigarette – Parush had already procured both the lighter and the cigarette before picking her up. In a short denim skirt, quite short by Calcutta standards, a long vest top which almost covered her skirt, long leather boots, legs crossed at the knees, sitting and puffing out rings of smoke, she was quite a sight in the sparsely populated ice-cream parlour at Outram Ghat.

'Ma says,' she started speaking, still looking out through the closed glass window overlooking the Ganga, 'if you're true to your emotions and sentiments, you can start loving anyone in the world, no matter who he or she is. She believes love initiates with a simple and innocent liking for certain qualities in a person. You get attracted to the person because of these qualities, which you think an ideal human being should always possess.'

She turned towards Parush, looked into his eyes and rested her hand gently on his knees. 'Once you start knowing the person, slowly, you get passionate about, or rather obsessed with these qualities. You start feeling your association with this person is bringing in some positivity, some happiness in your life, which no one else can bring. In other words, the person gradually *seems* to be indispensable. That's when you feel something different. You feel an intense passion, a sexual urge, a lust or simply love, in a more common term. Ma feels that in this entire process the gender of the person or the social relation is so irrelevant that at the end you may land up loving a guy, or a cousin, or a friend's wife, or a sister-in-law…'

Parush tried to recall what exactly in Ru had attracted him to her. Perhaps, he thought, it was the way she would treat him, not like a kid, but like anyone else around her. Or was it the gentleness and tenderness in her behaviour, her touch, her hug, her kisses, which he never got from his mother? Not a single day, Parush remembered, would he forget running to Ru's house after school. He liked everything about Ru, the way she dressed, the way she talked, the way she walked, the way she sat at her desk, the way she kissed him every day, the way she became an inseparable part of his life.

Had he not seen Ru through the key-hole in that state, Parush thought, would things be different?

Arav, his best friend, had called him a pervert after hearing everything about her.

'Isn't it perversion?' he asked Bitasta.

'Ma feels it's not perversion if it happens naturally and spontaneously.' She pushed the butt of the burnt cigarette into the ashtray and held Parush's hands. 'Porus, let me assure you, you're not a pervert. And you should thank Ru for handling you so well. Amazing lady.'

'Do you accept Kakima's views?'

'Not really, not till I met you and...'

A few guys had entered the parlour. They came and sat very close to them, ogling at Bitasta.

'Bits, why don't you put on your jacket?'

'Why? I'm comfortable without it. Even the summer in Nova Scotia was colder than this...'

'Put it on,' Parush said sternly.

Bitasta was smart enough to figure out the context. She smiled and put the jacket on. 'What's the problem if they ogle at me?' she asked him softly.

'Bits, I can't explain more. It's not only the ogling – they will later think about you and...'

'And what? They will jerk?'

That was something about Bitasta Parush had started to develop a strong dislike for. She was too direct at times when he would prefer a little diplomacy or untruthfulness. He didn't speak for some time. 'Let's go,' he said suddenly, pulling Bitasta by her hand. He walked with long strides, making it uncomfortable for Bitasta to keep pace. 'Porus,' she asked, 'what happened? Why are you suddenly behaving like this?'

Getting inside the car, Parush sat quietly, leaning against the seat. Bitasta dragged his face close to hers. 'Look into my eyes,' she said. 'I told you, you're no pervert. Those guys could be...'

Parush looked up and for the first time, embraced Bitasta.

***

Lately, Parush had been cherishing an idea in his mind that perhaps, yes *perhaps* in 'bold italics', Bitasta might have started thinking of him as the man in her life. He was aware that girls never 'propose' first, but then he didn't have the smallest iota of guts and courage to even bring up the topic in front of her, forget proposing. After some serious introspection, which mainly comprised just a few minutes of arguments with Arav, his best friend, he finally concluded that he was heavily in love with Bitasta. He saw her everywhere. 'Even in the resistance and capacitance?' Arav asked him once in the lab, considering all the visible and audible – Parush had lately started talking too much about one particular thing in his life – symptoms in him. He didn't have any answer.

Knowing that Bitasta knew all about Ru, Parush was hesitant if she would accept him the way he was. When Panchali asked him to teach her physics and mathematics he managed to get Arav in his place arguing that Arav would be a better tutor. In reality, he didn't want three more hours every week to be vulnerable in front of her. But he couldn't resist from going to Prembajar whenever possible either.

'If my man two-timed me, I would kill him,' Bitasta said one day, banging her closed fist on Parush's legs. Parush felt as if the warning was directed at him. Parush felt helpless. But Panchali came to his defence.

'Arca,' she said, 'it depends how you define two-timing. Someone may really need two persons in life, because both may have complementing qualities.'

'Ma, why do you always have such weird views of everything?'

'Didn't you read Tagore's *Shesher Kabita*?' she argued. 'Amit loves both Ketaki and Labanya, but marries Ketaki. In his own words, Ketaki is like water in a pitcher, to be collected daily, and used up every day. But his love for Labanya remains a lake, its waters not to be carried home but meant for his consciousness to swim in. I always felt, a love which develops like a poem, naturally, gradually, within the realms of a meter, is always a true love, irrespective of everything else. Amit says, "Long live my Labanya, long live my Ketaki, and long live Amit Raye *in all his dimensions*." Would you call it two-timing?'

Parush had already realised that whichever lake he swam in on a hot summer afternoon, he would have to always return to Prembajar, to quench his thirst with the cold waters of a well. He needed the lake, and the well too.

Bitasta looked at him suspiciously. Had she got wind of what was going on in his mind?

***

'Do you have lab tomorrow in the afternoon?' Bitasta would ask Arav at the end of the tuitions. 'Yes,' Arav would inform her, 'but we can leave early if the experiment is done.' And then Arav would come to Parush's room. 'Behen ka lauda,' he would start a conversation with Parush, addressing him as the dick of his sister, 'what more indication are you waiting for? I'll take care of the lab. Go and meet her tomorrow.'

And that was how Parush would spend most afternoons in Prembajar. They would often read out Panchali's favourite poems collected in an old diary. In the absence of a direct way of expressing love, Parush felt the poems served a very important role. The poems would arouse erotic fantasies in him, placing Bitasta in the place of the ladylove, to whom most of the poems were addressed, as though, by the same guy, like a string of letters written by him.

Somedays Bitasta would read out a Vidyapati, Parush lying on the sofa, eyes shut, his head resting on her lap.

Let the earth of my body be mixed with the earth my beloved walks on,
Let the fire of my body be the brightness in the mirror that reflects her face,
Let the water of my body join the water of the lotus pool she bathes in,
Let the breath of my body be air lapping her tired limbs.

And then, Parush would read out a Hafiz on some stubborn summer afternoon, Bitasta making a painting of a dull day, not a single leaf fluttering on the trees, not a single bird chirping around, only a few people lingering on the lazy alleys and a lonely girl looking out at the pathway with expecting eyes.

Though I be old, clasp me one night to thy breast,
And I, when the dawn shall come to awaken me,
With the flush of youth on my cheek from thy bosom will rise.

Bitasta would keep aside the drawing book and sit beside Parush, lolling her head on his shoulder.

'I've asked Ma many times,' Bitasta said one day, 'who offered her all these poems as gifts of love. I knew it couldn't be Baba. He's not the type that would make love with poems.'

'This may be an anthology she created with her favourite poems,' Parush argued.

'That's what she claims, which I don't believe. I discovered this diary one day from a heap of old stuff and Ma was very uncomfortable, despite the openness we share… None of these are complete poems. They're just a few lines, culled so wonderfully, surely with a purpose. And Porus, just see the passion in each line, the fantasies, the subtle eroticism… These are typical guys' stuff, things that would titillate a guy, make him drool... See these lines from Tagore: *Wet with sea-water, with loose dripping hair you sat on the rocky shore. Your flowing yellow skirt rolled and curved around your feet. The tender dawn wrote in glistening gold on your naked breasts and unadorned skin…'*

Leaning against Parush, Bitasta circled her index finger on Parush's thigh. He felt a very familiar and pleasing strain within. 'Any girl would go crazy if a guy recited these lines daily to her,' Bitasta muttered, as though talking to herself, 'no matter how unromantic or weird she were... As a memento, Ma would have written down the lines in her diary…'

***

With every passing day Parush felt more hopeless. He hoped that Bitasta would take the initiative, as she always took in everything else, and would tell him someday that he was her man. Her indications, which Arav claimed to be more direct than saying, 'I want to have sex with you and become the mother of all your children,' confused him a lot.

Then one day, on the way to Calcutta, Bitasta said something, just when the train jerked to a stop at Jakpur. Parush had always found the name of the station very weird. With so many hawkers and passengers suddenly jumping into the train and drowning even a loud shriek into the cacophony, like a whisper, he wished he could annihilate the station totally. 'I didn't know how I would say this to you,' she said exactly when the train stopped at the next station and more people pushed inside the already crowded train. Someone slipped a kid between Bitasta and Parush. Parush added Madpur to the list of stations he would annihilate. When she again spoke at Haur, keeping quiet through four stations he really became irritated. 'Why do you have to speak only when the train stops?'

Finally, when they reached Howrah, his list of stations to be annihilated included Narain Pakuria Murail, Nandai Gajan,

Ghoraghata, Abada, Andul... Parush wondered how he hadn't noticed all these kinky names earlier.

'What should I do for you to tell me what you wanted to tell?' Parush whispered in the taxi they had taken from Howrah station. 'Do I have to kiss you in front of Kakima?'

'Ma will throw you out,' she whispered back.

***

Then came the Mahalaya, the day that reckons the beginning of the biggest carnival of Bengal – the Durga Pujo. Parush reached Prembajar in the afternoon. Bitasta sat on the revolving chair in her room. Parush pulled the chair close and placed it between his legs. He dragged her face down and kissed her, on her lips, suddenly. She remained indifferent, as if he had done something very normal, like touching her mother's feet on the last day of the Durga Pujo. 'Tell me now,' he said firmly. 'You stayed a few days in Calcutta and then returned to Prembajar. A week has passed since then. You've been avoiding telling it all these days. You've to tell it now.'

Bitasta kept quiet.

'I'll leave if you don't tell,' he warned.

'Don't go,' Bitasta pleaded. 'I'll tell.' But still she didn't say anything. When Parush got up from the bed she held his hand. 'Porus, I'm in love.'

Parush behaved as if she had said something as humdrum as, 'Porus, you never say "fuck" or "shit"'. The reality was altogether different though.

'Who's the guy?' he asked casually.

She didn't say anything.

He pushed her and left the room. Panchali was reading a magazine in the living room. 'Kakima,' he told her, 'I'm leaving –

have to attend the last period.' Panchali was surprised to know that they even had such a period which started after five. Parush took his bike, opened the iron-gate on the boundary wall and sat on the bike. Bitasta had followed him to the gate. Just before he pressed the pedal she threw the words, 'You dumbo, it's you, idiot.'

Parush turned back and saw Panchali standing at the door, a little puzzled. Bitasta winked at him. He knew it would be too awkward to descend from his bike, come back and suck off the last drop of saliva from Bitasta's lips, which she was presently biting, not so hard.

'Bye Kakima,' he said and pedalled the bike at the least possible speed needed to barely keep the balance of the two-wheeler.

***

Parush came back to his hostel and directly went to Arav's room. In his characteristic way, he showered the choicest abuses on him. Parush wanted to call Bits and talk to her, but Arav asked him to meet her the next day and say everything in person. And then Parush spent one of the longest nights of his life ... not sleeping a bit... rewinding the scenes from the last evening in Prembajar again and again in his mind... thinking how else he could have reacted, what else he could have done ... feeling happy in a way he never had felt before ... feeling relieved ... feeling restless... He missed her terribly. He felt like running to her.

Parush called up Ru in the middle of the night and kept her awake till morning, talking to her, telling her every titbit of the evening... 'So, now you're not going to marry me anymore,' she said, before hanging up.

PROSODY

Parush was amused to see Bitasta blush for the first time.

After spending a never-ending night Parush had eagerly waited for the afternoon to appear directly, skipping the morning, like the semester exams, which seemed to appear suddenly, skipping the days just before. Even before he could knock on the door, Bitasta emerged from inside the house, dressed in a light blue long skirt and a milk white shirt, her cascading hair set free, her eyes lowered and her hands joined near her waist. She moved to the side, allowing Parush to pass by her.

'Someone was thinking you wouldn't come here again,' Panchali said, sliding her feet into the sandals kept by the door. 'Hope you don't have the evening class today. Have dinner with us. I'll be back in a few hours.'

Bitasta closed the door and stood in front of Parush, her eyes still lowered. He raised her face. 'Bits, you look so beautiful when you blush,' he said, putting his hands around her neck. 'You look like a girl.'

'How do I look otherwise?' Bitasta whispered.

'You look like a woman.'

'Do you like the girl more?' Bitasta slid the words into his mouth, slithering her lips inside, sucking his tongue. Parush pushed her against the wall, inserting his tongue deep into her throat. Gradually, the coquettish and timid morning sun relinquished all the prudishness and emerged as a fiery ball. She pushed him into the sofa and placed herself on him, her legs folded backwards, her hands wrapped tight around his neck.

'Dumbo, can't you say it even now that you love me too?' she asked, biting his lips hard, restricting even the slightest labial movements to allow any sound to emanate from his vocal chords.

'Speak with your eyes,' she rumbled and then suddenly let him free, spreading herself languidly on the sofa, as though like a tree, readying to shed its leaves at the onset of the fall. Parush felt as if he were reading from Panchali's diary or listening to her reciting one of those poems which would unleash in him the untamed fantasies about Bitasta. As he pulled her blue skirt, it slid from her waist, receding down her thighs and unravelling in front of him her bare legs. He stared with amazement at the naked slender limbs.

Having removed her blue water garment, – which, dropping from her bank thighs, by her reed branches, as by hands, is somewhat firmly held, – then O friend, if thou art gliding down to her, thy departure will be difficult; for who that has known their taste, would be able to leave a girl whose garment has slipped off her thighs?

He pulled down her underpants, the isolated piece of cloth which lay stuck below her waist, revealing the furry oasis amidst a barren landscape of alluring curves. She spread her legs apart and he dipped his head between them, rubbing his nose tenderly over the fur. For a moment, something he had stealthily seen through the key-hole of Ru's room many years ago flashed in his mind, like a spark of a lightning, which tore apart the darkness of a stormy night just for a wink, but whose rumblings never died.

With his teeth he snapped open the girdle and let it fall on the floor with a tinkle. Unbuttoning her shirt, he licked her navel and laid his hands on her heaving breasts, setting them free from the shackles of the brassiere. She closed her eyes, her suspires speaking the million words through the silent tremors of her lips, the rhythmic rise and fall of her breasts, the tightening embrace of her hands and the trembling copula of her legs.

Her girdle-band of a row of birds tinkles, and gracefully gliding, flows away, leaving her whirlpool navel exposed to view. She can't talk, for the first word of love in a woman is confusion in presence of a lover...

Drowning his face into the warmth of her bosom he shut himself off from the world, listening only to the sound of beating of her heart, his fingers fondling her hardened nipples and her perspires drenching him with the joy of the first shower of monsoon.

The massive black-clouds glisten like the blackened nipples on bosoms of pregnant women, ready to rain elixir of life on the lips of about-to-come offspring...

Love is like a poem and lovemaking the prosody, he remembered Panchali saying. 'Love,' she would say, 'like a poem, is a thought, a feeling; and lovemaking is its expression, like the meter, the prosody, which expresses a thought physically in the form of verses.'

Perhaps now he realised what she really meant. Each of the lines in the poems she had written in her diary – the words, the rhythm, the caesura and the pause – aroused in him a fervent craving to possess Bitasta, to make love to her in the most wonderful ways, in the same way, perhaps, each line itself exalted the theme, the thought, the feeling of the poem.

Bitasta slowly removed all the covers from Parush's body, throwing each piece of cloth across the room, one by one. 'Now make me feel like a Queen,' she spoke into his ears. She stretched herself again on the sofa, drooping her hands down, like a creeper slipping off its support. 'Decorate me with chandan.'

Parush got the small bowl filled with sandal paste, perhaps made by Panchali in the morning, from the thakur ghar, the small shrine in the house. He rubbed the pulp on her breasts, mixing it with her sweat.

And wet with sweat are the musk and sandal…

He removed her necklace and placed it between her breasts.

I promise by the golden pitchers of your breasts and by your necklace snake, which now I gather in my hands, if ever I touch anyone but you, may your necklace bite me… Bind me in your arms, bruise me with your thighs, choke my heart with your swollen breasts…

Lying entangled on the sofa, they allowed the moments to pass by silently, like a night. Parush explored every nook and niche and every curve and bend of Bitasta's bare body with wonderment. He wandered like an aimless traveller, mesmerised by the beauty of the landscape at every new turn. He played with her body like a kid playing with dough. He tried to smell her fragrance from every part of her body. He tried to feel the life flowing within her from every nerve of her body. He draped himself with her sweat. He kissed her, cuddled her, fondled her, fiddled her, caressed her and she allowed him to be his muse, his toy. When he got tired, Bitasta asked him, 'How's it?'

'It's like that poem of Tennyson you love so much.'

I chatter over stony ways, in little sharps and trebles,
I bubble into eddying bays, I babble on the pebbles.
I steal by lawns and grassy plots, I slide by hazel covers;
I move the sweet forget-me-nots that grow for happy lovers…

'Get up,' she whispered. Sitting on the floor, she lowered her face on his groin and started flicking her tongue against the hardened thing. She took it deep into her mouth, bobbing her head up and down as far as she could. When Parush felt it was about to happen he wanted to pull out, but Bitasta held it deep inside, till Parush could no longer control the surge. He had never felt so rhapsodic.

'Yuck, how could you swallow it?' Parush asked, once he had overcome the sudden rapturous excitement.

'Dumbo, deep inside the throat you don't have taste buds,' Bitasta said, resting her head on his thighs. Parush tenderly played his fingers through her hair.

'Bits,' he said after some time, 'there's nothing special about me and everything about you is so special. It's a wonder that you have flipped for me. If I had to compete, I wouldn't have any chance to win you. But now, I don't want to lose you…'

Bitasta got up and sat on his lap with her legs folded backwards. She threw her hands around his neck and drew herself as close to him as possible. 'Do you know why I fell for you?'

'Seriously, I don't have any idea.'

'I was jealous of you. You snatched a big part of Ma from me. Rather than fighting with you, I thought it's better to call for a truce and fall in love.' She sealed his lips, making sure he couldn't say anything. But he didn't speak even when she released him.

'What?' she asked, finding him burying his head into her shoulder. 'Why do you behave like a girl so often?'

Someone opened the iron-gate outside. Bitasta jumped up. 'Oh shit, Pishu might have returned. I had managed to convince her to go to Midnapore and meet her relative.' She collected her skirt and shirt from the floor and ran out of the room. 'Take your bra,' Parush shouted, gathering his robes scattered all around. She picked the white brassiere curled under the sofa and kissed him again before running into the bathroom. 'Courier,' someone said, knocking on the door.

Sometime later, when Panchali returned, Bitasta had to again run to the bathroom, assembling her dresses from the floor. Panchali was surprised to see the dark room. 'Why is it smelling of chandan?' she asked looking around the room. Parush noticed, to his horror, Bitasta's underpants, lying under the sofa. He sat on the sofa, guarding it behind his legs. While he mined for a convincing answer to Panchali's query, she herself rescued him. 'Was she again trying to make colours out of chandan and holud?'

'Yes,' Parush almost jumped on the sofa, 'yes Kakima, she has wasted so much chandan paste and almost half a packet of turmeric.'

When she went inside he picked up the stuff from under the sofa and hid it inside his pocket. Bitasta came out of the bathroom soon and showed him a pair of closed fists and a gesture with her eyes and lips. 'I'll kill you,' he heard her shout in supersonic pitch. 'Arca,' Panchali called out from the kitchen, 'you've to immediately get some stuff from the market. I can't start cooking otherwise.'

'Ma, Porus can go.'

'No,' Panchali rebuked, 'he doesn't know the shops.'

'I can come with you,' Parush said with a devilish smile, which perhaps only Bitasta understood.

Walking by his side, Bitasta spoke the moment their house vanished beyond a turn. 'I'm not going to spare you for making me come out without my panties.'

***

'Paedophile,' Arav said that night, after hearing everything. 'Come on,' Parush defended, 'she is almost eighteen.'

Bitasta's best friend Meher was surprised. 'You guys haven't yet made out?' she exclaimed. 'I can't believe it.'

But by her eighteenth birthday, they had actually *made out*, many times.

Bitasta would always come up with ingenious plans which often scared the hell out of Parush. She figured out many relatives of Pishu, their live-in maid, along the Kharagpur line of the South-Eastern Railways and very often encouraged her to meet them. 'Ma,' she would argue with Panchali, 'I'm no longer a kid that she has to always babysit me. She never goes out and meets her relatives. Next year when we move to Calcutta she can't come here so easily.'

Parush never came to know if Panchali ever suspected Bitasta's intentions. She herself would be out most of the afternoons. 'How do you manage it with Kakima?' he asked her one day.

'I don't have to manage. She goes out herself. Do you think she intentionally goes out to make it easier for us?'

Parush was embarrassed. 'Come on, I didn't mean that.'

'Don't think so much, baby,' she whispered, throwing him on the bed.

'Are you sure you keep track of the safe period? We never use any protection.'

'Porus, why are you so scared?'

'If we're caught some day?'

'Trust me, I wouldn't do anything that would bring disgrace to us. Porus, do you realise I love you? I can't stay a moment without you. I want to gulp you…'

She was already all over him. Other days too, whenever they got a chance, Parush's apprehensions would fizzle out in no time.

It was not possible that Panchali didn't get any wind of what was happening between Bitasta and Parush. With the way they behaved, even in front of others, they left very little to imagination. With the ICSE exams approaching fast, Bitasta had very little time beyond her studies. Whatever time she could manage to spare, she would spend it with Parush, either at home or outside. People would see them at various places in the campus – Tech Market, Chhedi's, Sahara, Harri's, Vegie's – and even at places like Woldies, which were outside the campus. Parush was often seen giving *doubs* to Bitasta on his bike. In the RK Hall Day it was Bitasta who greeted all of Parush's guests, including the professors, with Panchali always by their side.

In a small place like KGP, such a thing never stayed under wraps. People started talking about it. The girls were curious to know about this guy who flaunted such a girlfriend. A few guys were jealous of how a dumbass *thoka* could get such a *hep* girl. But folks in RK had a special liking for Porus and Bitasta. Porus was the current GSec SocCult. When Bitasta was seen in RK a few times before the next Illu, no one was surprised. RK again won the Illu and after the VP Bitasta joined a large gang of RKites at Chhedi's for the celebration.

***

Parush spent the longest night of the year – the night in the middle of the winter vacation when Bitasta entered the nineteenth year of her life – in KGP, arousing a curiosity in Sairandhri, his mother. That was the first time perhaps, Parush felt, his mother was showing concern or interest in something related to him. A few months later, on a visit to his home in Calcutta, Sairandhri called for him. Parush was again surprised because till that day there had been a handful instances when his mother had called for him.

'What's happening with your studies? I hear you are always seen with Bitasta now-a-days. When do you study?'

Parush was more shocked than surprised. He wouldn't have been surprised at all had it been for Panchali to ask him something similar.

Little did Parush know then that more surprises were awaiting him. Little did he know then that his mother, who had been always indifferent to any matter concerning him, would suddenly take so much interest in his relationship with Bitasta.

That was, he would realise not much later, the beginning of the end of his relationship with Bitasta, a relationship which lived with him for many more years than it actually survived.

Much later in life did he realise that poems live forever, but somewhere the prosody may lose its control over the verses or a new type of prosody may take charge.

FALL OF THE METER

'Prosody, I feel, is an indicator of Social Anthropology,' said Panchali, on the way to the Santal village.

Panchali hadn't been there lately, due to Bitasta's ICSE exams. Shaunak had been at home too, after a long time, to be with his daughter during her exams.

Holi fell in between and Bitasta wanted Parush to embellish every part of her body with colour, like a lush meadow sprawled over a curvaceous mountain slope. That was next to impossible, given that there was no way he could get her alone at home. The evening before Holi she asked him to meet her at the Tech Market. 'Take this,' she said, handing him a packet, 'and put colour on it, thinking it's me. I'll collect it tomorrow morning before you come to Prembajar.' Getting back to his room in RK he opened the packet to find a white lace shaping-slip, which she wore under the white salwar kameez the next morning – Parush spent the whole night putting colours on it.

Shaunak threw a lavish party the day Bitasta's exams ended. Bitasta, unnoticed by everyone, always drank from the glass half-emptied by Parush. 'The scotch is more intoxicating when mixed with your "suspires",' she told him later in an inebriated state, holding the iron gate, when everyone else had left. Shaunak left the next day. Seeing him off at Kharagpur station, Panchali wanted to go to the Santal village.

'Even if you don't speak any language, you can still communicate through prosody,' she spoke as they walked leisurely through the wooded trail. 'A mother talks to her child through the prosody of her speech. Her comfort speech has a legato quality. In marked contrast, she uses a strong staccato for prohibitions. She expresses encouragement, approval, prohibition and comfort through a nonsense language, the prosodic patterns of which are the same across cultures and geographies.'

They sat on the trunk of a fallen tree. The tender rays of the vernal sun sieved through the strainer of a mesh of sonajhuri and sal leaves and fell on them in filtered pieces.

'I can't believe a poem without the meters, the rhythm, the rhymes,' she continued. 'A poem without the shackle of the meter is like a love without the bondage of passion and obsession. The structure of a scale binds a raga. The structure of movements binds a symphony. A providential omnipresent force binds the billions of particles in the universe. Rabindranath says meter is like binding the strings of a sitar, without which the musical notes can't be liberated, can't be released freely to the world. Anything that binds is the meter to me, and anything that rents, breaks down and tears apart is the fall of the meter.'

When it was getting dark, they got up and walked towards the village. Panchali, Parush felt, hadn't spoken like this for quite some time. 'People like Ezra Pound were against the entrapment of poets by the iambic pentameter – A **thing** of **beau**ty **is** a **joy** Fore**ver**. The modernists wanted to loosen the shackles of the meter. It may be symbolic to the rise of the welfare states. Traditional poetic forms could no longer give expression to the modern free world. I love the entrapment … the shackles … not the freedom.'

Bitasta clung to Parush and held his hands tight while Panchali walked a little ahead of them. Parush felt he wanted Bitasta to bind him like this, keep him close to her like this, forever. This bondage, he realised, was more liberating than anything else. Unlike Bitasta, he didn't like a poem without the meter. He never felt *any* sound could be music. The fall of a meter was a total breakdown to him too.

'But Ma,' argued Bitasta, 'don't you think Keats would write differently if he were born today?'

'Might be,' said Panchali, 'but then I wouldn't love his poetry...'

Parush felt he too wouldn't love poetry if the meter ever broke down. But, he knew, for sure, Bitasta would still love.

***

The first indications of breakdown were visible at Rupsa, during a party thrown by Srinjay, Parush's father, to celebrate the completion of the first major project undertaken by the *Indus Planning and Consultancy*. Sairandhri totally ignored Bitasta, who along with her mother had recently shifted from Prembajar to their house in Calcutta at New Alipore, not very far from Rupsa. 'Does she want you to sleep with Raka?' Aru pulled him to a side and whispered, referring to the aberrant level of importance Sairandhri was giving to Raka. Sairandhri had always been a very bad host and it didn't elude anyone's sight that she was suddenly being very guest-friendly, going around and asking if the starters had been served properly, making sure everyone's glasses were refilled on time, enquiring if anyone needed anything more.

Sairandhri ignored Panchali too – Ru and Aru, along with Parush, didn't fail to notice that.

Since that incident in the launch at Achipore more than a year back, the relationship between Aru and Parush had taken an unusually pleasant turn, mainly with Bitasta taking a keen interest to repair it. Aru gradually opened up to him. 'Do you feel awkward?' she asked him one day.

'No Aru,' he assured, 'I don't feel awkward. I feel bad for you. Why do you have to ruthlessly turn down so many guys?'

'Get me one like you – I'll not turn him down...'

Parush never brought up the topic again.

Aru called him upstairs. He found Bitasta in the balcony, alone for the first time since she had come in the evening. Very strangely, whenever he had wanted to talk to her, Sairandhri would emerge surreptitiously from somewhere. He knew Bitasta would be very upset, but she didn't show it in her face. 'Lucky guy,' joked Aru. 'Girlfriend waiting alone upstairs, mom *setting* up another downstairs, and I'm here too ... mediating.' She left, giving Parush and Bitasta the most precious thing they had been yearning for – a few moments of loneliness.

'Bits, I'm really sorry. I've no idea what Ma's up to.'

'Forget all those,' Bitasta dragged him close. 'Raka is so hot even I feel something whenever I see her. Your mom just wants a hot babe for you. Now the question is what the guy wants...'

He kissed her on her lips, so sudden and hard that she almost lost her balance. He stopped her from falling. 'The guy doesn't want his girl to fall...'

'Dada,' Parush heard his sister shouting from her room where she and her girlfriends had been creating a ruckus all through the evening, 'Ma is calling you downstairs...'

He sighed. 'Have to do something.'

'What?'

'Have to tell my mother, I don't mind screwing *your babe* Ma, but still, *my babe* will be the mother of my child...'

Parush left. Bitasta stood in the balcony alone, perhaps wondering since when Parush had started talking like that. She smiled.

Parush met Raka on the stairs. She looked totally different. Gone were her flirtatious mannerisms, her coquettish and frivolous attitude, her winks, her enticing body language and all her provocative ways. 'Bitasta is upstairs?' she asked. He stared at her, knowing well that she was feeling uncomfortable, perhaps for the first time, in front of him.

'I'll go … and talk to her.' She tried to pass by. He pulled her hand.

'Rai,' he addressed her by her daknam, something he rarely did, 'I'm sorry for Ma's behaviour. I know how awkward you felt. I love you the way you are, not the way you pretend to be. You're more beautiful like this…' He rubbed his hand on her delicately designed hair and undressed the few strands in the front, something he would often do to irritate her when they had been kids.

Raka kissed him on his hands. 'Porus, I just care for what you say to me, what you think of me … and now perhaps I care for what she thinks too.' She pointed up.

Parush watched her climb the stairs slowly. Once she reached the landing upstairs, she looked down. Parush left only after that.

***

'What does your mother think of herself?' Bitasta asked Parush angrily, the moment he entered their house in New Alipore – it was a big campus with independent houses belonging to the different siblings of the Roy family.

'Arca,' Panchali intervened, 'don't talk like this.'

'Ma,' she shouted, 'you don't have any fucking business interfering in what I say. Do you understand?' Parush remembered the last time she had uttered the word "fuck" in front of her mother. But this time her mother didn't slap her. She just pulled Parush by his hand. 'Arca, don't shout like an animal. Baba will wake up.'

Parush had made it a practice to stop by New Alipore almost every day, on the way back home from his summer internship at a company in Salt Lake. Shaunak, Bitasta's father, hadn't been keeping well since his return from a hectic trip to the Americas with his two other partners.

'What happened?' asked Parush, as Bitasta banged the door of her room.

'Parush,' Panchali pleaded, 'she is a little short-tempered. It's nothing. Your mother had been here today during the day. I had a heated discussion with her on something...'

'About what?' Parush interrupted.

'Parush ...' Panchali took her time, 'why do you care? We're old friends. Can't we fight?'

'Kakima, why are you trying to defend her?'

'I'm not, Parush. Please try to understand. We fought after a very long time. And I feel as if we've gone back to those days...'

'Shut up Ma,' Bitasta shouted, running out of her room. 'And Porus, just remember,' she turned back, 'I love you. If she's going to think I just want to get screwed by an IITian, to hell with her...' She broke down, wailing loudly, first clinging to Parush and then gradually embracing him tightly. Parush felt awkward in front of Panchali – he was perhaps still not comfortable with PDA.

'Come inside,' Panchali walked into the guest room. Parush pulled Bitasta by her hand and followed Panchali. She sat on the bed and Bitasta on the floor, embracing her legs, still crying. Parush stood by the door, confused, watching the mother-daughter duo. He hadn't seen Bitasta cry.

'Ma, you know all,' Bitasta said, sitting straight, resting her back against the bed. 'I should have told you earlier. I didn't expect to tell you like this.'

Panchali gestured Parush to sit by her side.

'I know everything,' she said, once Parush sat on the bed, 'even though neither of you told me anything.' She paused and looked ahead. Parush stared at Bitasta. Sitting quiet with her eyes closed, she looked like a giant tree which hadn't wavered during the storm, but presently appeared withered, water dripping from the drooping and tired leaves.

'I'll say only one thing to both of you: *the pleasure of love is in loving, and one is happier in the passion one feels than in the passions one arouses in another*. You love someone you think is the ideal person, someone who has all those qualities you don't have. Love makes you forget everything you don't have. Love makes you feel complete. You're fortunate that you can love. Don't look back. And don't care about the world, about the people...'

***

Parush pushed the door of Sairandhri's room hard. The door opened and banged on the wall. Shocked, Sairandhri got up from her desk and found Parush standing in front of her.

'Sit,' she pointed to the bed. He didn't sit and looked straight into her eyes. 'What did you say to them?'

Sairandhri became cautious. 'Nothing,' she tried to be normal, hiding the anxiety.

'Ma,' Parush shouted, 'you've got to go there tomorrow and apologise for whatever you said.'

'Apologise?' she was surprised, 'For what? Do you know whatever I've said?'

'I don't care what all you've said. Kakima didn't say, neither did Bitasta, and I don't want to know. But I know they are hurt, they are angry, they are...'

'What's your relationship with Bitasta?' she interrupted.

'I want to...' Parush mined for the apt words to say it directly, and wondered why he faltered to compose even the simplest figure of speech. 'I want to marry her ...' he said finally, surprised how hard he had struggled to avoid the use of the simple word "love" in front of his mother. Simple things, he realised, couldn't be said so simply in front of *strangers*.

Sairandhri was more shocked than surprised to see the newly attained firmness in Parush, something she had never seen in the past. His body language, his looks and his tone – everything exuded an unfamiliar obstinacy. 'Okay,' she said casually, 'I'll go there tomorrow.' She went back and sat at her desk. 'You want to come with me?'

'No,' answered Parush firmly and left the room.

***

Lying on the upper bunk in a first-class coupe of Darjeeling Mail, Parush wondered what could have happened earlier the day when his mother had been to New Alipore, supposedly to apologise to Panchali. He had called Bitasta in the evening, before leaving for the station. She was not at home and her obnoxious cousin sister, taking the call on a parallel line from the adjoining house, asked the same irritating questions she would ask every time she picked the phone. Parush banged the receiver on the phone, cursing the telephone department for taking so long to give a new connection at Bitasta's house. He knew this trip to Gangtok and Darjeeling, entirely planned by his sister for the first time, would be his worst vacation. But he didn't know that this was the last time his entire family would travel together.

Parush was irritated to find Bitasta not at home when he called her some more times, first from Gangtok and then from Darjeeling. When he could finally talk to her, he shouted over the phone. Everyone around the small STD booth turned towards him and stared at him with a mixture of amazement and amusement.

'Are you nuts?' Bitasta shouted back. 'Why do you screw up things like this? Who told you to ask your mom to come here again and apologise? What the fuck do you think about yourself? Do you realise you have fucking made the situation even worse? She came here and created a ruckus leaving very little to the imagination of my fucking relatives who already have problems with everything I do – the way I dress, the way I talk, the way I eat...'

'Parush,' Panchali interrupted, snatching the phone from Bitasta, 'don't listen to her. Sairi is my friend. I know her more than anyone else, more than you, more than your father, more than anyone…'

The miles of cables and the complicated network of switches Parush had read about in the telecommunication classes, which were meant to transmit only tiny electrical stimuli, didn't fail to carry the pulses of emotions from Calcutta to Darjeeling – Parush could hear Panchali's heavy breaths.

'It's not about you and Bitasta. Don't you fight with people you love? We've known each other for so long. We've been by each other's side for so long. Sairi is my dearest friend, someone I love the most, someone who has all the right to fight with me, shout at me…'

The line got disconnected. Parush tried a few more times.

'It doesn't get through at times,' said the owner of the telephone booth.

***

Parush would often go to Raka's house in Salt Lake in the evening, directly from the place where he was doing his summer internship in Calcutta. Dropping her home after her swimming sessions in the afternoon, their driver took their car back to Ballygunj, to her father's office. Parush took a lift till Ballygunj, from where most of the days he would go to New Alipore to meet Bitasta. 'Come a bit early today, if possible,' Raka called him one afternoon and said. There was an unusual indifference in her voice.

'Everything okay?' asked Parush.

'Will see you in the evening…' she kept the phone down.

More surprise awaited him in the evening when Raka opened the door. She looked forlorn and melancholic. But totally contrasting to her looks was the stunning white chemise she wore. The double layer of chiffon sprawled tenderly across the landscape of her body with sheer elegance. Bold appliqués highlighted the bodice with a low scoop neck. She sat on the sofa with crossed legs. Leaning back, she gestured for him to sit too. He sat in front of her and stared at her with curiosity and bewilderment.

'In this lingerie nightwear, am I not looking like a perfect mistress?' she asked, uttering each word discretely. Parush was too perplexed to say anything. 'Stunned, right? This is supposed to be a birthday gift from you.'

'What?' Parush's reaction was involuntary. She removed a paper-weight from a side table and pulled a piece of paper. She held the paper in front of her for a while and then handed it to him. As she leaned forward her bare breasts swayed under the flimsy bodice. Parush took the paper in his hand and read the few lines scribbled on it. He didn't take even a moment to realise that it was his mother's handwriting. He sat quiet on the sofa, stunned.

'Your mother called me yesterday afternoon saying that she would send me a packet through your driver,' she spoke softly, as if she was talking to herself, staring out through the open window. 'In an hour I received the packet which contained this dress and the letter. Thank God, I'm not as dumb as she might have thought I would be. But Porus, what if I really believed it was you who wanted to give me this gift on my birthday, which I'm sure you forgot this year too? Porus, I'm a human being. I too have emotions, sentiments. I too have temptations which I must fight. Porus, how could she do this?'

Parush got up and sat beside her. He took her head and lapped it on his shoulder. He wiped the tears off her eyes. 'Porus,' she wailed silently, 'how could she do this? I feel like a whore who bares everything for the world but is shattered when the guy she loves brutally rips off her clothes...'

Parush pulled her up and took her upstairs to her room. 'Where do you keep your clothes?' he asked. She pointed towards one of the wardrobes. He opened it and selected a homely white dress. 'I'll be downstairs. Wear this and come down ... fast.' She ran to him and hugged him, burying her head in his chest.

Sitting on the sofa he felt an extreme hatred for his mother, a hatred which wouldn't subside ever in his life, not even when, many years later, he would be standing in front of her, unperturbed, unshaken, and she would be trying to say something desperately to him, through her slowly shutting eyes, in the last few days of her life.

Yes, he realised, somewhere, the meter had fallen. For that matter, he thought, had there ever been any meter in his life? Didn't he always feel others' lives were so ordered, so structured, and his so disorganised, so unmethodical, so imprecise? Ever since he could remember, he had always yearned for an entrapment, be it the bondage of an embrace or the shackles of a rebuke.

A thing of beauty is a joy forever ... the lines reverberated in his mind. The beauty of something entrapped in meter – that was all he had always craved for.

THE STAIR ROOM

The side entrance to Bitasta's house, leading directly upstairs, was through the most neglected part of the house. Shirir ghar, the stair room, as it is commonly called, is a narrow claustrophobic chamber nested under the staircase which rises by a floor in two steps, bending like a hairpin at a landing midway – the entrance was under the landing. In the absence of any other designated place in the house to preserve things like old magazines which would never be read again, old footwear totally unworthy of use, an old toddler bike and many other queer historical objects, the stair room acted as the default dumping space for all useless stuff which should have been thrown away.

But despite the incongruity and inconsequence, the stair room became a very significant part of Bitasta and Parush's love and its making. Unlike Prembajar, New Alipore never provided any lucky chance to be home alone. Even a simple kiss had to be meticulously planned and executed with perfect timing.

Under the prevailing austere and celibate circumstances, the sudden invention of the other aspect of the staircase was no doubt a progeny of necessity. Henceforth, Bitasta would artfully unhook the bra while descending the stairs and in those few precious moments before opening the door they would tear apart each other. She would arrange herself properly while climbing the stairs up.

Perhaps with some providential interference, she finally managed to be alone at home on Parush's birthday on 21st June. 'I'll be alone. Come and collect your birthday gift,' she told him over the phone. 'It's the longest day of the year… Don't waste the day… Bunk your internship and come right now.'

Bitasta hid behind the door when Parush pushed it. She switched on the bulb once he shut the door. She stared at him seductively, leaning her head to the left and biting the corner of her lips.

'Happy birthday, Porus,' she whispered, slipping the outer layer of white chiffon.

'Where did you get it?' he spoke into her ears, pulling the strings one by one and letting the pieces of the robe slide down her slippery body.

'Dumbo, what do you think? I've stolen it from Raka?'

The clumsiness of the stair room had become so familiar to them. Out of habit they did it all so fast, as though they were in the same hurry, like the other times. Exhausted, they lay on the dirty floor, entwined and entangled. He collected all the dirt and dust stuck to the sweat of her body and decorated her breasts with it. She rubbed her breasts on his body and mixed her dirt with his sweat. '*Take a lump of clay*,' she recited a poem from her mother's diary, '*wet it and pat it, make a statue of you and a statue of me. Then shatter them, clutter them, add some water, and break them and mould them into a statue of you and a statue of me. Then in mine, there are bits of you and in yours there are bits of me. Nothing ever shall keep us apart…*'

***

'Has Baba said anything?' Bitasta had asked Panchali.

'When has your father shown any interest in such things?' Panchali said casually. Bitasta wondered how her father could remain so calm and disinterested, even after all the commotion that had happened. He might have been asleep in the adjoining room. But it was hard to believe that he had not got any wind of it. Sairandhri's voice that day, when Parush had asked her to go and apologise, would have been audible even from her cousins' houses and Bitasta knew they already had their own theories about the entire episode.

She was more surprised when Srinjay, Parush's father, called her one day. 'We'll all be coming tonight. We'll have dinner at your place. And you know what Panchali has to cook for me?'

'Colocasia shoots?' she laughed out loud, calling kochur loti, one of Srinjay's favourite East Bengali dishes, by the name which sounded nothing like what it was in reality.

Srinjay opened a bottle of Cristal in the evening. 'The night today is for the lovely young lady, Bitasta Roy,' he announced. Neither did he explicitly say what the celebration was for, nor did anyone ask. In no time Srinjay and Shaunak were too drunk to say anything that would make sense. They left the room and sat in the balcony with their glasses. Inside, it was an awkward situation, with Panchali spending as much time in the kitchen as possible, Pushi, Parush's sister, listening to her Walkman with her eyes shut and Sairandhri reading a months-old *Anandalok*. After a while Bitasta went to help her mother and Parush joined Srinjay and Shaunak.

Before leaving, Srinjay embraced Bitasta. 'The next big party is on my son's birthday,' he announced, 'and you would be my chief guest. Who knows where he'll be from next year...'

On his birthday, on the longest day of the year, when Parush was leaving Bitasta's house, a few hours before the big party, Bitasta called him from behind. 'Porus, wherever we stay, I need a stair room like this...'

Parush rushed to his room to open the packet Bitasta had given him as his birthday gift. He removed the wrapping paper tenderly. When the last fold had been undone, the gift emerged – the white slip he had spent a whole night colouring before holi, unwashed, folded loosely as though not to crush his emotions and sentiments and the scent and sweat of her body. On a piece of paper was written: *Wash it, only when you want to wash me off.*

***

Raka, Ru and Aru made sure that all the guests had a blast at Parush's birthday party. That Sairandhri was not talking much didn't appear unusual to anyone. But, that she and Panchali exchanged glances, appeared very unusual to Bitasta, who caught a sight of it by chance. When everyone was busy putting cream on Parush's face she noticed them slowly moving away from the crowd and talking to each other.

On some pretext Raka took Bitasta and Parush upstairs. 'I wish both of you all the happiness, all the success and all the good things in life,' she embraced them together. 'Don't misunderstand me. I'll always love Porus in a way I wouldn't love anyone else. Let me live with that. Don't snatch it.'

She kissed both and left, leaving them alone in the balcony.

Bitasta was indifferent. 'What?' asked Parush.

'I don't think I'll ever understand your mother. But the strange thing is that Ma too may be equally incomprehensible…'

***

Parush returned to KGP after the summer break. The afternoons seemed unending to him. He had the duplicate keys for Bitasta's house in Prembajar. Since they had moved to Calcutta few months back, after her ICSE exams, the house had been lying vacant. He would go there and stay alone in the empty house for hours. He would sit on the revolving chair in Bitasta's room and stare at the books lying haphazardly on the desk. A pen had been left open on an open note book, as if she would return soon and resume writing on the open page. A painting had been left half done, the dry palate with a hardened paste of sandal and turmeric lying by its side. The bed still had a bedcover, crumbled from the last use. The wall still had the calendar, fluttering the page of an older month, the month when they had moved to Calcutta. Parush would wonder if Bitasta had meticulously planned to preserve her presence in everything he noticed. He would lie on the bed where they had made love so many times. He would sit on the sofa in the living room for hours, staring at the wall. He would ride his bike slowly on the way back to his hostel.

In the night he would spend hours sitting at his desk, keeping Panchali's diary open in front of him. Every poem bore memories of their togetherness, their unspoken love, their unexpressed vows, their untold admissions, their withheld yearnings.

The poems enlivened his loneliness and solitude, taking him back to those blooming days, when long before they could speak or express, the poems would unfurl them on their behalf.

Before you were coming, I was I...

So shrinks from Love the tender heart
As if from threat of being slain,
For when true Love awakens, dies
The Self, that Despot, dark and vain...

You who do know all the heart's turns,
Say, is it love now that in me burns?

Each poem would arouse the fervour in newer ways every time he read it anew. He would let loose his fantasies and allow her thoughts to possess him as if they were real. He would burn in the inferno till that moment of exhilaration, after which he would lie down listlessly on the bed for the rest of the night. Even then he wouldn't allow her thoughts to leave his consciousness.

He would call Bitasta at odd times when the calling rates were low. 'Bits, the silent moments of nights are the most intolerable. The silence kills me night after night. I feel like running away, but can't move a bit. I feel like you've hypnotised me…'

'Porus, why don't you just forget your fucking classes and come here? I just want to eat you up…'

Most of the times they would hang up suddenly suspecting someone was eavesdropping on the parallel connection.

'Can't you get a girl to make the call?' she asked one day. 'I hate my fucking cousin picking your call and then making obnoxious statements later.'

Parush started getting Sweti, his classmate, whenever she would be available. His friends, especially from SN and IG, the ladies hostels, would often tease him that Sweti had always had a *thing* for him and that Bitasta had "screwed up" her prospects. Though he didn't believe that it could be true, he would be extra cautious in dealing with her because he knew that his best friend Arav liked her a lot.

'You're so mean Porus,' Sweti complained one day. 'You remember me only when you have to call Bitasta. You haven't even bothered to introduce her to me…'

'Come on Swets,' Parush interrupted, 'a friend in need is a friend indeed…'

'Shut up,' Sweti slapped him.

'By the way,' Parush said, 'why do you always avoid Arav?'

'He is so gross. Does he ever speak anything other than slang?'

'How many times have you talked to him?'

Sweti stopped walking and stared at him. 'Everyone should have a best friend like you,' she smiled. '*Chalo*, the queue at the

STD booth is growing longer ...' she pointed at the line of people assembled in front of the telephone booth ahead of them.

***

Bitasta started writing letters to Parush, filling them with their favourite poems and simple titbits of her days.

'The world is full of folks, it's true, but there was only one of you... I missed you a lot at the fest. I miss KGP, I miss Prembajar, I miss you. The classes are boring...

'I'm having my cycle. I'm getting irritated with every small thing. Ma has become very quiet now-a-days, like your mom. I fight with her almost every day...

'Your sister and Aru pick me up in the morning. We all are in the same class. Aru has become my best friend...

'Your sister is just a facsimile of your mother. I don't know why she hates me so much. What's the problem with your mother? That day our driver told me, "Didi, why are you after Sairi madam's son? Don't you know he will finally marry Raka didi? He is playing with you." I asked him who told him this. He said your driver had heard your mother saying so to someone...'

Parush would write to her in the lonely nights, when he burned the most.

One day, Bitasta shouted at him when he called her up. 'Don't you know I stay in a public place where there's no privacy? Even my letters are opened and read. How could you write such a filthy letter? Do you have any idea how I felt when my aunt said to Ma that had she raised me in the proper way, boys wouldn't have written such obscene letters to me? She said I'm a *bajar girl...*'

Parush hung up the phone and ran out of the STD booth. He shut the door of his room and banged his head on the wall. He cried for some time and then fell asleep. He woke up with the sounds of loud knocks on his door. When he opened the door, he was shocked to see Bitasta and Aru in their Modern High school uniform. Bitasta pushed him inside and threw him on the bed. Aru quickly shut the door. Bitasta started beating him randomly. 'What the fuck do you think of yourself? Do you know how many times I tried calling your hostel last night? Your room was always locked from outside. Where the hell were you all night? Why didn't you think even for once that I could call?' She broke down. 'How could you do this to me? Do you've any idea how we managed to come here? And here you're sleeping so peacefully in your room. I'll kill you…'

Half an hour later Parush took the two girls to Sahara for lunch. It was already twelve and they didn't have much time if they wanted to get back to Calcutta by evening. When Aru had come alone in the morning to pick Bitasta up, she decided then and there to go to KGP, bunking the whole day at school.

'Your mother keeps calling her, asking her to break the relationship with you,' Aru informed, when Bitasta had gone to wash her hands. 'She tells her that you two can't be happy if she is so against it. Bits anyway was very upset and then that episode with your letter happened…'

'By the way,' Bitasta asked him at the station, 'how did you manage to lock your door from outside?'

'You might not have noticed there's a small window in the door. Hanging the lock through the window is a way to say "Do Not Disturb"…'

Bitasta started beating him again. Aru didn't stop her.

***

The final year was quite hectic. Parush couldn't go to Calcutta that often. Bitasta continued to write letters regularly. He too would write. But when he realised that not all his letters were reaching her, he stopped writing. The phone calls also reduced because Bitasta hadn't yet got a separate telephone connection. Whenever he would go to Calcutta there would be some new complication thanks to his mother.

Sairandhri's persistence became a matter of mental torture to both Bitasta and Panchali. 'Why do you entertain her every time?' Bitasta asked her mother one day. Panchali couldn't give any proper justification for her reluctance to cut Sairandhri off. Whenever she came to their house, Panchali would receive her as if nothing had happened. Most of the times, she would talk only to Panchali. But she talked to Bitasta too whenever she would be at home. Bitasta learned to ignore her totally. Panchali often cried in the night, not knowing that Bitasta was awake. Finally, Bitasta would burst in front of Parush, whenever he came. The only time they would forget everything was when they would be at the stair room for a short while. Returning to Rupsa, he would fume in front of Ru and Aru. But he never talked to his mother. Increasingly, he started hating her.

'Do you want me to talk to her?' Ru asked one day.

'No,' he said firmly. 'I just don't care.'

Shaunak threw a lavish party, again at Achipore, on Bitasta's nineteenth birthday. Amidst all the arrangements, the costly wine, the barbeque, the wide spread of food, the song and dance, the bonfire, there was something amiss. Standing at the edge of the bank Bitasta kept quiet for a long time. 'What's the problem, Bits,' Parush asked.

'Porus, something is terribly wrong… I don't know what, but I'm sure there's something between Ma and Sairi Auntie. It's not that she hates me or Ma. Every time she looks at me, I get confused. It's not what I may think…'

'I hate her,' Parush interrupted. No one talked for the rest of the time they were alone.

***

Parush had been to New Alipore to meet Bitasta the day before he left for Noida, to join the company he had got an offer from. When the time came to leave, Panchali had hugged him for a long time at the landing where the staircase ended upstairs. She kissed him many times. 'Be happy, Baba,' she kept on repeating. She wiped her tears and went inside. Bitasta and Parush remained in each other's arms for a long time in front of the closed door of the stair room. Bitasta wept copiously as though they wouldn't meet ever in their lives. Parush was a little confused as to why the mother and daughter were behaving in such an over-emotional way. He too was feeling bad, but then he had felt worse to return to KGP alone after the summer break the previous year.

The last one year had acclimatised him to staying apart from Bitasta. He had got used to the loneliness, the void, the insecurity of not having Bitasta always by his side. What he would miss in Noida was perhaps Prembajar, her house, the Hijli forest, Tech Market, Chhedi's, his room in RK – everything that had something of Bitasta in scattered bits and pieces.

Later, Parush wondered if Bitasta had had a premonition that evening that they would meet at the stair room just two more times, but none of those meetings would have any loving memory.

***

A week before Durga Pujo, Parush called Bitasta from Noida. He wanted to surprise her by saying that he would be in Calcutta the very next week. He had expected an excess of emotions and reactions from Bitasta. Ever since he had decided to go to Calcutta during the Durga Pujo, he had been finding it tough to contain the excitement of seeing Bitasta unexpectedly in a few days. He had expected a similar excitement in Bitasta too. But her reaction was anything but that of excitement. She appeared extremely cold over the phone. Only upon reaching Calcutta and hearing everything from Ru did he realise what had happened in between.

One day, Bitasta had returned early from school. The door of the stair room was not shut. She saw Sairandhri's sandals at the landing of the staircase. Walking up the stairs she tried to hear the conversation between Panchali and Sairandhri – they were in the bedroom.

'Kalyani,' she heard Sairandhri's firm voice, 'it has to stop. You know it.'

'I beg Sairi,' Panchali pleaded, 'please don't separate them. Do you understand Sairi, they are in love…'

'Kalyani, this is wrong, this is wrong. They can't be in love…'

Bitasta remembered Sairandhri had addressed her mother as Kalyani the first time she had come to Prembajar. She also recalled how Panchali had given a flimsy justification for that. Who was Kalyani? Why did Sairandhri address Panchali as Kalyani?

'Please Sairi,' Bitasta heard her mother weep, 'let us forget all those…'

Bitasta entered the bedroom and was shocked to see her mother sitting on the floor, holding Sairandhri's legs. In a moment, she lost control. She pulled her mother up and made her sit on the bed. She held Sairandhri by her hand and dragged her towards the door. 'Just get out of here, you bitch,' she shouted. Sairandhri lost her balance with the sudden drag and fell against the wall. Panchali ran to her. Bitasta came in between and blocked her way. She pulled Sairandhri up and pushed her hard towards the door. 'Stop,' Panchali shouted at the top of her voice. Bitasta left Sairandhri's hand. Panchali slapped her. 'Not a word more. Apologise to her,' she said firmly. Bitasta looked at her in disbelief. She shut her eyes and gathered all the energy she had. 'Fuck you all,' she ran out of the room. She ran down the stairs, kicked open the door and came out in the main road in front of their house, barefooted. She stopped an auto. 'Rupsa,' she told the auto driver. Fifteen minutes later, she alighted from the auto in front of Ru's house.

***

Parush ran to New Alipore to meet Bitasta. Panchali behaved normally, as if nothing had happened. Parush couldn't understand if Shaunak, Bitasta's father, knew anything. 'Let's go out,' Bitasta said. She came down the stairs fast, opened the door of the stair room and waited for him on the road. While shutting the door from outside Parush remembered the last time they had been at the stair room, the day before he was leaving for Noida. Things had changed a lot, he realised, in these few months.

Bitasta didn't talk much in the car. Neither did they talk like before in Scoop, the familiar place overlooking the Ganga they had been to so many times in the past. No one brought up the topic of the recent fiasco. They talked about trivial things. 'How are your studies going on?' he asked her. 'Fine,' she replied. 'And, how is your work?' she added.

'Fine…'

'Didn't have any problem getting leave?'

'No…'

'Have you guys finally got a good cook in Noida?'

'Yes, and she's a Bengali too…'

The conversations were short, in staccatos. When Parush dropped her home, she didn't ask him to come inside.

***

A few months later, when Parush called Bitasta after her ISC exams, he was shocked at what he heard.

'Porus, I want to break-up with you,' she said directly.

Parush couldn't respond. 'It's not going anywhere,' she continued. 'I give a damn about your mother. But I can't fight with my mom. Even she feels I should break-up...'

'No, I don't believe it,' Parush shouted over the phone, attracting the attention of the other people in the queue behind him. 'Kakima can't say that.'

'Porus, forget about what she says. I'm saying I want to break-up, and I'm saying this after a lot of thought. My decision wouldn't change. And if you think practically, this would be good for you too...'

The next day Parush was in Calcutta. The return flight fare was more than his monthly take-home salary of six grand. His bank balance, like that of his friend Arav too, after eleven months of working, was surprisingly nothing. Many a time he and Arav would wonder why their condition was like that of daily wage earners, even after close to a year in job. Month ends would completely deplete their cash, month after month, while the beginnings would be lavish. Arav arranged for the money required to buy the tickets.

It was Rabindra Jayanti, Tagore's birth anniversary, and Calcutta was decked up in festivity. Popular Tagore songs, heard so many times, seemed like a loud cacophony in some unknown language. Parush's eyes were burning. When he reached Bitasta's house at New Alipore it was seven in the evening. He had called Bitasta from Delhi airport to say that he would be in Calcutta in a few hours.

Standing in front of the closed door of the stair room, he anticipated Bitasta would emerge from behind the door. He pushed the door – it was open. Every step he climbed he expected Bitasta would come down and hug him, like she would always do. He reached the landing upstairs, removed his shoes and sat on the sofa.

Bitasta emerged from the bedroom and sat on a chair, facing him. Parush drank a few glasses of water, but still felt thirsty.

Bitasta spoke first. 'You're cheating on me…'

'What?' Parush interrupted.

'Yes,' her response was calm and short.

'With whom?' Parush was more puzzled than hurt.

'With Raka…'

Parush wanted to react, but felt numb. He just sat quiet, his face turned down, his eyes hovering over the alternate black and white squares of the floor mosaic which had always appeared to be in a proper pattern but presently looked all random. He listened to everything Bitasta was saying, not reacting at all. Her voice seemed familiar, but her words incomprehensible, like the Sanskrit mantras uttered by the priest at any religious function.

***

A few hours later, when Parush came down those stairs for the last time, Bitasta walked behind him. She had an eyesore and was not able to see properly. She walked holding the railing. Neither did Parush notice that she was struggling to descend the stairs.

Parush opened the door, turned back and stared at Bitasta. He looked up, hoping Panchali would call him back. She didn't. She hadn't even come out of her room to talk to him. She was not keeping well, Bitasta had said. He stared at the stair room for the last time, the heaps of junk items, the dirt, the dust, the stairs, and

Bitasta. Parush suddenly started coughing. He felt breathless and thirsty. Bitasta came forward, but he moved back. 'Want some water?' she asked.

'No,' he managed to say, still coughing. 'Thanks, no, I'll manage.' Bitasta looked directly into his eyes, his burning eyes, his dry eyes, his deep eyes.

'*Bhalo thakis*,' he said and turned back.

'You too stay well,' Bitasta said from behind.

The stair room was visible for quite some time from the main road. He felt like turning back many times to see if Bitasta was there at the door.

That was the last time they saw each other.

KGP

I looked at my watch. It was close to five. The chill in the air increased suddenly, along with a shivering wind which whirred through the trees. Parush started coughing and feeling breathless. 'O shit, I've forgotten my puff...' He tried to stand up, but couldn't. He fell on the fallen tree trunk we had been sitting on for a while now. He started shivering. I removed my muffler and wrapped his head with it. As he struggled to breathe I felt nervous. 'What should I do?' I asked in a tizzy.

'Don't worry,' he tried to assure me, 'I'll be fine. I've got used to it now.' He rubbed his chest with his hand.

'May I?' I offered. I held him straight by putting a hand behind his back and rubbed the other on his chest slowly.

'The first few times were really bad. It started from that day, when I was returning from their house. I was allergic to dust and pollen. I would often carry cetrizine with me. But I was not asthmatic, though doctors had warned that I might become one sometime...'

'Are you feeling better?'

'Ya... I told you... I'll be alright. Let me continue...'

I felt he might not have spoken about all these in years and was feeling lighter pouring out everything which had accumulated over a long time, like clouds, sucking the waters and coalescing into dark monsters. His life was all clouds.

'... I had been already panting and finding it difficult to breathe when I left Bitasta's house. When I arrived in front of Ru's house it was quite late. The auto driver helped me walk to the door. A few hours later Ru and Aru took me to Calcutta Hospital and I was put on a nebulizer. Next morning, I saw Baba sitting by my side in the emergency ward. I looked around, not to see if Ma had come, but to make sure she hadn't… I saw her again many years later, a few days before she died...'

'Let's go back Parush. It's getting very cold.'

'The Santal village is close by. Someone may still remember me…'

He got up with my support and led me to the village through another forest trail. He couldn't walk for more than a few minutes at a stretch. It was quite dark, but he strode confidently, not getting confused at any turn. Gradually, the forest cleared up and opened into a small village veiled under the thick morning mist. At a distance I could see the silhouette of a woman cleaning the courtyard in front of a hut. Parush rested against a tree and took a long breath. 'Henda ho,' he shouted. I waved my hands at the woman. She kept the broom and came towards us.

'I want to meet Boma Kisku,' he shifted to Bangla. 'Does he still live in this village?'

The woman stared at him for some time. 'Parush Dada?' she exclaimed. 'You don't remember me? I'm Lokkhi. I was a small girl when you would come here with Ajin and Didi. Come with me. Noa atoren mukhia hor kanae, he is now the mukhia.'

'Edaina, note hijukme,' she asked me.

'Lokkhi, she doesn't understand Santali,' Parush clarified. 'Saoli, she's asking you to follow her.'

While walking behind her, Parush told me that they would call Panchali ajin, elder sister in Santali, and Bitasta didi. The woman talked to Parush in a mix of Bangla and Santali, but in chaste Bangla to me.

'Chetleka menama?' Parush greeted the village headman. The woman had left us behind to inform him of our arrival in advance.

'I'm fine. What a surprise to see you my boy.' Boma Kisku embraced Parush. He figured out from Parush's condition that he was not well. He took him inside his house. He got him an anga, a long-quilted coat. Parush lay down on the bed. Another woman, the same age as Lokkhi, smiled at him and got a blanket, which I laid properly on him. He felt a little better after drinking a glass of warm milk. His breathing became normal.

Parush felt awkward that the people at Boma Kisku's house were treating me as though I was his wife. 'I'm sorry for the confusion,' he apologised to me when we were alone.

'It's fine. Should I ask them to get some medicine?'

'No, I'll be alright soon. Outside it was very cold. Now I feel very comfortable. After that day, when I had been to Bitasta's house for the last time, I never had such a bad breathing problem. To be very frank, at one point I doubted if I would be fine without a nebulizer… Saoli, I still remember that morning, in hospital. Staring at Baba, I felt a sort of camaraderie with him – we were both victims of the indifference and insensitivity of the same woman, my mother.'

'Did your mother know that you were in hospital?'

'I can't say. When I told Baba that I wanted to stay at Ru's place he didn't say anything. I was there in Calcutta for another three days and Baba would come to see me every day. Ma never came. I cried the whole day after returning from the hospital. It was not that people don't breakup, or relationships don't work out. You may think I had overreacted. I thought about it so many times later, when I would try to introspect, and analyse everything. No Saoli, I didn't overreact. It was not that I lost my girlfriend. It was not that I felt terrible to be dumped. It was not that I felt betrayed though she had claimed that the final nail in the coffin was her feeling that I was cheating on her with Raka…'

'Did you believe that?' I interrupted.

'No, I didn't. I was always in touch with Raka and she knew it. She knew that I would write letters to Raka. She claimed that Raka herself had told her that I was cheating on her.'

'You didn't confront Raka?'

'No. I didn't know whom to believe. She said Raka was interested in one of her cousins whom Raka had met at her place when he was visiting them from the US and that Raka didn't like my insinuations. To add to my suspicion, Raka too hadn't replied to the last few letters I had written to her from Noida. Whatever, I didn't care for anything. For me the end of the relationship was like the end of everything. She and Kakima had created a world, which I had always craved for but which I had eventually learned to live without. I yearned for the love and tenderness I never got at home; I yearned for loving care, a feeling that someone's there to feel for me, to be happy and sad with me, to shout at me, to be angry with me, to be soft with me, to hug me, to cuddle me, to give me the strength to feel strong, to give me the courage to fight the world…'

'Wasn't Ru there too?'

'I believe Ru was more like an ointment to the scars of a kid who grew up with multiple fixations, and multiple deprivations at home. Without her I would have been a psycho. She saved me. But she was cautious too. After all, she was a cousin, albeit distant. If she weren't cautious I would have been swayed. Ru made dough out of a lump of washed away soil, but Bits and Kakima moulded the dough and gave it a proper shape. Ru was like a fantasy, they were the reality. In those few years Bits brought a drastic change in me. The sense of void at home, the weird relationship between my parents, my indifferent mother who rarely touched me, my silly sister with whom I didn't share any relationship for a very long time – all these perhaps gave me a feeling that I was a deprived person, that I couldn't get anything from life. Unconsciously, I wanted to tell the world, "*Hey, you bunch of assholes and fuckers, here I am, look at me. I'm not what you see.*

I'm at the top. I've got everything..." But I didn't know how I would do that. When I came to KGP I was an immature, romantic kid and when I left KGP, perhaps unknown to myself, I had already learned all the tricks I needed in life. And it was Bits who had taught me everything, I don't know exactly how. Losing her was like losing all those tricks... losing me... I hated the insecurity I had always had... I didn't want to be insecure again in life...'

He started coughing again. I sat beside him on the bed and gently rubbed his chest. I wondered how he had so efficiently performed his own psychoanalysis.

'I changed the day I met her at the NCC camp. My friend Arav perhaps noticed it even before me. Earlier, I had cooked up something to avoid standing in the sun. I had taken a job in the kitchen. That was how I had been before I met Bits. I would always prefer the shade. I met her and the very next day I started going out in the sun...'

Boma Kisku returned in a few hours. Parush had already freshened up. We were getting ready to leave.

'Chetleka jiwi jati menakpea?' he asked Parush. 'How is your health generally?'

'Boge gean, apart from this problem I'm generally fine. Adi johar, thanks for everything.'

'Don't embarrass me. Ajin was very close to us... We were shocked when...'

'Do you know about her?' Parush interrupted.

'Yes, Bitasta had come here to do the bhandan ceremony after her death...'

***

'So, what do you think is the real reason why she broke up?' We were sitting on the gallery of Gyan Ghosh stadium.

After returning from the Santal village Parush had slept the whole afternoon, waking up in the evening. While he was asleep I had sat by his side, watching his crumbled contour moving up and down under the blanket with the rhythm of his life. The silent slumber of the lazy afternoon was interrupted only by the sound of his breathing, which was no longer heavy. From the way he was sleeping, so comfortably, so cosily, could anyone comprehend anything of what his life had become in reality? Did he always sleep like this or was it only now, when the ruthless world of his had sunk into oblivion under the aegis of this house in Prembajar, where, many years ago, he would come for peace, solace and love?

I couldn't but keep staring at Parush. He reminded me of his sister, someone whom I missed badly. She slept just like her brother. Flashes of that night, when I had stayed over at her place for the first time, after the conference at the Jadavpur University, came in front of my eyes. We were reciting Sappho's poetry to each other. The summer night had cooled down after the drizzles. Her bedroom was filled with the aroma of lavender candles. That night, lying side by side on the bed, her breath falling on my face with the rhythm of her heaving breasts, Parushni talked a lot, things which she wanted to speak out. She delineated her happiness as I was with her, but somewhere, she was hesitant, rather, scared. She confided in me her childhood traumas, her loneliness, her hooded eyes revealing the hidden pain as she looked at me.

I was abstracted in the thoughts of Parushni. When Parush woke up, he felt shy to see me staring at him.

'Had a nice sleep?'

'Ya, nicer than any I can remember of late…'

'Want to go out? We can take a walk in the campus.'

I drove his car around the campus, showing him the new buildings Vikramshila and Takshashila, grandly inserted between the *ghasi dep* – the Department of Agricultural and Food

Engineering – and the Tata Sports Complex. 'What was here earlier?' Parush asked, looking around the sprawling Srinivasa Ramanujan Complex in amazement. 'Wasn't here a wasteland covered with a sort of a jungle?'

'Ya, I think so…'

He stretched his arms, shut his eyes, looked up at the sky and spun around like a kid enjoying the raindrops falling on her face. A few people who passed by us threw a perplexed gaze at him. I hoped no one would recognise him. In this age of Twitter and Facebook it wouldn't be surprising to see my own picture along with his in the newspaper or some television channel the next day, with another interesting story.

He sat on the grass and then lay down on it, attracting the attention of few more people. A guard started walking fast towards us. With his eyes still stuck to the mobile held in both his hands, the guard almost fell after stepping on the threshold created along the side of the pathway. No one needed to be told that he was playing a game on his mobile and that it was very likely a GameIT creation – such was the impact of GameIT on the masses.

'Don't say anything,' I requested the guard. 'He is one of the most famous ex-students of IIT. He is visiting KGP after fourteen years. If anyone objects please call me – I'll take care.' He stared at Parush suspiciously and started walking back, his eyes on the mobile. I called him from behind. 'Which game are you playing? Can I see?' He proudly passed on his phone to me. I saw the familiar graphics of *Kismat*, a game recently launched by GameIT, targeting the mass Indian market – it was a stripped-down version of *Luck*, the epoch-creating mobile game from GameIT. Parush had been accused of passing on insider information about GameIT to its competition. 'He has created this game …' I pointed towards Parush, lying on his back, taking deep breaths, his eyes closed. He didn't arouse any curiosity in the guard, who left in no time, concentrating on the game.

I sat beside him. When he opened his eyes, they were glowing. 'We would play a very childish game,' he said excitedly. 'I would take Bits to some place in the campus on my bike. She was supposed to open her eyes only after reaching the place. If she identified the place within the first five seconds she would win. And if she couldn't, I would lose… The loser had to kiss the winner then and there… The last time we had played the game, I had brought her here … where we stand now…'

We walked out of the campus. I sat with Parush on the pebbles by the railway track which skirted Chhedi's, the 24x7 trackside joint which had been witness to more success and failure, union and separation, love and hatred, jubilation and mourning than anything else in KGP. He plucked a leaf and placed it on the track. 'She would often place a petal of a rose on the track when a train approached. She hoped that someday the petal would fly off the track and not get crushed under the wheels of the train. It never happened. She would say, "Dumbo, my petals are not crushed; they just get hitched on to the wheels." After she had left, I would place a leaf on the track and it always flew off.'

After having dinner at Billoo's Parush took me to his room in RK. Many people identified him. Few took photos with him. 'Do we still win the Illu?' he asked.

We walked through Vegie's, one of the few places which vibrated with the pulse beat of the campus till late in the night. We sat on the open gallery of the Gyan Ghosh stadium which otherwise had more dark corners than the few IIT couples could look for.

'…You never wanted to find out why she did it?'

'Yes, I would call her from Noida, any time of the day, whenever I couldn't control myself, not caring if the calls were at full rates. She never dragged Raka's name again. She put the blame entirely on Ma. She said Kakima too wanted her to break-up, which I never believed. But Kakima never talked to me again. By the time I talked to her for the last time, I was a complete broke. I had borrowed money more than a few times my monthly salary from my friends and withdrawn the maximum cash allowable on my credit card. Just the phone calls at full rates were more than a few grand.'

We took a stroll along the Scholars Avenue as the IIT gradually fell asleep in the wee hours of the night. The mist grew thick and hung under the streetlights.

'The only good thing that happened around that time was that I got really close to my sister Pushi. A week after I had returned to Noida from Calcutta, Ru, Aru and she came to stay with me for some time. Aru and Pushi were anyway free after their ISC exams and Ru had to meet a few people in the ministry for a few clearances for the low-cost housing project IPC had undertaken. One night I woke up to see Pushi sitting on the bed by my side. Leaning against the wall and stretching her legs, she too had fallen asleep, her hands still on my forehead. I embraced her legs and cried the rest of the night. That was the first time perhaps I understood how sweet it was to have a sister...'

We sat on a bench in front of the Alumni Guest House. He took a puff. 'Want to get back to the car? It's getting very cold.' He pulled me by my hand and started walking towards Tikka's.

'They took me to Lansdowne, as if I needed a sanatorium to recuperate from some terminal illness. It was no doubt a charming diversion. Perched atop an isolated hillock, the small hotel run by UP Tourism was connected to the desolate backside of the small town with a collapsible wooden bridge across a deep gorge. The bridge would be pulled up in the night to prevent tigers approaching the hotel in the night. The night fell suddenly on the hills. I went out to take a stroll. I don't remember how I finally landed up at the downtown, in front of the only STD booth. Any visitor at Lansdowne was a V.I.P. The booth owner came out running. "How did you come?" he asked me excitedly. I myself didn't know how I had come. Seeing me silent he called a few other people. They took me with them, walking cautiously as we approached the narrow-wooded pathway leading to the backside of the town. They created a racket with their sticks and flashed their torches all around. When we arrived at the collapsible bridge they were shocked to see it had been already pulled up. "How did you cross the river?" they asked me again in utter surprise. We could see lights on the other side of the gorge. I saw the silhouettes of three women and one man running around hastily. My escorts shouted at the caretaker of the hotel. He pulled the bridge down. The four people on the other side came running towards me. Ru held me hard with her hands and slapped me. Pushi embraced me from behind. Aru stood at a distance, biting her lips, burning me with her stares. Back at the hotel Ru put Dettol on my bruises. The watchman and the other people who had escorted me were awestruck. "How could he manage to cross the river in the night? It's so deep and dangerous. And there's a man eater in the jungle. Even we don't dare to go out alone in the woods in the night..." Next morning even I was shocked to see how deep the gorge was...'

***

I got used to this new routine. We would talk the whole night and he would sleep the whole day next. On the second day I caught up a bit with my own work. In the evening he drove his car. Instead of taking a right towards the IIT, he took a left on the main road. 'Where are we going?' I asked.

'Subarnarekha... I'm sure you haven't seen this place too...'

We ate dinner at a jhupri in Bhonsraghat and drove towards the river. He took the car on the river bed and parked it at a place where a solitary narrow stream snaked on the dry bed. We sat on the upturned hull of a broken boat. I had brought enough warm clothing this time. I wrapped a Manipuri shawl around him and gave him a scarf to cover his head. The barren river bed flanked by the silhouettes of the tall trees and a single stream meandering silently on it, bearing the pulse of a river that could be ferocious some other time, gave me an eerie sensation. The lifeless stream was so much like Parush.

'One day I almost came under the wheels of a Blue Line bus in Delhi. The gujjar conductor pulled me up from the road, kicked me and threw me off on the pavement, shouting the choicest abuses. I lay on the pavement, I don't know for how long, not bothered at all by the suspicious looks of the passers-by. I stayed awake the whole night, waiting for the same bus to pass by again. It came the next day in the morning. I boarded the bus, avoiding direct eye contact with the conductor. It was a *mudrika* vehicle, going round the city along the Ring Road. It stopped for some time at Sarai Kale Khan and the driver and the conductor took a break. I befriended the conductor saying that I wanted someone like him to take care of the logistics of an IT company I was going to start. Keeping him distracted with my high promises of fat bucks I took him behind the Humayun's Tomb complex, close to the railway lines on the fringes of the Nizamuddin railway station. Suddenly, I pushed him hard. He fell on the tracks. Even before he could react I slammed his head on the track and kept it pressed till a desperately honking train approached so close that we could be run over by it in just a few blinks. I pulled him at the right time and threw him on the shrubs. He didn't even try to attack me…'

Parush held my hands tight and started coughing. I gave him the puff. I opened the flask and poured some hot tea into a paper cup I was carrying.

'Next day, when Kratu came to see me, Arav told him there couldn't be anyone better than me to help him in his operations.'

'Who's Kratu? Isn't he the CEO of GameIT?'

'Yes. He was our neighbour in Rupsa. He's two years older than me. He went to IIT Delhi and I went to KGP. He has been always quite close to me. Our families had known each other for long. Apparently, we were from the same village in Bangladesh before coming to India after partition and settling in Rupsa. He had been in touch with me for the gaming start-up he had co-founded in the Bay Area but I didn't want to leave Bits and go to the US. At that time, after my breakup with Bitasta, he was visiting India for some personal work. He had met Ru at Rupsa and learned everything about me. He insisted I join him. I was least confident. But it was Arav who kept pestering me. He reminded me again and again that I was no longer the same Parush I had been in the past...'

Yes, it was true. Parush was a new person, waiting at the threshold of a new life, a life where Bitasta would be conspicuous and omnipresent in everything, even though she would be nowhere around him.

PART II

"WITHOUT"

BAY AREA

Tista waved at Parush emerging from the arrival gate of the SFO airport. Parush couldn't locate her in the crowd. She came running towards him. 'Ei Parush,' she patted him from behind. 'Chintei parchhis na?' Parush was embarrassed. 'Sorry Tista, nothing like that. Can anyone forget you?' Parush tried to smile. He was perhaps correct. The families of Tista and Kratu, Parush's neighbours in Rupsa, had had a very close relationship for long and Tista was well known to everyone in Rupsa. Till Kratu got married a year ago to someone he had met in Stanford, many at Rupsa believed he would one day marry Tista. Even the unnamed mudi, the owner of the small grocery shop at the entrance of Rupsa, exchanged pleasantries with Tista whenever she passed by. Ever-smiling, she was as good looking as she was sweet-tempered and gentle. Parush had known her forever and now he would stay with her, in Berkeley, for some time.

Tista stared at him. 'What the fuck have you done to yourself?' She slapped his face gently. That was exactly what Parush would expect of her –loving and caring in a gesticular way, unique to her. 'Chal, let's go.' She pulled him by his hand. 'By the way,' she stopped, 'where's your luggage?'

'That's it. I haven't brought anything else,' Parush said hesitantly. He realised very well that the single midsized suitcase he had found sufficient to pack all his belongings into would surely evoke surprise. Most people from India who had travelled with him on the same flight passed by him, cautiously pushing their carts loaded with inflated bags and suitcases packed beyond their warranted capacity.

Tista removed her jacket. 'Wear it. October may be quite chilly in Bay Area compared to India. You're shivering.' Parush wore the jacket and walked silently behind Tista. He noticed subtle changes in her. Had she toned down a bit? He wondered. She had accessorised a bit too. In his Calcutta neighbourhood of Rupsa, everyone would call her 'mishti meye', a sweet girl, the Bengali *mishti* being an epithet for a combination of a plumpish physique, simplicity and an amiable disposition. She was still a *mishti meye*, he affirmed to himself.

'Pocha has warned me not to tell you anything,' Tista said, on the way to Berkeley, calling Kratu by his nickname, 'but still I'm saying this because I just can't hide it all. I don't know how much you're aware of the current situation.'

'I know everything,' Parush said nonchalantly. 'Arav told me before I left India.'

'What do you know?' Tista was suspicious.

'That GameIT has run out of funds and that all the VCs have ditched it at the last moment…'

Tista slowed down the car a bit and someone honked from behind. 'And you still came here? To work for GameIT?'

'Yes.'

'Do you know Pocha is looking for a job for you? They are pulling in some cash just to pay the severance package to the five guys they have.'

'I've already figured out what those guys are working on. I alone can manage that.'

'And who is going to pay you?'

'No one … till they get the funding.'

'Are you out of your senses or what? Do you know what you're saying? How're you going to survive? Without any money?'

Parush smiled. 'If you don't charge anything for allowing me to stay with you and cook some more food daily … that will solve a major part of my problem. And the rest … don't worry Tista, I'll survive. Do you know I almost came under the wheels of a bus in Delhi? I survived…'

***

After completing their undergrad from IIT Delhi, both Kratu and Tista had got good scholarships to pursue Masters and PhD in the US. They wanted to be in the same school, but finally Kratu went to Stanford and Tista to Berkeley, both quite close by. In his leisure time, Kratu created a gaming software based on one of the folktales his grandmother would tell the kids of his family. When the game became very popular among the students of Stanford, Tista gave a copy of it to Sam, a spoilt kid of a rich businessman and a software geek who many believed would someday do big in Bay Area. Sam was in Berkeley too, doing his PhD. He dreamed of founding a company which would revolutionise the world of mobile games. He already earned a good amount of money as a freelancer, coding complicated algorithms for various Bay Area startups and the popularity of his games had spread much beyond the Bay Area.

Finally, a year back, Sam had founded GameIT, with Kratu as the co-founder.

Given Sam's popularity in the Bay Area, everyone expected him to raise good money for the startup. His idea of GameIT initially did create a good buzz in the Bay Area. Many people were ready to make the seed funding. But when it finally came to business, Sam's arrogance and stubbornness to accept the terms and conditions of the VCs jeopardised the prospects of GameIT. Eventually, when Sam and Kratu were giving up on the idea of GameIT, they bootstrapped with Sam's savings of a hundred grand. Soon a seed corpus of half a million was raised with investments mainly from Kratu's rich father-in-law and some from Tista's grandfather.

GameIT started out from a garage in Berkeley, with Sam as the Chairman and Kratu the CEO.

Parush met Sam for the first time that evening. Tista had wanted him to take rest after the long journey from India, but he wanted to meet Sam. Tista asked Kratu and Afsar, Kratu's wife, to come to Berkeley and stay the night. 'Anyway, it's weekend,' Parush heard Tista. 'Let us celebrate the arrival of such an important person...'

While Tista talked to Kratu over the phone Parush thought of Bitasta. Was she also *celebrating*? Did she know that Parush had literally run away from Delhi? From the place which bore the burns of the *loo* in the scorching hot afternoons, like the burns within him? Sitting at the departure lounge of the Indira Gandhi International Airport at Delhi, he had suddenly felt very weary, very insecure. He was finally leaving Bitasta behind forever. The prospect of the dreaded void was looming large in his mind – the void he had totally forgotten to deal with.

***

'Are you sure of what you're talking about?' Sam asked Parush. Sam's appearance was exactly what Parush had visualised, from whatever he had heard about him – shabbily dressed, not too different from Parush, his stoic face and tall and lanky structure adding to the arrogance exuded through his body language and speech. But Parush liked him the way he was. His confidence was contagious.

'Yes,' replied Parush confidently. 'I can manage for a few months. I'm sure you'll raise the funds.'

'Parush,' Sam's irritation was clear, 'I *don't think* I can raise funds so easily. These assholes don't understand anything. They ran away from me just because I told them I'm going to work only on mobile games. Last year the total games-software revenue in the US was a mere 3.7 billion, of which almost nothing came from mobile games. But it's my gut feeling that playing games on PCs would soon be obsolete. There will be more and more portable devices and I'll bet my life that in fifteen years, just the mobile games software industry would be close to 20 billion. If we start early GameIT can be the biggest player in this space. I'm looking at ten billion in fifteen years. The VCs don't see this…'

'So, you want to say,' Parush interrupted, 'you can't ever raise money and you'll give up?'

Sam looked directly into Parush's eyes. Tista was arranging the table for dinner. She too froze and looked at Parush.

'I'm not going to give up. We'll do it later,' Sam said.

'But the fire may not last that long…'

Parush might have meant something else. He knew for sure the fire burning within him now would lose its intensity with time. But he hated to see the wasted unburnt wood pieces buried under the white cold ashes of the bonfire from the previous night. If there were a bonfire, he felt, let the wood burn completely, rather than lying wasted till the next morning.

It was settled that Parush would stay at Tista's place. Sam gave him an ATM card and bought a fifteen years old Toyota Corolla for a few grand. His needs were limited and he rarely needed to use either the ATM card or the car.

***

At that time the principal of Kala Bhavan in Shantiniketan was the famous painter and muralist Binod Bihari Mukherjee. By then, he had almost lost his eyesight completely. Sairi and I would often go to his studio and watch him work. We felt he had an inner eye with which he could see everything better than us. I was the one who would talk more and Sairi would remain quiet most of the times. One day he told us, 'You two are like the two sides of the same coin – one head and the other tail, but still it's the same coin.' Another day he told us, 'You're like the two sides of the beautiful Pir Panjal Mountains. Panchali, you're perhaps like the Kashmir valley, expressive – green, full of blue placid lakes; and Sairandhri, you're like the Lahaul and Spiti Valleys, silent and quiet – miles and miles of barrenness. You two are so different, but so alike.'

We had then decided that I would name my girl Bitasta, the older name of Jhelum that originates from the Kashmir side of the Pir Panjal; and Sairi would name her girl Parushni, the older name of Ravi that originates from the Lahaul-Spiti side. And yes, we believed that we both would have girls.

When you were born, Sairi named you Parush, supposedly the male form of Parushni, which later became the name of your sister.

I didn't have any problem in Bitasta's case.

***

Parush was accompanying Kratu, Afsar and Tista to Napa Valley for a weekend day-out. When Afsar had asked him about the origin of the names 'Parush' and 'Bitasta', he narrated the story he had heard from Panchali.

'That's interesting,' Afsar exclaimed. 'You Bongs think so much before choosing a name, and still you guys give such *horrible* daknam. Parush, do you have any pet name at home like Pocha?' She poked her husband Kratu, who himself had always been ashamed of the name Pocha, which meant rotten in Bangla.

Parush had met Afsar the first time at Tista's place, the day he had arrived in the US. Her Pakistani origin, Parush had felt, was quite obvious from her looks. Quite tall – with heels she would be taller than her husband Kratu, her longish face with sharp features matching her slim figure to perfection, she appeared to Parush like one of those rich Pakistani girls cheering for their team from the front row during an India-Pakistan cricket match in Sharjah or Islamabad. 'How clichéd and judgmental,' he had recalled Bitasta telling him many a time for such generalisation.

'By the way, Parush,' Afsar continued, 'often the name of a person defines his personality too. The Sanskrit word parush comes from the root "pri", which stands for fullness, completeness, mukammal in Urdu. Parush is akin to purna in Sanskrit, plenus in Latin and "full" in English. Parush, you'll have a fulfilling life…'

'Please Afsar,' Tista interrupted, 'Parush is still new. You can take his linguistic classes later. Otherwise he will run away…'

'Come on, that's what I do for my living,' she said with a wink. 'When you guys have tolerated my lessons till now, so would he…'

Perhaps Parush was not listening. As Kratu drove the car across the Carquinez Bridge, he was staring out at the San Pablo Bay, merging at a distance into the void of the Pacific Ocean.

Seeing him silent, Tista realised the topic shouldn't have been brought up. Afsar gestured an apology to Tista. Tista gave an imperceptible nod, assuring them that she would take care. She had already *taken care* many times in the past few weeks. 'Ei,' she pushed Parush, 'when are your sister and Aru coming here?'

'During the Thanksgiving weekend,' Parush replied.

'Which college are they going to?' Kratu asked.

'Sewanee,' Parush answered.

'That's near Nashville, isn't it?' Afsar asked.

'I think so – they had a flight till Nashville.'

'Have they got a scholarship?'

'Yes.'

'What's their major?'

'English.'

The conversation continued with staccato responses and monosyllables from Parush. When Parush realised that his companions were trying hard to make him feel comfortable, he felt embarrassed. He tried to crack some jokes to lighten the situation. 'The other day I was wondering why Tista has so many thin straws in the kitchen. I tried to drink coke with one of those. Later she told me those are stirrers. Why the hell do you need holes in a stirrer?'

Tista had been observing Parush very closely for the past few weeks. She caught his lame attempt.

The next few hours they hopped from one vineyard to another, taking tours and tasting wine. The sprawling greenery, the expansive views of the hillside and the laid-back old countryside soothed Parush. It was long since he had been out like this, roaming around leisurely, unwinding the senses and savouring the taste of the cool air – the scorching loo in Delhi had become more unbearable towards the end.

They had lunch at a café in the small picturesque town of Yountville and took a stroll along Washington Street. When they passed by French Laundry, one of the costliest and most famous restaurants of Napa Valley, Kratu said prophetically, 'One day we'll hold the most exotic party of the town at a place like this…' Afsar hugged him and quipped, 'Sweetheart, just buy the most exotic diamonds for me, and the rest will fall in place.'

Parush smiled, unpretentiously. Tista pulled him by his hand.

They entered a souvenir shop at the V Marketplace. A large dazzling blue wine glass attracted Parush's attention. He proceeded towards the shelf where it was the lone exhibit. But coming close, he froze instantly. He stared with a jolt at the big red mark of a pair of lips near the edge of the glass and the four lines engraved inside. Nearby, Afsar, Kratu and Tista were absorbed in a conversation which appeared like distant rumblings to him.

'The wine at Sullivan was the best...'
'Kuleto had the best ambience ...'

Parush had been already transported thousands of miles away, to the empty house in Prembajar. Bitasta and Panchali had already moved to Calcutta and he was spending one of those torpid afternoons in the solitude of the house, trying to sense any sign of Bitasta's existence in the fluttering of the old calendar hung on the wall, the drops of water dripping monotonously from a leaking tap, the monochromatic noise of the fan suspended from the ceiling – nothing seemed to have changed for the calendar, the tap and the fan. He was frantically opening each of the empty cupboards, as if a sixth sense had told him that he would come across a hidden treasure, carefully kept for him to chance upon someday. And then in one of the cupboards he found an empty wine glass with the mark of a pair of lips. He lifted the glass from the wooden shelf and stared at the thick red marks of lipstick, the same marks Bitasta would artfully put on his naked body in bountiful abandon and then fudge with her body, painting both in passionate red. A piece of paper flew off the shelf and fell on the floor. He picked the paper from the floor and read the four lines written by Bitasta:

Drink to me only with thine eyes,
And I will pledge with mine;
Or leave a kiss within the cup
And I'll not ask for wine.

Parush took his stare off the glass displayed at the souvenir shop. Afsar, Tista and Kratu had moved away. Parush could hear faintly that they were still talking about the various vineyards they had visited since morning.

'Signorello had awesome views...'
'I heard Del Dotto has the best tour…'

Parush lifted the glass from the shelf and read the four lines again and again. 'It's one of the best-selling items,' someone said from behind. 'It will be a great souvenir.'

Parush turned back. 'Yes,' he said, holding the glass tight in his hand, 'it's a great souvenir…'

'It's twenty-five bucks… I'll pack it for you.'

As the person took the glass to the cash counter Parush suddenly pulled out his purse. He had only three five-dollar notes with him. He looked up and saw Tista standing in front of him. He kept his purse in his pocket and looked down. Tista slapped him hard on his face. Everyone at the store turned towards them, but she didn't seem to care. She held his hand and dragged him behind her. Kratu and Afsar came running towards them. 'What happened?' asked a surprised Afsar.

'Pocha,' she said loudly, 'ask him why he's not carrying the ATM card.'

'Believe me, I forgot. And I really didn't know I wasn't carrying enough cash…' Parush offered a lame excuse.

'*Ek thappor marbo*,' she almost slapped him again. 'You forgot? Okay, how much money have you drawn till now?'

'Few hundred…'

She pulled out the purse from his pocket and flipped it open. A few coins slipped on the floor and rolled under the shelves. She pulled out the three five-dollar notes and flashed them in front of Afsar and Kratu. 'Pocha, this is what he has been surviving on for the past many days. The rest all he has spent on groceries.' She turned towards Parush. 'Do you think I don't understand?'

'Tista,' Parush tried to defend, 'it's not like that. You too know I couldn't have bought groceries worth few hundred bucks…'

Tista looked disgusted. 'Pocha, I don't take this crap. Please tell this idiot I don't need money to buy groceries. Wasn't it a deal that he's going to withdraw as much as he needs? Then why do I see this horrible scene that he doesn't have the money even to buy a souvenir that's just twenty-five bucks? Pocha, I'm very serious. If he does this again I'll kick him out of my house. Let him go back to India or find a job which pays him a salary. He doesn't have to act like a saint...' She left the shop, leaving behind the three of them and the handful of people inside the shop puzzled. Kratu went to the counter, made the payment and picked the packet.

Afsar hugged Parush and kissed him. 'Porus, we all love you so much. Do you understand that? Why do you hurt us, hurt yourself? Chalo...' she held his hands and walked him out of the shop.

Tista was fuming, leaning against the pole of a street lamp. Parush walked to her. 'Tista, I'm not good at all this. I can't say sorry in a good way. Believe me, I really didn't know that I wasn't carrying much cash... I do have sufficient money... Only the other day you made me buy so many shirts...'

Tista looked up at him. 'Was that for that sweet girl who came once to pick you up? That classmate of yours who's in Stanford?'

'Tista, come on, Sweti is a good friend...' Parush felt uncomfortable.

'Oh. Stop it...' Tista gestured a punch.

***

'That's what I call Murphy's Law at its best,' Sam said. 'Bill has been lately showing interest in giving us the first round of funding. I went to meet him yesterday. While talking to me he got a call. Apparently, his daughter, who has just come out of a six-month rehab, was again seen at a rave. The cops didn't arrest her again, realising she's William Valentine's daughter. That's it. Suddenly, Bill asked me to meet him later.'

'Was she arrested in the past?' Parush asked.

'Yes, that's why she had to go to rehab. There's something called a deferred entry of judgment to beat marijuana possession charges in California. You plead guilty of the charges and go through six months of treatment. After remaining arrest-free for an additional twelve months, the case is dismissed. I learned she's a drug addict. When she was arrested even her rich dad couldn't save her. Finally, with the best lawyers in the country she managed to get along with a six month stay at a rehab.'

'How old is she?'

'She's a sophomore at Stanford, from which I can guess she would be nineteen-twenty. Her father being one of the biggest VCs in Bay Area, even Stanford can't throw her out that easily.'

'When has Bill asked you to meet him again?'

'He just said "later". I'm going to get in touch with him again next week.'

That night Parush stayed awake for a very long time. By the time he had gone to sleep, it was already early morning. Next afternoon he called Sweti.

'I'll see you at Stanford this weekend. I'll tell you everything then. For the time being please find out everything about Bill Valentine's daughter. And let me clarify, it's not what you're thinking.'

ECSTASY

'Why are you doing this, Porus?' Sweti asked sadly. They were sitting on a bench by the Oval Park in Stanford.

'It's a chance I'm taking. And if not me, who else?'

'Do you understand the risk?'

'Swets, I'll do it anyway. If you don't help me, it will just take me longer... Swets, you've always helped me whenever I needed...'

'And you remember me only when you need some help,' she interrupted. 'In our final year in IIT you would call for me only when you needed me to call Bitasta...' She stopped suddenly, realising that dragging Bitasta's name was perhaps not the apt thing now. Parush looked at her but didn't say anything. 'I'm sorry Porus. I didn't mean to hurt you. I'm just concerned.'

It was not that Parush didn't understand the risk involved, but nothing appeared dreadful or shocking any longer to him. He realised he had acquired an unprecedented daring, an impulsive daredevilry, a reckless gut, which bordered on insanity, and that he cared very little for himself, his own life, and unfortunately, his own loved ones too. He could have been killed by the man-eater at Lansdowne. He could have been in jail for threatening to kill the conductor of the Blue Line bus in Delhi. It didn't bother him that he had been a broke for the past many months.

During the last few months in India he had rarely called Ru or Aru, and as they had no way to get in touch with him other than writing letters, which anyway he had stopped replying to, he remained incommunicado for weeks, and then months. Aru and Pushi had desperately tried to talk to him before they left Calcutta, but Parush never called. Ru was almost in tears when he finally called her a day before leaving India to inform her that he was going to the US the very next day. He didn't call his father. Srinjay and Ru took the early morning flight to Delhi the next day and saw him off at the airport in the night. Srinjay was unusually calm. 'We're there, my son, we're still there …' he had managed to say just before Parush entered the cordoned area not accessible to visitors. Parush turned back to see Ru, holding the railing tightly, staring at him. He turned back again many more times and saw Ru standing there, in the same posture, holding the railing. Now, it was Tista who routinely made him call Ru and his father in Calcutta and Aru and Pushi in Sewanee, where they were doing their undergrad.

'Kya hua? What are you thinking?' Sweti asked.

Parush kept quiet. He just stared at Sweti.

'Okay, this is what I've got till now. Her name is Alina Valentine. She's majoring in American Studies. She has a room in Casa Zapata in the Stern Hall though she rarely stays there. Lately, she has been found visiting the Cyber Café at the Stern Dining late in the nights with a group of her girlfriends.'

'And could you get *The Mercury News*?'

'Yes….' She pulled out the folded newspaper from her bag. She opened the front page and read the excerpt.

Police Captain Jason Marty raided a rave organized at the Maritime Hall in the SOMA neighbourhood under the pretence of a normal rock show. Alina Valentine, the daughter of William Valentine, a noted alumnus of Stanford University and one of the biggest names in the Bay Area Venture Capitalist fraternity, was among the many detained. She was later released as she was reportedly not in the possession of any Class A drug like MMDA, better known as Ecstasy, and marijuana. The residents moving into the new upscale lofts in the neighbourhood have been urging the police to shut down all major nightclubs in the locality…

'Are you free this weekend?' Parush interrupted.

'Yes.'

'I want you to meet Jason Marty.'

***

'Porus, do you understand how much it hurts to be party to something which I'm sure will screw up your life like nothing else?'

'Swets, why do you think in that way? Who else can I go to?'

'Ya, you remember me only when no one's around…' She didn't talk for a long time while Parush drove his old Corolla to an upscale neighbourhood in San Francisco – South of Market, better known as SOMA. 'Porus, think again,' she pleaded, when Parush parked the car in front of 850 Bryant Street, the Southern Station of SFPD, San Francisco Police Department. Parush opened the door for her.

'All the best…' He hugged Swets, for the first time. 'Sirf tu hi hai… *yes, it's only you*, who's there for me for all these…' Sweti smiled and walked confidently towards the Police Station. A short stature, always with a studious look with a pair of old fashioned round specs that she had lately replaced with lenses, Sweti, or Swets as Parush called her, had always been by his side since his IIT days. It would be unthinkable, a few years back, of her to do something like what she was going to do now. He knew she was nervous. He recalled how she would always chew the end of a Reynolds pen whenever she would be nervous, before the exams.

Captain Marty was waiting for her. She showed him her Stanford identity card and the Indian passport. 'It's a very unusual request, I would say, young lady,' he said, returning her the documents.

'Officer, I've lost my brother in India,' Sweti repeated for the final time what she had practised so many times before Parush all through the previous night. 'He was a drug addict and finally died of an MMDA overdose. I don't want a single young life to end in that ignominious way. I want to create awareness in schools and colleges about the evils of raving. I also want to help the cops bust such parties…'

The Captain listened to Sweti's memorised speech with rapt attention. 'I'll tell you everything I've gathered till now,' he assured after Sweti had completed her long speech. She poured one glass full of water into her throat and took a deep breath while the Captain spoke passionately. 'I need support from people like you. Raves are gaining momentum though most are still underground, relegated to old army bases, condemned buildings and underground warehouses. Tom Loar, a freshman at the San Francisco State University, has become Bay Area's biggest promoter of raves. In the rave circuit he's known as Happy Kid. The party I raided last week at the Maritime Hall was also organised by him. He's kinda smart to go legit in most cases, though I know not everything he does is proper. If you can get him, he will spill out more secrets about raves…'

That evening Parush and Sweti went to the Stanford Shopping Center to buy a few things Sweti had never worn in her life. Parush drove her to her apartment in Escondido Village after dinner. 'Swets,' Parush held her hands, 'I don't want to humiliate you by saying sorry and thanks at the same time, though I don't find any other word more apt. Guys like me always need people like you…' Sweti hugged him for a long time. 'I wish things really happen the way you're expecting,' she said before leaving.

***

Sweti removed her jeans in the car. Underneath she was wearing the denim cutoffs and the black stockings with suspenders she had bought the previous evening from the Stanford Shopping Center. She pulled the oversized tee to cover the tiny shorts. Along with the story of the raid at the Maritime Hall, *The Mercury News* had carried a picture of the revellers from which Parush and Sweti had got an idea of the attire Sweti should wear.

No one talked as Parush drove the car to SFS. Sweti put on a thick red lipstick and sprayed a generous dose of a strong perfume all over her. At ten thirty on a Sunday night they reached the University Park South Apartments. Sweti switched on the light inside the car, pulled the jacket from the backseat and slipped her legs into the tall black leather boots. Parush stared at her while she leaned to fit the boots properly. 'Porus, I'm ready,' she said, opening the door. Parush leaned over her and pulled the door back. 'Enough, you're not going anywhere dressed up like a whore. We're going back.' He ignited the engine and pressed the gas pedal.

'Porus, stop,' Sweti shouted. Parush stopped the car on the driveway. 'Who told you I'm looking like a whore? Don't be judgmental. Many girls dress like this. And let me clarify, I'm doing this not under any obligation. I'm doing it, because I decided for myself. And one more thing ... like you're concerned about me, please be concerned about yourself too.' She patted Parush on his cheek and got off the car. Parush parked the car properly and walked with Sweti.

'I hope he has been informed that I would be coming now,' Sweti said, once they reached the entrance of the apartment. 'I did pass on the message through a common acquaintance in my department.'

Parush stayed back, watching Sweti stride into the apartment.

Sweti expected Happy Kid to be some crazy funky chap. But he turned out to be a very normal guy, a rather timid freshman. Without wasting time, she came to the point, settling on the only chair in the austere room, while Happy Kid, sitting on the bed spilled over with books, looked at her unsuspectingly.

'The rave scene in Stanford sucks. I heard a lot about you. We would like to have some fun at our place too.'

'You can join our legit events.'

'Where's the fun there?'

He looked at Swets, sitting cross-legged on a chair in a dimly lit room. A thick smell in a dimly lit small room made it really uncomfortable for her. 'What do you really want?'

'The real rave...'

'Why should I risk giving you the details?'

'Okay,' she got up, 'I'll come again. Someday you'll trust me.'

'Wait a minute,' he called her back when she was about to leave the room.

'Take this number. Call him and just say you want to have fun. He will give you a code, which you've to crack to find out the venue. The folks who regularly go to the raves would crack it in no time. You have to do it yourself.'

When Parush reached Berkeley after dropping Sweti at Stanford, it was one thirty in the night. Tista had gone to LA to meet her sister. The house was empty. The phone was blinking. Parush heard Sweti's message.

'Colonel Edward D Baker. Battery by the beach,' he wrote down on a piece of paper. He called Sweti.

'What was Alina's reaction?' he asked. 'Was she shocked?'

'Not at all. Rather I was shocked to see her at the Cyber Café. I didn't expect it. I just took a chance. After you had left I called the number and got the code. Then I went to the Café. It was around twelve thirty. She was there with two other girls. She was alone just for a short while when her friends had gone to get some stuff from the counter. I went to her table and passed on a chit of paper to her. She read the code, the date and time, and winked at me. I left immediately saying, "See you soon."'

***

'Tista, there's a get together at Sweti's place tonight,' Parush said.

Tista winked. 'You and Sweti are getting together?'

Parush smiled. 'Tista, I wouldn't hide anything from you. If anything like that happens, you'll be the first to know.'

She came and sat beside Parush on the sofa. 'You've changed a lot over the past few weeks. I know she is the reason. I just pull your leg, like people would always pull mine. Love doesn't mean you should sleep with her. I do love Pocha, and sorry, he's not "just a friend". Afsar knows that too. It's a privilege that he's there in my life. If Sweti happens to be someone like that, don't feel shy about it.'

For a moment, he thought he would tell everything to Tista, about what he was going to do tonight. But then somehow, he couldn't manage to spill the beans. He drove to Stanford in the evening.

'Are you sure you've cracked it correctly?' Sweti asked him.

'I think so. It seems to be very simple. The Captain had said that raves are generally organised at old army bases, condemned buildings or underground warehouses. The code was: *Colonel Edward D Baker. Battery by the beach.* Battery can be associated only with army bases. I searched for all the old batteries in and around San Francisco in the library. Few of the batteries, I found, were part of the old Fort Baker, named after Colonel Edward D Baker, someone who was killed in the American Civil War. It's now a part of the Golden Gate National Recreation Area. Two of the batteries of Fort Baker were at Kirby Beach and Gravelly Beach which, I've figured out, are actually side by side. So, it was quite trivial. By the way, have you got the chemicals?'

'Yes. You've to treat my friend who managed to get the stuff from the Chemistry department.'

'I hope the amounts are correct.' He pulled out a chit from his pocket. 'To reduce the neurotoxic effects of ecstasy,' he read out, 'you need a post loading supplement consisting of 200mg of 5-Hydroxytryptophan, up to 100mg of Vitamin B-6 and up to 1000mg of Vitamin C.'

'Yes, I had asked her to check it properly.'

Parush mixed the chemicals together and wrapped it with a small piece of white-paper. 'Okay, time to leave now.'

'Porus, mujhe dar lag raha hai, *I'm frightened...*'

Parush hugged her. 'Don't frighten me.'

They left Stanford at nine in the night. Parush found it hard to merge into 101N. People honked him from behind. His hand was trembling. 'Swets, I can't drive.'

'Okay Porus, take it easy. Take the next exit.'

Parush took the Marsh Road exit and parked the car at the Chevron gas station. He drank some water and relaxed for some time. They started again at ten. When they crossed the Golden Gate Bridge, it was close to eleven. Parush took the first exit and came to the other side of the road through an underpass, which led to the entry to the bridge from the northern side. He turned right from the main road, keeping the bridge to his left, and took the uphill narrow pathway treading along the steep hillock overlooking the Golden Gate. Soon the top of the towers of the bridge appeared at their level, from where the bay loomed like a dark void below, and the bridge hung like a colourful necklace across it. The sky was exceptionally clear and the air extremely chill. The breathtaking view of the bridge and the San Francisco city lights at a distance mesmerised Parush as he drove cautiously along the crest of the steep hillock. Soon, they left behind even the few over-enthusiastic vista seekers, who had braved the cold and parked their cars along the narrow road to get the best possible view of the bridge. Parush took a left downhill, leading to the Kirby Cove Campground, overlooking the Kirby and Gravelly beaches.

The campground emerged suddenly from the darkness. Parush took a U-turn and parked the car off the road on a small clearance at a curve a little away from the campground. Most people had already arrived. Parush and Sweti entered the site, which looked like a cosy private party. They paid a hundred and fifty bucks each at the entrance. The bouncer handed each of them a small packet, which they knew contained what. People were dancing to hard metal music. Sweti got a strong smell which appeared familiar to her. She realised she had got the same smell the previous Sunday in Happy Kid's stuffy room in SFS. She coughed a few times. She found Alina, dancing with a guy. She walked to her. 'Hi,' she said, patting her on her back. She turned back. She was already high. She left the guy and stared at Sweti for some time. 'Oh, ain't you the girl who met me at the Café?'

'Ya, how're you doing?'

'Fine, fine … oh ya, thanks … thanks for the invite…' She called someone. 'Hey, take care of her … she's my guest today … everything she asks for is on me…' She turned towards Sweti. 'Enjoy yourself…'

By twelve, when almost everyone was high, Sweti slipped out and made a call from her mobile. She came back and whispered to Parush, 'They'll be here in half an hour. I've asked the Captain to let me know when they cross the Golden Gate.'

In fifteen minutes, Sweti got a call. Parush swung into action. He went to Alina and whispered into her ears, 'I think there's going to be a raid, come with me, we've to escape before you're caught again.' Alina was not able to react. Parush dragged her out and walked fast towards the road. Alina leaned against his body. She could barely walk. Parush dragged her off the road and entered the jungle, making their way up cautiously against the steep slope. They stopped at a place from where the entrance of the campground was visible between the trees. Soon he could hear the siren. Three police vans screeched to halt in front of the campground. Parush gave Alina some water. He pulled out the paper wrap and fed her the post-load supplement. He gave her some more water. Then he opened one of the two packets the bouncer had handed over to him and Sweti while entering the place. He swallowed all the tablets. He looked at the campground below. When he was sure that no one was outside, he pulled Alina and moved towards the road in the direction where his car had been parked.

By the time he reached the road, he suddenly felt the surge of the drug. He felt a rush of blissful euphoria. He felt his heart was pounding. For a moment, he felt as if Bitasta was by his side, gradually dragging him deep inside the jungle... He felt as if Bitasta was making love to him like the first time... He felt her passionate touches everywhere on his bare body. He breathed heavily. When he reached the car, he felt he had a high fever – his body was burning. He opened the door for Alina. She entered the car and sat silently while he took some time to reach the other side and get to the driver's seat. He ignited the engine and pushed the gas pedal hard. The car trembled into action but moved unsteadily – he was not able to hold on to the steering properly.

Somehow, Parush managed to drive till the road which led to the bridge. His hands were trembling. 'Hey, you okay?' Alina asked.

'No, I'm not. I can't drive any more. You should be fine – I've given you the anti-dope. Just get off the car and hide there.' He pointed towards the Battery Spencer. 'Looks like, there's something to hide. When the cops leave and when it's safe, call someone to pick you up from here... Get off the car before the cops arrive...'

'But you'll be caught...'

'It's no time to argue... Get off before the cops arrive. You shouldn't be arrested for a year if you don't want to go to jail... Do you understand that?'

'Why do you want to save me?'

'Not every question has an answer. For God's sake, there's no time ... Please leave the car if you don't want to be arrested...'

But it was already too late. Cars came from behind. The cops surrounded his car. They recovered one packet of ecstasy drug from the car. Parush was arrested.

FIRST ROUND

'Do you know why I'm one of the most successful VCs?' Bill Valentine asked Parush the next day when he came to meet him at the holding cell of the South Station of SFPD.

'Because you always find the right place to put your money in,' replied Parush calmly.

'Yes, that's true. And I'm now convinced that GameIT is the right place to put my money in. I saw the fire in Sam. Now I've seen the volcano in you. I'm convinced you guys will go to any level and do anything for GameIT. I'll do the first round of funding for GameIT.'

'Thank you, Sir.'

'I've heard everything from my daughter. Now tell me the truth. You gave her the anti-dope and she came clean, but why didn't you take it yourself. The medical report says you took the drug sometime around twelve thirty – that's when you might have left the party. That means you didn't take it during the party. Then why did you take it at all? When you were running away from the party, supposedly to prevent arrest, then why the hell did you take a packet of drug with you? If your intention was to attract my attention, you could have just saved my daughter. Why get arrested?'

'Sir, if I were not arrested, would you spend so much time with me? Would you be convinced that I can go to any level?'

Bill smiled. 'Smart boy,' he patted Parush on his back. 'I'll arrange for bail ASAP.' He got up and started walking. Just before leaving the room, he turned back. 'By the way how did you know that this very place would be raided?'

'Sir, I just took a chance. That's what you also do, isn't it? Take chances?'

'I like it. You'll do things in life.' He turned back again. Parush felt uncomfortable. What was he going to ask next?

'And, when did you see the cops?'

'I had gone to the restroom when I saw the three cars zooming down the hillock.'

Left alone in the cell, Parush tried to recall why exactly, in the first place, had he decided to get arrested. Was it just to prove to Bill that he could go to any level? Or, was it something else? Perhaps, he felt, it was something else. '*When there's a bonfire, let the wood burn completely* ...' he said to himself.

***

Sweti had been the first to be arrested and bundled into the police van. 'I'll be back soon,' the Captain assured her. She waited in the car alone for some time till the cops came out with everyone else in the party. Two cops waited at the campground with the revellers while the others got inside the other two cars. The Captain drove the car she was in. The three cars jerked into motion and zoomed through the darkness. Soon Sweti saw the lights of a car, moving slowly up the road, little ahead of them along a curve. Sweti's heart started pounding. Soon the lights vanished in the darkness. The Captain pressed the gas pedal harder. The car suddenly appeared just in front of them, not moving, parked haphazardly off the road in a clearance which gradually broadened into a small parking lot. The cops came out of the other two cars and surrounded Parush's old Toyota Corolla. The Captain didn't wait there for long. He drove her up to the bridge where a Yellow Cab had been waiting at the entrance of the bridge. 'The cab will drop you home,' the Captain said. 'Thanks for your help. No one will come to know about it.'

She wanted to call Tista immediately, but didn't want to speak from the cab. She left the cab the moment it entered the Escondido Village and called Tista from her mobile phone. Tista lifted the receiver when the phone rang for the third time. 'Tista,' she shouted, 'I'm Sweti. Please come here immediately… Porus is in trouble…' The phone fell from her hand and disassembled on the ground. She sat down and tried to locate the scattered parts, but couldn't find them in the darkness. She got up, but felt dizzy. She waited for some time, trying to regain the energy to walk to her apartment. This time she managed to walk to her apartment. She ran towards the phone but fell again on the ground. Someone appeared at the open door of her apartment. Her eyes shut… She felt sleepy… Her body loosened…

When she woke up she found a young lady sitting by her bedside, staring at her.

'I'm Afsar,' the lady said. 'How're you feeling?'

'I'm fine…' Sweti tried to recall what had happened. She looked around the room suspiciously.

'Don't worry. I'll tell you everything. First tell me if you're really fine.'

'Yes, I'm fine.'

'Okay, this is what happened. You called Tista saying Parush is in trouble, but disconnected the phone abruptly. Tista tried calling you back, but your phone was not reachable. She called us. We too stay in Escondido. We got your apartment number from the directory. When we came here we found you lying on the floor.'

'Did you say you're Afsar?'

'Yes, do you know me?'

'Yes, Porus often talks about you and Kratu. Somehow, we never met. Thanks, Afsar…' Suddenly she remembered something. She sprang up on the bed. 'Porus… He'll be in jail … and it all happened in front of me…' she broke down.

Kratu came running into the room. 'The cops have no information…'

***

'I can't call the Captain and enquire about Porus,' Sweti argued. 'That'll make him suspicious. If it comes out that the whole thing was orchestrated, all the planning Porus did will go down the drain. I think the best thing would be to wait for his call. I'm sure he'll call. We've studied the drug laws. Given that this is his first offence, it's very likely that he'll get bail. He'll surely call me with some update.'

Kratu, Afsar, Tista and Sam were sitting on the bed, surrounding Sweti. Tista's eyes were shut, her face resting on the tip of her folded hands. Afsar nested Sweti's face on her shoulder, rubbing her hand gently over Sweti's back. Kratu was motionless. Sam was getting restless.

'How the hell could you keep quiet all the while?' Tista yelled at Sweti. 'How could you do this? That's what you do to people you love?' Tista covered her face with her hands. Kratu embraced her. 'Tits, calm down. What's her fault? Do you think he couldn't have done this without her? Please, don't blame her.'

Tista got up and sat beside Sweti. 'I'm sorry… I didn't mean to hurt you. I'm really sorry…'

And then they all waited, for hours, staring at the phone, hoping it would ring any time.

Finally, it rang around noon. Sweti ran to lift the receiver. She switched the speaker on.

'Woh funding karega,' everyone heard Parush's excited voice as he spoke in Hindi. '*Can you believe he's going to do the first round of funding for GameIT*? It worked! Yeh … it worked! Thank you, thank you…'

'Porus,' Sweti shouted, 'stop it, stop it I say. Just tell me if you're fine...'

'Yes,' he calmed down suddenly. 'Yes, I'm fine. Bill is arranging for my bail...'

Everyone else left immediately for the SFPD South Station. Sweti stayed back as she didn't want the cops to realise that she was known to Parush and that everything that had happened had been all orchestrated.

***

'Let me introduce you all to the executive team of GameIT,' Bill announced to a big gathering in the lawns of his palatial house spread across two blocks in Atherton, one of the most upscale neighbourhoods in Bay Area, which was home to many millionaires like him. He invited Sam, Kratu, Parush and Sweti onstage, introducing them respectively as the Chairman, CEO, COO and Director of Engineering of the newly refurbished GameIT for which, he had recently completed the first round of funding of $5 million and committed another $5 million in two years. Sam and Kratu had insisted Tista be the CTO, but she didn't want to take up such a big responsibility. She just remained a shareholder in the company, proportionate to the seed funding her grandfather had made the previous year.

'I would like to share a story with you,' Bill said, once they came down from the stage. 'It's the story of GameIT. You all know I'm very conservative when it comes to putting my money. I just look for two things – right opportunity and right people. Sam first came to me more than a year back with glittering eyes. He talked excitedly about a mobile games company which could make Ten Billion in fifteen years. My team did the research and we did find his speculations were not baseless. But I was not sure if he had the right people. Then I met Kratu. I was still not convinced. I asked my folks to keep a tab on them. I knew they were running out of money. Still I didn't jump on it. Sam kept meeting me. Then someone did something really crazy.' He paused and stared at Parush. 'Ladies and gentlemen,' he continued, 'what I'm going to say now may not be something a dad would like to say about his daughter. But still, I've to say this, ladies and gentlemen. This young man invited my daughter to a rave and orchestrated a raid. He helped my daughter in every possible way to evade arrest but himself got arrested...'

Parush was stunned that Bill knew everything. He looked at Swets, who was also taken aback by the revelation.

'He took all precautions to make the whole thing look as if it was just by chance that he landed at the rave, and that he got arrested saving my daughter. The interesting thing is that when I found out the truth, I was not upset. Neither was my daughter, when she came to know that she had been used as a bait in the whole thing. Perhaps for the first time in her life she came out of a rave in all her senses because Parush had administered the right dose of anti-dope on time. He took good care of her as long as she was with him. When I look at the entire episode, I find he took a well calculated risk and treaded effectively on the thin line separating the realms of what you term as ethical and unethical – both are vital things in business. And when I asked him why he did all this, he told he just wanted to show that he could go to any level for the sake of GameIT. I knew Sam has the right folks now.

'Ladies and gentleman, I want to clarify one thing, I've made the funding not because someone saved my daughter, but because someone convinced me that he will keep no stone unturned to make this company earn big bucks for me in future...'

The sprawling lawn thundered with the sound of applause. The media hounded Parush, clicking photos and quizzing him about the whole episode. When they left him alone, suddenly he felt that void in him, yet again. Now that he had burned himself so much, what would be next? What should he do now to burn again? He felt insecure, like he would feel before, when he hadn't yet known that there would be a place called Prembajar, somewhere in the world, somewhere nearby, yet undiscovered.

He heard someone say a 'hi', from some distant land. He jerked a bit and turned back. Alina was standing beside him. In a wonderful white gown, the long end of which lingered on the floor like the tail of a mermaid, she looked totally different. 'Hi,' Parush reciprocated, 'you look so dazzling today.'

'Thanks.'

The conversation ended there. They hadn't met since that night. Parush felt he should apologise to her.

'Is she your girlfriend?' she asked suddenly, pointing towards Sweti.

'No,' Parush was a little surprised.

'I wouldn't do as much for anyone,' she shrugged, 'as she has done for you.'

'Alina, I'm really sorry for everything. I didn't intend to do any harm...'

'That's fine. Now I can go partying without the fear of being arrested. You'll save me, wouldn't you?'

'I can't make you a bait every time...'

'I didn't mean that. I meant...' she paused and stared at Parush.

'What?'

'That you'll just save me...' she turned back and walked fast towards the house.

Parush stared at the trailing end of her gown fluttering behind her. He walked after her.

***

'Are you sure?' Bill asked Parush a few weeks later.

'Yes Sir, I'm sure.'

'I can understand she has fallen for you, perhaps, being overwhelmed by the situation under which she met you. After all she's still a kid, though she's twenty, but what about you? You still refer to her as "your daughter". You don't even take her name. I know you don't love her. Why are you playing with your life?'

'Sir, I'm not playing with my life. I just can't control my life. So, it's better I allow it to take its own course. It's like being in the middle of an ocean in a small boat without an oar. Rather than trying to control the boat, isn't it better to allow it go wherever it's taken by the waves?'

'That sounds philosophical. I know you don't take chances. Rather you make a certainty look like a chance. Tell me, what's the truth?'

'Sir, the last time you figured out the truth yourself. This time too, if there's any other truth, you'll find it out.'

'Yes, I will, I know. But still, isn't it simpler if you told it?'

'I told you. She asked me, "Would you marry me?" and I said yes.'

'And you want to sign a pre-nup? Should the marriage end, you wouldn't claim a penny in alimony from her?'

'Yes, that's true, just in case people thought I wanted her money.'

'I'm confused. I still don't understand why you consented to marry my daughter.'

'Because she asked me, and I didn't have any reason to say no.'

'You don't love her, do you?'

'I don't hate her too…'

'What would you do if anyone else made the same proposal to you?'

'No one has made one so far. There's no reason to assume someone would do so in future? Sir, you told, to assume is to make *ass* of *u* and *me*. I don't like to *assume*.'

'You seem to be very stubborn. Take some more time and think over it again. I never thought my daughter could ever fall in love with someone and want to marry. Ever since she started doping, she never did anything that would make me happy. I'm now happy for her, but sad for you. Still, I wish both of you all the best... I hope, against all hopes, this doesn't turn out to be the first round… After all, marriages are not meant to be like funding.'

Parush called his father during the Thanksgiving weekend to inform him about the marriage. 'Do you want me to be there?' Srinjay asked.

'Of course, Baba,' he said. 'But only you and Ru.' Aru and Pushi, who had come from Sewanee to spend the long weekend with him and had heard the news just the previous night, stared at him, stunned at the firmness they hadn't seen in him earlier.

'Whom are you punishing?' Aru asked him later.

***

The marriage took place at the plush Ahwahnee Hotel in Yosemite, a destination for queens and presidents alike, on a cold Sunday. It was 21st December. The reception started in the evening and extended long into the longest night of the year. It had been meant to be a *small* gathering of the closest acquaintances and friends. But for Bill, closeness was directly proportional to the prospects of making big bucks. His closed group comprised a fleet of bankers, senators, media barons and eminent lawyers. The old lady on a wheel chair, commanding over everyone, was Bill's mother, the only person from the Valentine clan other than Bill himself and his daughter. The sprawling lawn behind the hotel overlooking a mammoth rock had been bedecked and illuminated exquisitely for the occasion. Large heaters placed everywhere kept the guests comfortable in the freezing cold of a winter in Yosemite which had seen some unusual snowing that season.

Alina looked brilliant in the radiant red Benarasi sari Srinjay and Ru had brought with them from India.

Bill introduced Parush's father and sister to most of the guests. Apart from shaking hands with people he didn't know, Srinjay didn't play any other role in his son's marriage. He and Ru settled in a corner, close to a heater. They sat silently, staring at everything, but not watching anything in particular. Aru and Pushi stayed with Alina, helping her manage the sari. Alina asked them titbits about Parush. The GameIT family – all the ten-people hired in the last one month and the executive team, Kratu, Afsar, Tista, Sweti and Sam – sat close to Srinjay and Ru, making a small island of people on Parush's side. 'Pocha,' Srinjay asked Kratu, 'are you sure he wouldn't land up in jail?'

'Kaku,' Kratu assured, 'don't worry. He has the best lawyers fighting for him. From what I understand, he'll be charged with something called a misdemeanour drug offence for possessing drugs for personal use. That's much lighter than felony drug offences like drug trafficking and peddling. Also, given that this is his first drug offence, he's very likely to get PC1000, which is a deferred entry of judgment. Before pronouncing the judgment, the court will give him a chance to participate in a drug diversion program. He can't drive for six months. He must undergo counselling at a rehab for six months and then for the next one year he shouldn't be arrested again for a drug crime. So practically, there's no impact on him.'

'No impact at all?' Srinjay asked absent-mindedly.

***

Following the Bengali tradition of *phool sojja*, the bed of flowers, to commemorate the first night of togetherness after marriage, Tista, Afsar, Aru and Pushi had decorated the royal four-poster canopy bed of the Mary Curry Tresidder Suite with flowers. Ru was the last one to leave the room, and leave the newlywed couple alone. 'Was it necessary to choose this particular day?' she asked him quietly in Bangla before leaving. He hugged her and whispered into her ears, 'There's fun in burning. At least the flames come out... What would I do with those kept inside?'

Parush looked out through the door as long as he could see her.

'How do you feel?' Parush asked Alina later that night, the longest night of the year, the night which heralded Bitasta's twenty first birthday.

'I like doping. It's like a dope.' She took out a cigarette and handed one to him. She lit hers and, holding it between her lips, she came very close to him, closer than she had ever been in the past. 'I want to see where we land. It's the most intoxicating thing in the world – doing dangerous things without knowing what's next, isn't it?' She lit his cigarette with the burning tip of hers. 'At least for now, smoke her out...' She released a dollop of smoke into the warm air of one of the costliest hotel-suites of the world. She loosened herself gradually and lay on the huge bed embellished with the most beautiful flowers specially ordered for this night. 'The Queen of England slept in this room, on this bed... Now I'm the queen...' She didn't keep awake for long.

Despite the luxuries and warmth inside, Parush's mind drifted outside, in the shivering coldness, in the icy wind, which dashed against the pines and crashed against the other side of the large glass windows. He knew, the media in India would again publish the story of another Indian techie making it really big in the Bay Area, though not through conventional channels of hard work and growth. His orchestrated arrest for a drug offence, along with the associated story of saving the nubile girl of a prominent Venture Capitalist and the subsequent events had made a good read. They would write about this marriage too.

Parush felt cold and helpless, like one of those pines shivering outside in the snow. Did someone already know anything about it? Would she read it later when it would be published as a sizzling piece of news item? Would she finally break the silence of so many months and call him to say, 'Porus, how could you do this? How could you take all that seriously? Why the hell didn't you ask me even for once before putting the last nail on my coffin? How could you, Porus?'

He looked at Alina, lying on the huge bed, her body curved like an 'S', her hands stretched out beyond her head, her feet still bordered with the red *alta*, which Ru had remembered to get from Calcutta and which Tista had applied so carefully in the evening in an attempt to make her look like a Bengali bride. She had changed from the heavy Benarasi sari to a white gown which, Parush hadn't noticed earlier, looked so beautiful on her. He sat on the bed. He felt bad for her – after all, he had again used her as his bait.

But this time the bait hadn't worked.

***

Parush got up from the bed and walked to the window, watching the trees turn white, gradually, eradicating the signs of green, silently. He knew the white trees would again turn green the next morning, when the bright sunlight would make it hard to believe how pale they had been the previous night. Parush wondered when his own life would be green again. He turned around and moved towards the bed, where Alina was sleeping, calmly, her red alta adorned feet the only visible sign of their new association.

Parush stopped by a round table in the middle of the big room, staring at a rectangular jewellery box which, he recalled, he had seen his father place on Alina's hands the previous evening – it's a ritual in a Bengali wedding, known as ashirvad, which symbolises the blessings of the elders through gifts of gold. The picture on the lid of the jewellery box had attracted his attention. He picked up the box and looked at the lid with amazement. It had the picture of a boy hunting a bear. It resembled very closely the cartoon he had first seen on the door of Bitasta's room in Prembajar. There, the boy's face had been replaced with that of a baby Bitasta. The picture, he recalled, is a depiction of the Greek myth, where a young Arcas is about to kill, unknowingly, his mother Callisto, who has been transformed into a bear. Bitasta's mother, Parush knew, was much fond of Callisto's character, so the cartoon in her house, depicting the Callisto myth was understandable. Parush was also aware of the interesting anecdote behind that cartoon, how Panchali and everyone else started calling Bitasta by the name Arca after she, as a little kid, had played the role of Arcas in a theatrical depiction of the Callisto myth, where Panchali herself had been Callisto. But why would Parush's father buy a jewellery box with such a picture? Then, did the box belong to Sairandhri, his mother? Was she aware of Parush's marriage? Had she sent it as a gift to Parush's bride?

He opened the lid of the jewellery box. At its back was engraved, '*Ovid's Metamorphoses, by Johann Wilhelm Baur, 1639.*' He closed the lid and stared again at the picture on it. Like he had felt a few times in the past, he felt again that Sairandhri, his mother, and Panchali, Bitasta's mother, had a strange commonality, an alikeness, which went much deeper than their apparent differences or dissimilarities.

It was not possible that Sairandhri was not aware of the significance of the picture in connection to Panchali and Bitasta. She herself would sometimes call Panchali by the name Kalyani, the Indian Callisto. She would also know for sure that, for Panchali, the kid in the picture, who is about to kill the bear, signified Bitasta. Parush wondered why Sairandhri had sent the jewellery box with that picture, whose symbolism pointed so strongly to Panchali and Bitasta. When she had been lately behaving in a way as though she hated them so much, what was the point in dragging their references, that too at a time when Parush was getting married, not to Bitasta but to someone else?

Thinking of his mother, Parush suddenly felt a surge of hatred for her. When he went back to the bed and looked at Alina, the intensity of his hatred increased manifold.

COKE

Parush was staring at the calm waters of the bay through the large window of his office. Just a few days back they had moved to this building overlooking the bay on Beach Park Boulevard in Foster City. The three floors of this big house could accommodate fifty people and would be sufficient for the next one or two years. Parush stayed in the attic of the same house, thus enabling him to work almost anytime he would be awake. As none of Sam, Kratu and Sweti were full timers at GameIT – they were still in Schools – Parush was the only executive to have an office, which also doubled as the break room for the twenty odd employees, mostly recent college grads from Stanford and Berkeley. For weeks, Parush wouldn't leave the premise of GameIT, with Aru, like a routine, calling nearby restaurants from Sewanee and getting stuff home-delivered for his lunch and dinner. When Alina would visit him, they would sometimes go out. Strangely, or perhaps not, Alina never stayed back – they hadn't spent a single night together since their marriage. But Parush never failed to accompany her whenever she had to report to the rehab.

Sweti came and sat in front of Parush. He was still looking out, his gaze fixed on something distant. Sweti didn't talk for some time.

'Why do you always look so dull whenever you see me?' he asked Sweti.

'Porus,' Sweti looked straight into Parush's eyes, 'does it ever occur to you that you're leading the weirdest life? And don't think that just because people don't ask you any more, they're all fine with whatever you do. Porus, they've all given up. Tell me one thing, isn't it really odd that you don't stay with Alina?'

'She prefers staying in Stanford.'

'She's another weird person. Have you asked her to stay with you? Don't give me the crap that you're anyway fulfilling all your responsibilities. Just appearing together at parties or accompanying her to rehab occasionally is not everything – do you understand that Porus?'

'What more can I do?'

Sweti was going to say something. She closed her eyes and kept quiet. Parush got up and stood behind her. 'Swets,' he pleaded, 'please don't think so much. I feel awkward.'

'Thank God, at least there's something that makes you feel awkward.'

They went out and sat by the bay. Sweti pulled out an envelope and handed it over to him. 'Arav has sent it through someone visiting from India. He said he has already talked to you about it.'

'When is he coming here?'

'In July, after his sister's marriage...'

Parush had already opened the envelope. He was sifting through its contents – IIT degree certificate; mark sheets, admit cards and certificates of secondary and higher secondary examinations; an LIC policy document; salary slips and the complete set of employment documents of Intersoft; the last few letters written by Ru and... He stopped. He tried to recall if he had thrown away *all* her letters. Yes, he assured himself, before coming to the US, he had indeed thrown away everything – all those letters he would read many times, every time, whenever they came from Calcutta. But then, suddenly he remembered he had kept aside a few of Bitasta's letters in this envelope – he had become fond of the poems she would scribble sometimes as go-betweens, as though to broker temporary peace amidst the ongoing aggression of hostile words...

The pages slipped from his hand and scattered on the sand.

***

'Bill, Java's going to be really big in the future. It's going to be the platform for all mobile games,' Sam prophesied in March 1998. The executive team of GameIT – Sam, Kratu, Parush and Sweti – and its biggest investor William Valentine were having lunch at the Moscone Center in San Francisco on the first day of the JavaOne conference.

Sam removed the Java Ring – it had been given as a memento to all the participants of the conference – from his index finger and placed it on the table. The jewel of the ring was the "JAVA" logo, engraved on the round stainless-steel casing of a robust single-chip microcomputer with a powerful Java Virtual Machine. 'One day, this simple device is going to change the world, opening new doors of opportunities,' Sam said, pointing to the ring. 'It was really symbolic when Sun's CEO, Scot McNealy, actually opened a door on stage with a prototype of the Java Ring last year in the Java Internet Business Expo. Its greatest promise is its capacity to interact with any internet application and possibly run any Java applet on it, both of which can convert a simple mobile phone into a really smart thing. Today's phones are not smart at all, but when they get smarter day by day, we've huge prospects with mobile games. I want to make smart games for tomorrow's phones. I don't want to compete with the silly Tetris and Snake which appeared in the Nokia 6610 phones last year…'

Parush had been greatly fascinated by Sam's confidence. It was perhaps this contagious confidence which gave Parush the strength to remain awake for nights and work like a robot. Or, was it just the thrill of destroying himself? 'People who take poison or jump off the cliffs are not the only ones who commit suicide,' Sweti often told him agitatedly.

***

Later that day, when Sam, Kratu, Parush and Sweti had assembled at the GameIT office in Foster City for a regular review meeting, Parush brought up the topic of the game based on the white-paper he and Kratu had jointly created two months ago.

Ever since Kratu had told him the story of a group of people breaking into a heavily guarded round fort, he had been highly intrigued by a particular aspect of it. He learned that Kratu's grandmother had a repository of many such interesting stories. Even before co-founding GameIT, Kratu had already created a game based on this story of his grandmother's. In this story, the invaders, having failed many times to break into the fort, finally study the pattern of events in the lives of the defenders and find the correlation of these events with the positions of stars and planets. Next, they do a similar study on their own people and select only those who have a higher probability of breaking in on a date and time when the positions of stars and planets would be favourable to them.

What was intriguing here was the astrological connotation, from which it could be conjectured that astrology is nothing but a simple statistical dependence, the correlation between two sets of seemingly unrelated events – one, the events in the life of a person and two, the positions of stars and planets. Kratu's game was quite simple though, it didn't have any astrological aspect. But in July 1996, he, Tista and Sam, along with Kratu's advisor at Stanford, published a paper titled *Mathematical Modelling of Astrology Based on Statistical Dependence* in the *Mathematical Modelling and Numerical Analysis,* a part of the *European Series in Applied & Industrial Mathematics.* A year later they filed an eponymous patent on the same subject. When Parush came to know of the story and the paper, it suddenly flashed in his mind, why not bring in the astrological aspect in the game by allowing the users to *train* the invaders, or rather choose them aptly to improve the chance of their success? In other words, he wanted to *control the fate of the invaders.*

Eventually, he and Kratu jointly wrote the white-paper on *Using Statistical Dependence to Train the Characters in a Video Game.*

'Porus,' Sam said, 'I've been thinking about it a lot lately. Yes, you do have a point here. It can be our answer to the popular Tamagotchi games released recently by the Japanese company Bandai. In a typical Tamagotchi game, an alien species drops an egg on Earth – egg is *tamago* in Japanese - and it is up to the player to raise the egg into an adult creature. You're also talking about a similar concept, where you're going to give an option to the players to raise their own team, in this case, to break into a heavily guarded fort. That's a novel idea, but I don't think the infrastructure available in mobile phones would be able to support it. Don't worry, we'll do it one day and, yes, we'll do it big, really big.'

Sam looked out at the dark waters of the Bay. 'We'll call it "*Luck*"', he said, still staring out. 'Everyone wants to have the luck of his choice and that's what we're going to give them: *Analyze luck and choose what you want...*'

***

When everyone left, Parush pulled out the envelope with Bitasta's letters from a locker, perhaps the only space in the entire house, which could be designated as private. Along with the envelope, the otherwise empty locker also preserved the only other important possession of Parush – Panchali's notebook. He kept aside the loose papers, printouts, open books, floppies, the unopened box from a nearby Indian restaurant Aru had made an arrangement with to deliver his dinner every day, and some other insignificant things which comprised his work place paraphernalia, and created space on his desk. He spread the letters neatly on the desk and stared at them for some time. He touched each letter tenderly with his fingers and tried to erase the marks of its folds. The scattered lines of the poems written by Bitasta floated around him in the room like the notes of a haunting melody.

Kiss, kiss me a lullaby,
Kiss me a love song under the deep blue sky.
Kiss, kiss me a memory,
Kiss me a lifetime that belies memento mori.
Kiss, kiss till daybreak,
Kiss me a hypnotic....

As he read the poems again for the umpteenth time since he had got them, he could see the changing tones in Bitasta's voice. The later poems were devoid of the rhymes and the meters and the earlier exuberance of the yearnings of a lovelorn lonesome young girl. Along with the maturity came the despondency, the frustration and the angst.

I am caught here –
Between hopes, dreams and despair,
Where you live with me too...

How would this story end?
By ticking off the remaining boxes
Of worldly achievements?
Or by going through the last bits of anguish,
Which seem to have been kept aside for me?

Bitasta had written the poems over a span of just a few months, but still it appeared, as though, they were written in two different ages, in two different worlds, by two different people. He threw the letters and jumped on them to tear them off, but he couldn't. He sat quietly on the carpet, leaning against the wall, breathing heavily.

After some time, he collected all the letters scattered on the carpet and put them back into the envelope. His eyes were burning. He went to the washroom and splashed cold water on his face. He went out to the balcony and stood there for a while, staring at the void of the Bay. He returned to his desk. When the phone rang it was well past midnight.

'Haven't you slept yet?' Aru asked, knowing very well that Parush rarely slept.

'You're awake too...' Parush said, leaning against the chair.

***

'Christina Rossetti and Elizabeth Barrett Browning?' Parush asked. His sister had called him from Sewanee, as she would do once or twice a week, but this time she had asked something unusual.

'Yes, don't you remember seeing the books at *Ma's desk*?'

It was in many months that someone had brought up Sairandhri's name before him. For a moment, the very reference of her seemed to make the air around him so hot that he felt as though his skin was burning and his eyes were drying up. But then immediately he had a totally different feeling. He wanted to see his mother – he hadn't seen her for so long, much longer than the last one year. The very next moment he wondered if she at all realised that, had it not been for her, his life could have been so different. He felt the burning sensation again.

'Yes, you're right,' Parush said, trying to calm down. 'The books were there at her desk. Why do you ask?'

'I was preparing for a submission. I had to refer to an edition of *Sewanee Review* for an article on the handling of sexuality by the female poets of the Victorian Age. There I came across the names of Browning, Rossetti and Emily Dickinson, all of whom are said to have written on lesbianism, something quite unusual of their times. All the three names sounded familiar to me because I've heard Ma reciting their poems, especially Rossetti's *Goblin Market*. It was kind of weird to know that *Goblin Market* is about two sisters Laura and Lizzie whose relationship has strains of lesbianism...'

Later that night Parush pulled out the notebook – perhaps the only memento of his association with Bitasta and her mother he had retained with him. Turning the pages of Panchali's notebook of poems he felt as though it was a time machine which had compressed the innumerable moments of passion from the past into a few winks of time in the present. He turned the pages as slowly as possible, perhaps to decompress the moments and stretch the winks. He reached the page which had a few lines from *Goblin Market*.

Did you miss me?
Come and kiss me.
Never mind my bruises,
Hug me, kiss me, suck my juices
Squeez'd from goblin fruits for you,
Goblin pulp and goblin dew.
Eat me, drink me, love me...

He shut the notebook and ran out to the narrow shore adjoining the bay. He fell on the sand and rolled a few times till he hit a bench. '*Did you miss me*?' he cried, pouring out like a sudden burst of rain which wouldn't stop soon. 'Oh ... Bits ... eat me ... drink me ... love me...'

***

'Come to Stanford,' Sweti told Parush over the phone sometime in June, few days before his birthday. 'Today, around seven.' There was an unusual firmness in her voice. It was perhaps not unknown to many that Sweti had a special place for him in her heart. Her gestures and body language seldom hid the fact that she did love Parush. Many of their common acquaintances would often tease them in the past, but now not many joked with Parush, especially since his marriage the previous year. Perhaps Tista was the only one who still dared to be frivolous with him.

'You okay?' asked Parush, realising that Sweti had never called him like this. It was he who would call her anytime, anywhere.

'Yes, I'm fine. See you in the evening.' She didn't stretch the conversation.

Parush booked a cab – he was not yet allowed to drive – and reached Sweti's apartment in the Escondido Village a little before five. He was surprised to see Alina at Sweti's place. Somehow, he had never seen Sweti and Alina together. There were some unexpressed cold vibes between them – at least that was what he believed. Seeing them together, which appeared to be premeditated, was rather more suspicious than surprising. He sensed something was amiss. For a moment no one talked. He stared at Alina, looking pale. The dark marks under her eyes made her look very sick. When he had accompanied her to the rehab a few weeks ago, she hadn't looked so pale. Suddenly he felt guilty. Was he being unjustifiably ignorant about her? He had always tried to make himself believe that, for Alina, the entire marriage was perhaps only a whim, a post-dope fancy. And for him, it was just another way to hurt himself, kill himself, burn himself. But now, seeing his wife, looking pale and sick, sitting quietly, he felt bad.

Parush didn't want to ask Sweti why Alina was at her place. Expectedly, Sweti got up. 'You guys can stay here. I've some work. Just pull the door shut when you leave.'

'Swets,' Parush called her from the back, 'can you please call a cab?'

Sweti smiled and left the room. She first called the Yellow Cab and then Bill, Alina's father and the main investor of GameIT. 'Thank you,' Bill said. 'Thank you…Thank you…' he repeated a few more times.

***

When Parush got down from the cab and walked towards the entrance of GameIT, Alina by his side, the few recent college grads, who were working late on a Saturday evening, were a little surprised. They had rarely seen Alina with Parush, perhaps never with his hands wrapped around her waist. Parush directly went to the attic, the place officially designated as his home, but where he barely spent any time other than when he needed the toilet for ablutions and bath. Given that it was a guy's room, it was unusually clean. He made Alina sit on the bed, stretching her legs forward and leaning against the pile of pillows. He pulled the comforter over her legs and sat beside her. They kept quiet for a long time. On the other occasions when they generally met, during the visits to the rehab or the parties her father threw from time to time, the conversations would be always situational, without needing to ponder over any topic to chat on. 'Hope you haven't doped in the past few weeks,' he would always ask on the way to the rehab. And in the parties, she would introduce him to the guests he hadn't met earlier. But just now, the situation was different and hence they mined for words.

'You could have called me,' Parush finally initiated a conversation, without much emotion.

'You're busy with your work. And the doctor is known to us. Had I needed any help I would have called you.'

When Parush got up to open the windows, Alina talked again. 'This morning I bumped into your friend in the Escondido. I never liked her, but she has been always courteous with me. When she saw me today, she shrieked, thinking I was very ill. She asked me to come to her place in the evening. I couldn't say no.' She paused for some time and when Parush came and sat beside her again, she said, 'She still loves you and I'm not sure if that kid ever loved you like her.' Alina, Parush recalled, had a few times in the past referred to Bitasta as kid. Parush didn't react.

'You're indeed ill. Are you taking the medicines properly?'

'There's not much medicine. And I too don't have a problem. I just can't sleep. The doctor had initially given me a strong sleep aid called propofol. Now he wants to wean me off propofol. He has started giving me other sleep aids known as benzodiazepines. But since I've stopped taking propofol, I'm not able to sleep. Perhaps that has made me look pale.'

Parush felt a peculiar camaraderie with his wife – both struggled to sleep. 'I too can't sleep,' he said.

Alina rested her head gently on his shoulder and he patted it tenderly with his hand. 'I want to dope,' she said suddenly. 'I want to sleep. Please get my bag.'

Parush hesitated for some time but then relented. Soon they were both snorting coke. Parush hadn't taken cocaine earlier. He started sweating. He felt a heavy palpitation. Suddenly, he felt as though an irritating pile of dark clouds had unexpectedly slipped off the sky and the sun had spilled into the room after a long time. He felt the dazzle of the sun, reflected against the thousand glasses scattered everywhere in the room. A sudden feeling of euphoria raised him high up in the sky and made him fly in the air. He felt elated.

Kiss, kiss till daybreak,
Kiss me a hypnotic, and doses of you which I take.

He heard Bitasta's voice reverberating around him. He threw the comforter off Alina's body. He jumped on her and pulled her dress up, slipping it off her body from above. He dragged her bra up, pounding on her breasts like a fierce animal, squeezing and crushing them with his hands. As he sucked the breasts hard, she tore apart his shirt, unzipped his pants and pulled her underpants down. No sooner did he start biting her lips wildly, than he inserted himself into her, rocking violently against her trembling body. She held him tight with her arms, scratching his back, moaning, tears dropping off her eyes. With a sudden jerk the rocking movement stopped and he lay flat on her, perspiring and breathing heavily. He felt sleepy, really sleepy, after a really long time, so long that he couldn't recall when he had last felt like this, so calm, so tired, so peaceful. Even when his eyes would etch, he never felt sleepy. But now, he wanted to sleep.

'Take me to the tub...' Alina mumbled. 'I want to sleep in the water ... with you.'

Parush took her slowly to the tub, filled it with water and soon a soothing slumber drowned him into a deep and peaceful sleep he hadn't had for months.

When he awoke the next day, a roomful of anxious faces looming on him, Alina had been already dead. Later he learned that Alina had died in the tub due to cardiac dysrhythmia caused by a cocktail of cocaine and a fatal dose of the prescription drug propofol, which her doctor had given her as a sleeping aid. When someone came to work on Sunday morning, the entire carpet in the first floor had been soaked badly with the water overflowing from the tub. He ran upstairs and banged on the door of the attic. When no one opened, he called 911. The cops pulled out Alina's corpse and Parush's almost lifeless body from the water. Parush survived as he hadn't snorted much coke.

VOLCANO

Had it not been for Bill, Alina's father, who stood like a wall guarding his son-in-law, the world would have come pounding on Parush's home and life. First, it was the legal implication, his role in Alina's death, given the fact that the doctors at the rehab had testified that Alina hadn't taken drugs for quite some time till that fateful night when she died of drug overdose. Then there were the questions raised about Parush's sense of responsibility as a husband. Parush had been in the news a few months ago too, when he had married the only daughter of the most prolific VC of Silicon Valley under unusual circumstances. Bill's name and fame brought the media glare again on Parush in the US and India. 'How could he allow her take drugs again?' questioned *Aajkal*, a Bengali tabloid from Calcutta which broke the news of a broken affair, which had wrecked Parush's life not long ago, being the reason for his indifference towards his wife.

'Do you think you still love her?' Sweti shouted at Parush, banging the door of the attic of the office of GameIT on Beach Park Boulevard in Foster City. 'For God's sake, don't have such terrible misconceptions. People like you can't love. It's just your hurt ego that someone has ditched you; that you couldn't get something in life; that you couldn't get someone whom you had desired so much. And now you've become vicious. You just want to take revenge. You just want her to feel terrible, feel responsible for all the shit that's happening to you…'

As she shouted, Parush sat quietly on the bed, expressionless. She pushed him hard and slammed him on the bed. She stood at the edge of the bed for a few moments, breathing heavily, her eyes shut. Then, suddenly she pulled him up, dragging him by his shirt, and pushed him against the wall. She tore apart his shirt, and then slowly collapsed like a magnificent ivy plant nimbly losing all the strength in its roots with which it had clung to the grand university walls. Sitting at his feet, she cried for some time, Parush not uttering a single word.

Parush went incommunicado, Bill handling the media and the cops. For weeks he didn't come out of the room where he had had sex with his wife for the first time just before her death. He spent days and nights thinking about the girl whom he had always used as his bait, whom he had never thought of as a human being with heart and flesh, who had been a mere necessity for him to keep his angst, his pain, his grief alive within him. He wondered if he was feeling guilty or helpless. Now that she was dead, who would be his next bait? Who would be so effective in burning him completely, torturing him every moment he lived and killing him with every wink of time that passed? He remembered Sweti's words. Did he really want to take revenge on Bitasta? Would he lead a normal life if he knew she was not able to lead one, burning every moment in repentance and guilt? Would he burn himself more if he knew she gave a damn about whatever happened to him?

There was no denying the uncomfortable truth that he was indeed missing Alina, whatever the reason. He wrapped himself with the comforter which he had placed on her body that night. He filled the tub with hot water and lay inside it for a long time. He laid her white dress on the bed, straightening the creases and folds, as though someone would wear it soon. He looked around for the bra he had violently opened that night during a very short and fierce foreplay, but he couldn't find it – someone would have removed it from his room. He upturned her bag from which she had taken out the coke. The bag was empty. He held the bag close to his chest.

Sweti, Tista, Aru, Pushi, everyone would come to meet him by turns. He rarely talked to anyone. He hadn't even attended Alina's memorial mass.

The day before Aru and Pushi left for Sewanee, Aru had appeared in his room, alone, late in the night. She shut the door behind her and leaned against it, staring at him, as he remained seated quietly on the bed. She came and sat beside him for a long time, silently, staring at the floor. Parush never talked. Before leaving, she did something that she hadn't done ever in the past. She kissed him, on his lips. 'I'm leaving,' she said, holding his face tenderly with her hands. 'Don't burn yourself anymore…'

She left abruptly, keeping the door open, not turning back.

***

'Why're you trying to save me?' Parush asked Bill one day. 'I killed your daughter.'

Bill stared at Parush. 'Well, I would say, you couldn't make her live, like me. And anyway, you're suffering for that, like me.'

Bill left the room.

Parush felt a weird sense of kinship with Bill. They both had ignored the same woman. Alina was only five when Bill's wife had run away with his brother and died in a car accident soon after. Bill moved to the Bay Area, little Alina tagging on to him like one of the many unnoticed pieces of household belongings. She lived her short life with Bill's indifference and died with Parush's.

He thought about his mother, to whom he had attributed everything bad that had happened to him in the recent past. He hated her more than anyone. He hated her for her lifelong indifference towards him and his father. He hated her for ruining his life. But now that he himself could be held responsible for killing Alina, for being so indifferent and insensitive to her, was he any better than his own mother? That was when a very awkward thought peeked into his mind. What had his mother been burning with all her life that she had turned so indifferent, so silent, so ruthless, so solitary, so distant?

He thought of calling his mother, for the first time in so many months. He lay down on the bed for hours and then fell asleep. When he woke up, it was morning. He climbed down the stairs slowly, staring at the empty cubicles, the blank screens of the computers, the piles of papers on the desks, the half-empty coffee mugs, the scribbling on the white boards, all familiar signs he suddenly started missing. He went back to his attic, freshened up and returned to his office, after many weeks, which seemed like ages. Someone noticed him at his office and called Sweti. 'Thanks,' she said. 'Call for a status update meeting this Friday. I'll be there...'

***

On a weekend in July, Parush and Sweti went to SFO to receive Arav. Parush located him in the crowd, pushing a cart, coming out of the arrival gate. He too had seen them, waiting for him at the arrival lounge.

Arav came and hugged Parush for an unusually long time, while Sweti stood by the cart, staring perhaps at a different Arav she had never seen before. It was not unknown that he had a thing for her. But neither had he ever expressed it to her, nor had he told anyone about it. It was true that Sweti too never allowed anyone to come close to her. Somehow, it was also known to all that Sweti had a special feeling for Parush, despite knowing that his relationship with Bitasta was rock solid. Perhaps, she thought that was the reason why Arav might not have expressed his feelings to her. When he unnecessarily fought with her over silly things, she always knew it was a lame attempt to hide his real feelings. To say the truth, she had been waiting eagerly for Arav to come to the US and join GameIT.

'Sala kutta,' Arav said to Parush with tears in his eyes, '*aren't we there in this world*? If you want to die, tell us. We'll kill you...' As he rubbed his eyes, Sweti pushed the cart, smiling. She knew if there was anyone who could control Parush, it had to be Arav.

***

'This year seems like a Meteor Shower of dot-com start-ups,' Sam said on September 4, 1998, the day when Larry and Sergey, two of Sam and Kratu's acquaintances from Stanford, incorporated their start-up, started recently at Susan Wojcicki's garage in Menlo Park. The previous year they had rechristened their BackRub search engine as Google, a play on the word *googol*, a mathematical term for the number represented by the numeral one followed by 100 zeros.

'Go.com, Kozmo.com, Pets.com... Oh, how could I forget Boo.com?' Kratu joked.

'You forgot one,' added Parush, 'Whoopi Goldberg's Flooz.com.'

'Bill is smart enough to not put money in any of these,' Sam said. 'I don't think this concept of "Get Big Fast" works. They're now giving free services and running under huge losses just to create brand awareness. They hope to charge later, but are you going to pay for something that's free now? Guys, I'm very particular about this. Nothing should be free. We've to make money from day one. Let's hit the gas hard...'

The next three years were hectic for all at GameIT. Kratu, Sam and Sweti completed their studies and became full timers. With a target of going public by 2002, Bill ensured that no one had much time for outside work. Bill also ensured that there was enough buzz around GameIT. 'It's all perception,' he would always say. 'If they *think* you are good, you are good. And if they think so, they should talk so. A big mouth is not always bad…'

Pushi and Aru would come to Bay Area more frequently in their freshman and sophomore years. But when they were in their junior year, their visits became more and more infrequent. Gradually, Aru started calling Arav to enquire about Parush. 'Make sure he doesn't sit at his desk for very long,' she would instruct. 'I'm reading a lot about ergonomic problems. He should take small breaks in between…'

Whenever Ru would visit the US, she would make sure she spent some time with Parush. That would be the only time Parush wouldn't work for eighteen hours a day. 'Why are you looking old, Ru?' he asked her one day, when she had just come out of the arrival gate of the SFO airport. She looked pale and forlorn. Allowing him to push her cart she walked by his side. 'Don't you think I'm already forty?' she said, smiling coquettishly.

'What rubbish,' Parush scoffed, 'you're still the same one I would run to see after my school every day. What happened?' He stopped walking and looked at her, a few strands of grey hair falling on her face, her eyes looking tired, her lips dry.

'Nothing… I think the lonesome days in Calcutta are making me look pale.' She paused to see Parush's reaction. 'Don't worry, with the life you're leading, you too will get old soon. Get someone, otherwise…' She didn't complete. Parush left the cart and held her with his two hands. She embraced him and buried her head into his chest. 'I wonder how your mother always looks so young, despite being stranded in life…'

'How's Ma?' Parush asked in the car, after a long silence. This was the first time he had asked about his mother in all these years.

'Wouldn't you ever talk to her?' she asked.

Parush didn't say anything for the rest of the journey.

***

'I believe the introduction of the WAP browsers two years back has brought better prospects for mobile games,' someone said, when Sam was talking about the latest offerings from GameIT at the JavaOne 2001. 'Last year there were very good games from companies like JAMDAT Mobile, Ludigames, nGame and Digital Bridges. This year too Digital Bridges and Sega have demonstrated new games on prototype Motorola phones, which are running a micro version of the Java programming environment. Where do your games stand against these?'

'I personally liked a lot *Steve Jackson Sorcery* from Digital Bridges. *Alien Fish Exchange* from nGame was an interesting Tamagotchi rendition. This year the Java 2 Micro Edition has showed us that fast games are possible on mobile phones. We too have released our games on Java 2 Micro Edition. But the resolution of a mobile screen is still limited to 3000 pixels. We've a long way to go. This year I'm hearing a lot about games like *LifeStylers* and *The Lord of the Rings* from Picofun and Riot-E. We're quite well placed against our competition. But the best of GameIT games are yet to come…'

'Sam, to be very frank, I feel there's a lot of buzz around GameIT, all thanks to Bill's handling of the media, but I don't see much coming out of your company. On the contrary, this year Volcano had a much greater impact at JavaOne. What's your take on Volcano?'

Parush realised the journalist was intentionally instigating Sam. It was the talk of the town that Sam's equations with Rajesh Malhotra, the founder and CEO of Volcano, were not that great. In fact, their rivalry was quite old, dating back to their days at Berkeley. Both wanted to outdo the other but Rajesh, being short tempered and more arrogant than Sam, would always come about as the fallen one in School. But once out of School, things changed. Bill's rivals joined hands and promoted Volcano in a big way. And lately, Volcano had been really doing well. People did say that GameIT might lose to Volcano, eventually.

Parush came forward to respond. 'Our take on Volcano is that they're offering us good competition and we're thankful to them for that. Competition always leads to better quality...'

Parush pulled Sweti out of the crowd. 'Swets, I want to meet that journalist,' he said sternly. Sweti saw the sort of fortitude in his face she hadn't seen for a few years now. 'Come on,' she tried to pacify, 'leave him. That's his job.'

'Swets, you know, I'll do it anyway and without your help it will just take longer. Dinner tonight. Gary Danko. Me, you, Arav and him...' he left her alone and proceeded towards the crowd. 'By the way,' he turned back, 'what's our annualised revenue run-rate for this year based on Q1 revenue?'

'It would be close to six million.'

'And what's Volcano's?'

'Rajesh is claiming it's 7.5 million.'

Sweti stared at Parush as he walked ahead. Everyone, who cared a lot for Parush, had been happy that since Alina's death three years ago he had been so engrossed in his work that he had never got time to torture himself, kill himself. That deadly instinct, which would arouse suicidal streaks within him had been dormant all these years. 'Sweti,' Aru had asked once, 'don't you think he has moved on?'

'I hope so,' she had replied. But seeing that face again today, she felt apprehensive, as though she had seen the signs of a bad omen. She looked for Arav.

Later when Sam read the news item he was surprised. 'Swets,' he exclaimed, 'I thought he would write bad things about us...'

Sweti's gaze was fixed on the cars, stuck in the rush hour traffic on 101, visible from Sam's office at the new place in Sunnyvale they had moved into recently.

***

'I know what you're thinking,' Sam said to a big gathering at Bill's plush home in Atherton, a year later. 'Mobile game companies are running out of cash. *Riot-E* and *Vizzavi* have closed. *Picofun* has been bought by *Aspiro* for just one million. The dot-com bubble has exploded. *eToys* and *Flooz.com* have filed for bankruptcy. *Webvan* has collapsed. *Boo.com*, *Pets.com* and *Kozmo.com* have all closed. Is it a good time for an IPO?' He paused to check the reaction of his listeners.

'Well,' he continued, 'our times are not bad. We're the first to unlock the full potential of mobile Internet technology. We're the first so-called "wireless application" play to hit the market. We've turned mobile terminals, such as WAP-phones, into a platform for games and entertainment. We've changed people's perception of mobile entertainment. We believe entertainment will be a killer application for mobile Internet and that entertainment soon will account for at least 50% of the operators' revenues. Already most phone users in the US play our games. *We want all users to play our games ... only our games...*'

As Sam spoke to the unusually large gathering, taking questions and trying his best to make his point that GameIT was the strongest player in mobile games, Parush was turning the pages of a magazine.

As far as video games for mobile phones are concerned, you ain't seen nothing yet! Now the revolution's come. You can download them and change them as often as you want – they move, they vibrate and they play. What's happened? Well, at long last, Java's here!

He read the article on *Gameloft*. He turned the page.

With a VC investment of $30 million, mainly by Bill Valentine and partially by Apax, Benchmark and Qualcomm, and an annualized revenue run-rate of $20 million in 2002, the Sunnyvale based GameIT is slated for an IPO later this month…

Volcano is the biggest competitor for GameIT, which seems to have lost most of its earlier hype…

Rajesh Malhotra, CEO of GameIT's biggest rival Volcano, is confident that he can raise $80 million through its IPO, expected around the same time as that of GameIT. "We'll kill GameIT," he claimed at a recent press release…

'We're hopeful that we would raise at least $75 million through an initial offering of 5.5 million shares at a price of $15 per share.' Sam's announcement was greeted with a thundering applause. 'Our revenue in the Q1 of 2002 is $5 million…'

GameIT finally raised $80 million through its Initial Public Offering, the first ever for any mobile gaming company in the US, and paid back all its investors. It was valued at a decent $350 million.

Volcano raised $85 million a month later, during which there was an exodus of key people from GameIT to Volcano. It was rumoured that Rajesh Malhotra had poached them by offering lucrative pre-IPO stocks. GameIT stocks tumbled down to $10, a 35% dip within a month, from its peak of $15.5.

***

In the December of 2002, just a few months after GameIT had gone public, a disquieting news item created a sort of an unexpected tremor in the Bay Area. Parush had suddenly resigned from

GameIT. There were interesting stories about what had transpired on the day when Parush had walked out for the last time from GameIT's premise in Sunnyvale. People had claimed to have seen Parush coming out of Sam's office after a very long meeting, Sweti running after him. 'Porus,' she had apparently shouted, 'for God's sake, please don't do it again. Don't hurt yourself again. How many times do you want to kill yourself?'

Parush had embraced her, spoken something into her ears and walked out of the office, not turning back even once.

Arav overheard a conversation from the break room a few days later. 'Parush has taken drugs, got himself arrested, married a drug addict, and slogged his balls for eighteen hours a day for four years at a stretch – all for GameIT,' someone said. 'I don't believe he can walk out like this.'

'But he did walk out,' said someone else.

'There's something more to what we know, what we see…'

***

'Welcome,' Rajesh Malhotra greeted Parush at Volcano's office in Mountain View. 'Welcome to Volcano. Now we can kill GameIT for sure.'

Parush smiled. '*Yes, now you can kill GameIT…*' he said, shaking hands with Rajesh.

THE LITIGATION

'GameIT is losing steam,' Parush said to an excited Rajesh. 'Even the smaller players like *JAMDAT*, *Gamevil* and *Gameloft* seem to be more innovative. Sam is very stubborn at times.'

Parush paused to study Rajesh's expression, till there was a spiteful smile on the face of his eager listener. 'I've been telling him,' he continued, 'that the concept of controlling the fate of the characters would be a great leap in the evolution of video games. Shortly after joining GameIT, the idea came to my mind from a paper Kratu, Sam and others had written way back in 1996. The seed idea of this paper had in turn come from folklore which Kratu's grandmother used to tell.'

'But, I believe, you guys never worked on such a game, did you?' asked Rajesh, leaning on the table in front of him.

'Elaborating on my thoughts, Kratu and I wrote a white-paper in 1998. Yes, you're correct – we never worked on such a game. Sam feels that the required infrastructure for such an elaborate game is still not available.'

Rajesh pushed back on his chair and hung his head backwards, resting it against his crossed hands. 'Are you confident that this will be a killer game?' he asked.

'Don't you think so?'

'Yes, I do...' Rajesh said, fixing his gaze at the ceiling of his plush office. He sat erect and looked at Parush, sitting calm on the other side of the table. 'Get started,' he threw the words and got up. Parush didn't get up. Rajesh had started walking towards the door, but seeing Parush still seated, he turned back. 'But...' Parush asked, 'what about the legal implications?'

'It was your idea and they never worked on it. Neither did they patent the idea. There's no question of patent violation or theft or misappropriation of trade secrets. Don't worry, get started...' he left the room.

Later that day Parush sent an e-mail to Rajesh.

I can get started any time. Think about the legal implications once more. If you're confident of handling it, should there be any problem later, I've no issues ...

Rajesh sent a one-liner reply.

Leave the legal things to me. You go ahead.

The same week Volcano entered into a patent cross-licensing agreement with Stanford and Berkeley.

***

Two weeks later, GameIT sent a letter to Volcano enclosing a copy of Parush's employment agreement with GameIT and asking Volcano to confirm that it would not use any confidential GameIT information. 'No mention of the white-paper you and Kratu wrote in 1998,' Rajesh pointed out, reading the letter. 'As you said, Sam doesn't see much value in it.'

Within a month, Volcano filed a patent on "*Controlling the Fate of the Characters in a Video Game*". Volcano declared in the filing that they had used a prior art – a story mentioned in *From the Horse's Mouth*, a collection of Kratu's grandmother's stories compiled by Kratu's sister and published in 1996.

'Rajesh,' Parush said one day, 'I've got to know that GameIT has used my white-paper to file a patent on "*Using Statistical Dependence to Train the Characters in a Video Game*". Looks like, Sam has finally taken my idea seriously...'

Few months later, in May 2003, Rajesh said in LA, at the Electronic Entertainment Expo, 'It's my pleasure to announce a game that would change the world of gaming. You can now be Gods... You can control the fate...'

Around the same time, the editors of *Red Herring* magazine named Volcano in *The Red Herring 100*. 'According to a *Business Wire* release,' Rajesh sent out a mail to all his employees, 'this annual ranking recognises the top 50 public and the top 50 private companies whose services, business models, products and quality of management define business innovation...'

In January 2004, Volcano released the game *Changers*, based on the patent they had filed the previous year. Two months later, Patent 465 was issued to Volcano.

***

Rajesh threw a lavish party at his new house atop a hill in Saratoga to celebrate the success of *Changers*. He had invited all his close acquaintances from the Wall Street, media, engineering and legal fraternity and most of the Bay Area celebrities. Expectedly, his acquaintances from GameIT were conspicuous by their absence. Already known for his extravagance and fondness for costly wines, Rajesh's new house in a sprawling estate, comprising an entire hill and complete with a mini golf course, lakes, woods and large manicured lawns, was as decorous as his image. He took his guests on a guided tour of his house, spending enough time in the underground cellar connecting the two portions of it, talking about the bottles of rare wines he had collected from around the world. 'This is a 1990 *Louis Roederer Cristal Brut*... That one is a *1980 Moët & Chandon Cuvée Dom Pérignon* ... and then I've also got a *Pernod Ricard Perrier Jouet*, there...'

He talked about the paintings of famous contemporary world painters he had acquired at different auctions and adorned the various walls of his house with. 'Tyeb Mehta is my dad's favourite and I had to get that one...Those two are Husain ...That's a Takashi Murakami...That one is a Richard Prince...'

Opening a huge bottle of champagne Rajesh addressed the gathering. 'This year we've been ranked seventh on *Deloitte's* list of North America's fastest growing technology firms. In addition to ranking first on *Electronic Business's* list of *Best Small Electronics Companies* for the second consecutive year, we're listed second by *Forbes* on the list of the fastest-growing technology companies...'

Since joining Volcano a year and a half ago, Parush had tried to remain off the media glare as much as possible. That had fuelled more gossip and meaty news items, especially when the meteoric rise of Volcano in the recent past had been largely attributed to him. Presently too, he tried to stay away from the crowd. He had been sitting quietly all the evening, trying to avoid almost everyone. Perhaps the grandeur and extravagance of the evening was so overwhelming that even the most investigative journalist had ignored him till now.

'VLKN last traded at $31,' Rajesh continued. 'Last year it appreciated 35% and this year, already 45%. I'm sure my Wall Street friends will accept it's one of the best performing stocks. With a current Value of $27.20 per share, it's fully valued compared to its Price of $31 per share. VLKN has a forecasted Earnings Growth Rate of 38%, which *VectorVest* considers to be excellent. Our EPS and PE ratios are...'

Parush got up and walked slowly towards one of the three lakes, behind the white fortress which made up Rajesh's house. As he passed by groups of people, greeting them with mute and gestured hellos, he grabbed bits and pieces of their excited conversations.

'Lot of money is pumping into mobile games...'
'Digital Chocolate raised $13 million...'

'Mforma raised a whopping $44 million and bought UK studio Blue Beck for an undisclosed sum...'

'InfoSpace spent an amazing $26 million on German developer Elkware...'

'JAMDAT is going IPO in Oct...'

***

Parush sat on the white bench overlooking the lake. He leaned back and hung his head behind, closing his eyes. He didn't count the moments which might have passed by till he heard someone asking him in Bangla, 'May I have the pleasure of giving you some company?' He opened his eyes and turned back. A lady in a beautiful blue sari stood behind the bench. Her face looked familiar. 'You seemed alone all evening,' she said, walking from behind the bench and sitting beside him, so close that her bare arms brushed against his.

'You have been observing me,' Parush said.

'I've been trying to meet you for quite some time. You had rejected me two years back when you were in GameIT. I had applied for the position of Director of HR. I'm Piyali Sen, call me Piu...'

'How are you here?' Parush asked.

'Nem is a good friend of mine. I've come with him.'

Nem had been two years junior to Parush at KGP and had recently joined Volcano after completing his PhD from Stanford.

'I've always underestimated Nem. I never thought he could have a *friend* like you...'

'Every acquaintance is for a reason,' Piu interrupted. 'After all, any individual achievement is always a team effort. We need the right acquaintances to achieve ... achieve something really big.' She looked into Parush's eyes with a meaningful smile. For a long time Parush hadn't been in such close proximity of any woman. Since Alina's death six years ago, the only thing he had kept himself burning with was work. It was not that he wanted to achieve something. He just wanted to exhaust himself, wane himself, wean himself from everything else. People around him, people who cared for him, thought he had finally got a reason to live, but in reality, he had found another way to cease to live one day. Perhaps his detachment from everything, even from the outcome for which he worked, made him excel better than anyone in anything he did.

'Want to join us?' Parush asked.

'But you already have an HR head?'

'She will report to you...'

Later that night Parush drove her to her house in San Jose. 'Want to have some more wine?' she asked while getting out of the car, a brand-new Mercedes-Benz E Class Cabriolet.

Not much later, when Parush had let himself loose, sinking into the warmth of a woman's body, she hissed into his ear, licking the lobe, 'You wouldn't be lonely any more...'

As he sat warmly in the large sofa, she pulled his head into the daunting abyss of her ample bosom, quavering her body slowly, gently, pushing that exhilarating moment of ecstasy as far as possible, taking him deep inside her in a hypnotising rhythm. She pressed hard every time he was inside, so hard that it hurt her, and she moaned. As though she knew the exact moment, she suddenly stopped rocking and pressed even harder, shoving him deep into her innermost crevasses. 'Don't stop,' he groaned, biting her breasts. 'Calm, calm,' she uttered in jumbled whimpers, 'let it happen in its own sweet way ... just be calm ... leave everything to me...' He trembled, scratched her back and bit her breasts harder till he abruptly lost all strength.

***

When he woke up the next morning, he found himself still buried into her, his head nesting between her breasts, her arms wrapped around him, she still sitting in the same position. 'You didn't sleep?' he asked.

'I hope you are satisfied,' she said, licking his lips with the warm tip of her tongue.

Later that day when Parush mentioned to Rajesh about taking Piyali Sen as the VP, Human Resources, Rajesh was a little surprised. 'What do we do with Linda? She has been doing quite well for years.'

'She will do it better. I've asked her to meet us tonight. My favourite place – Gary Danko, Fisherman's Wharf.'

Parush brought Piu with him in the evening. She was dressed in a seductive beaded evening gown. With hip-high slits and a silhouette that tightened at the waist while cupping the breast – perfect for her svelte figure – the gleaming gown revealed more than just a hint of skin with its nude chiffon fabric.

'Would you mind dropping her home?' Parush asked an inebriated Rajesh after the dinner. 'He is still not convinced if you would be better than Linda,' he whispered into Piu's ears, as Rajesh went ahead and wrapped his arm around hers. In a few weeks, she joined Volcano.

***

Sometime back, Sweti and Arav had met Nem, their junior at KGP. When they were leaving, Arav told Nem, 'Be careful, don't get burnt. It's a real hot thing…' Sweti elbowed him.

Lately, the earlier uneasiness between Sweti and Arav had allayed a lot. Perhaps their common affection for Parush had acted as a binding force between them. 'Arav,' she said in the car, 'do you really think we care for Parush?'

Arav held her hand. 'He doesn't care for himself. What good would our care do?' He looked melancholy. 'Since that day, when he left us, we've been just working like robots...'

***

Parush couldn't recall anything when she introduced herself to him over the phone. 'Nimisha?' he couldn't suppress his surprise.

'I expected you wouldn't recognise me,' she said. 'You never liked me or my mother.'

Parush realised who she was. Yes, at some point of time he had really hated Nimisha and her mother Stuti Auntie, because he suspected his father was having an affair with the latter. Nimisha was just a year older than him and they had met many times as kids, Stuti being the wife of one of his father's friends. Over the years, he had approved of the relation, more because, perhaps, he wanted his mother to be deserted. Ru had told him, the last time she had called him, that his father had moved out of their house in Rupsa and started living in with Stuti somewhere else. He had known that something like this would happen sometime, but strangely, he felt bad for his mother after hearing that his father had *actually* left her.

'Where are you?' he asked Nimisha.

'I'm in LA. Can I come down to your place sometime?'

Few weeks later Parush received Nimisha at the San Jose airport. She stayed with him for a few days. They talked about themselves and discussed about their parents' divorce with their respective partners. 'I'm sure it's not a very enjoyable thing for them, still it may be their last attempt to be happy in life...' Nimisha said.

'First attempt for my father,' Parush interrupted. Nimisha looked at him with surprise. 'He should have divorced Ma long back. I don't think he was ever happy with her. The last time they might have had sex was when my sister was born...'

Nimisha hugged him at the airport, before leaving. 'Thanks …' she said hesitantly, 'I was really apprehensive about how you would take the entire thing. At least we're not enemies…'

Parush waited till she entered the departure hall, waving at her when she turned back.

***

'I want you to hire all the good people from GameIT,' Parush asked Piu the day she joined. 'I'll give you the list. Pay them 50% more than what they're making at GameIT. Do whatever it takes, *but I want them.*'

Few days later Piu dashed into his office while he was talking over the phone. 'I need to talk to you, now.' He asked her to sit but she kept standing. Parush kept the phone down. 'What's the matter?'

'Each of the guys you've asked to hire from GameIT has got an unexpected hike last week. Post-hike the salaries look ridiculous. Now if we've to pay 50% more that would be really crazy. Don't you smell a rat?'

'What?'

'It's obvious that someone has leaked our plan to them.'

'What plan?'

'That we're going to hire those people…'

'There may be other people too who got hikes. It's no secret that you joined us last week. Knowing your credentials, even an ass would guess that the first thing you would do here is grab the key people from them.'

Piu didn't say anything for some time. 'But, is it fine to pay such crazy amounts?'

'Just do it … I'll take care.' Parush picked up the phone. Piu left his office.

A few days later Parush called for a meeting with Piu in the evening. He wanted to understand how much she had got a hold on the key people at Volcano. 'Unless you know the people well,' he told her, 'it's always going to be a threat.'

Piu came to his office at six, as scheduled. He requested her to come an hour later. By the time he actually started the meeting it was well past seven. 'Who do you think wouldn't listen to you?' Parush directly came to the point.

Piu smiled. 'Generally, everyone listens to me, unless someone is…'

'Impotent?' Parush laughed.

'Is there a problem with Arash Hassibi?' she asked.

Parush stared at her for some time. 'We hired the right person to head HR. I want to sack him. But he is very close to Rajesh. He himself had hired him. Also, he is very strong technically. I can't fire him just because he doesn't get along with me…'

'Don't worry, I'll handle Rajesh,' she said very confidently. Parush smiled. Handling Rajesh had always been an issue.

He had a few more things to discuss. Parush had known that it would be late by the time the meeting would end. He had delayed it further. It was nine thirty. 'Why don't you join me for dinner?' Piu asked. Parush went to her house, had dinner, sipped some wine, but didn't stay over. 'Are you sure you want to go?' she asked, leaning over the window of his car, her lips fluttering very close to his ears.

'Have some more important work…' he smiled.

***

Next day Rajesh called him in the afternoon. 'What do you think about Arash?'

'If I could, I would fire him.'

'Okay, go ahead.'

In the next few weeks, Parush got rid of few more people. 'It's impacting our hiring Parush,' Piu told him one day. 'I hated all of them, but all of them were technically very strong. People are not happy that they were fired without any reason.'

'We want to keep our costs under control.'

'But Volcano is doing exceptionally well now.'

'We would do better.'

'Candidates don't accept that. Few people declined to join us. I talked to one yesterday. He told me Volcano's recent firings didn't go down well…'

'What's our present severance package?' Parush interrupted.

'Three months' pay.'

'Make it six months. People can make more money if they are fired. No one will decline.'

'Are you sure?'

'Yes, go ahead…'

***

One day, Arav and Sweti overheard something while passing by the break area. 'People are now looking for opportunities to be fired at Volcano?' Arav joked.

'If our old employees are fired, isn't it a great opportunity to hire them back?' Sweti quipped. 'By the way, I'm dying to see this woman. They are saying Volcano is already under her control, just in six months.'

'Strong women always have the control … in bed.'

Sweti pinched Arav.

***

Parush stared at Aru with a tired look in his eyes. 'What?' she asked, pulling the vacuum cleaner out of the closet.

'Thanks for coming here whenever you get time,' Parush said.

'Good that you still have some sensitivity alive within you.' Aru started vacuuming the carpet. 'Otherwise, you're just a lifeless, insensible, selfish giant…' She uttered each word discretely. 'Why can't you just move on, Parush? Shit happens in life. Accept it. How long will you remain trapped in the past and punish yourself? And, by the way, what are you punishing yourself for?'

'Aru, this is how I've chosen to live. Please let me live my way…'

'Are you living?' She didn't say anything more. For the next few hours, she vacuumed the entire house, arranged the lofts and closets properly, threw away the piles of old letters, bills and other useless things, made the bed, washed the dirty utensils lying in the sink and cleaned the toilet, as Parush sat quietly at the corner of a long sofa in the living room, not doing anything in particular.

'I want to see that woman,' she said at the dinner table, arranging the plates. Parush had wanted to take her out, but she preferred cooking, something she had taken interest in since joining CNN the previous year.

'So,' Parush asked, dipping his finger into the red gravy Aru had poured in a bowl he never knew existed in his kitchen, 'what all has Swets told you about her?'

'How many times did you sleep with her?' Parush sensed a hint of jealousy in her tone, something he had never felt, even when he would get cosy with Bitasta in front of her. He felt good, and sad too.

'How often do you meet Pushi?' he asked her after the dinner, while they were walking on the narrow beach in front of his house. 'She's enjoying Harvard?'

'Most weekends I drive from New York to Boston to meet Pushi. Yes, she's fine. Why don't you come to East Coast sometime?'

'Yes, I'll come… sometime…'

***

'GameIT has been recently issued Patent 446 on "*Using Statistical Dependence to Train the Characters in a Video Game*"', Parush informed Rajesh. 'I've got to know that they've also started working on a game which they claim is based on this patent, but which, in reality, may be a copy of our *Changers*. Looks like, seeing our success, Sam has realised the importance of the idea.' He kept quiet for some time, waiting to see Rajesh's reaction, something he could now predict in most scenarios. 'The idea was mine,' he added. 'Though I wrote a white-paper, Sam never used it as long as I was there. And now, seeing the success of *Changers*…'

'Sue them…' Rajesh didn't allow him to complete. That evening Parush sent an e-mail to Rajesh.

There may be legal implications. It was my idea, no doubt, but their Patent 446 is based on the white-paper Kratu and I co-authored during my tenure at GameIT…

Rajesh sent a one-liner reply.

Leave it to me. Go ahead and sue them.

In a few days, Volcano sent a legal notice to GameIT for infringing on their Patent 465. It claimed that the concept of "*controlling the fate of the characters in a video game*" was Parush's invention and that GameIT had indulged in the reduction to practice of an invention which was legally assigned to Volcano through its Patent 465.

GameIT didn't respond to the notice. But a month later, in September 2004, they filed a suit in Federal Court against Volcano, alleging it was the rightful owner of Patent 465, issued to Volcano, because of a *Proprietary Information and Inventions Agreement* Parush had signed with GameIT when he was employed there. GameIT further alleged that Volcano had misappropriated technology conceived at GameIT through the acts of Parush, a former employee of GameIT. It also alleged that Volcano's Patent 465 infringed GameIT's Patent 446.

The next month, Volcano announced it had filed an answer and counter claims in United States District Court in response to the lawsuit filed by GameIT. 'We claim full ownership of Patent 465. Parush has invented the concept, which was never used at GameIT during his tenure,' Rajesh said in a press release. 'GameIT wants to imitate Volcano's success with *Changers*. They have used Parush's white-paper, whose importance was never understood by GameIT, till now.'

Within a few weeks, GameIT filed a $100 million suit against Parush.

THE GAME

'California Labor Code Section 2870 says, "*any provision in an employment agreement which provides that an employee shall assign, or offer to assign, any of his or her rights in an invention to his or her employer shall not apply to an invention that the employee developed entirely on his or her own time without using the employer's equipment, supplies, facilities, or trade secret information*". This implies that the invention, the idea of the game in this case, which Mr Parush made and which he captured in a white-paper while being a part of GameIT, should be assigned to GameIT, as per his employment agreement with GameIT...'

Maryam Kheradmand from *Susman Godfrey L.L.P.*, one of the best and costliest law firms in the US, had been explaining the various aspects of the litigation to the executive team of Volcano. 'Susman Godfrey would cost a bomb,' Parush had warned Rajesh. 'Go ahead...' Rajesh had said. But now, Rajesh got agitated. 'Maryam, I don't have the time to listen to all this. If it were a simple thing, why would I hire you?'

Of course, Maryam didn't like the way Rajesh talked. 'Maryam, I'm sure you'll do something which wouldn't be obvious,' Parush took control of the situation. 'Patent violations are complicated cases. We're confident that you'll turn the outcome to our benefit...'

Parush was to depose in Mountain View and Maryam coached him thoroughly. 'The seed idea of my invention comes from the book *From the Horse's Mouth*, published in 1996,' he said in his deposition. 'I read the book in 1997 and conceived the idea of "*Controlling the Fate of the Characters in a Video Game*" even before joining GameIT...

'Volcano is responsible for the reduction to practice of my invention, which forms the basis of its Patent 465 and the successful game *Changers*. When I was in GameIT, no one found any value in my invention. Finally, I co-authored the white-paper, "*Using Statistical Dependence to Train the Characters in a Video Game*", which now seems to be the basis of Patent 446 issued to GameIT…

'Conceptually, the white-paper is very close to the implicit core idea behind one of the stories in *From the Horse's Mouth*. But, at the same time, it's not *exactly the same* as my invention. The core idea behind my invention is *controlling the fate*. It's the foundation of Volcano's Patent 465, but not that of either the white-paper or GameIT's Patent 446. There's no question of my breaching the *Proprietary Information and Inventions Agreement* I had signed with GameIT…'

When the transcript of the deposition appeared in the media the next day, an old employee of GameIT was shocked. 'These are blatant lies,' he said excitedly to Arav. 'He didn't know anything about it before joining GameIT. In fact, he got the idea from a paper written by Kratu, Sam and others in 1996 in the *Mathematical Modelling and Numerical Analysis*. Kratu had casually mentioned that one of his grandma's stories had triggered the thought, which finally crystallised into this paper. Parush had asked for the compilation of the stories and I still remember Kratu giving him a copy of *From the Horse's Mouth*.'

'There's also a patent based on this paper written by Kratu, Sam and others, isn't it?' Arav asked.

'Yes, it's the Patent 112, issued jointly to GameIT, Stanford and Berkeley Universities in 2002. Volcano surely infringes this patent.'

Few days later GameIT filed a claim of unfair competition against Volcano in California Superior Court in Santa Clara County as well as a complaint in the U.S. District Court for the

District of Delaware. 'Volcano infringes,' said a press release, 'not one but two patents – 446 and 112 – held by GameIT.'

***

Parush checked his mail again. No, the mail he had been expecting for the past few months was still not there in his mailbox. It was well past midnight. He came out of the house, the grandest one in the same neighbourhood as that of the old office of GameIT in Foster City, overlooking the Bay. Barefoot, he walked on the sand and sat on the only bench on the narrow beach. He stared at the shining waters of the Bay. He remembered the night of the reception of Sweti and Arav's marriage, a few months ago, when he had, for the first time in so many years, felt a deep yearning to reach out to Bitasta.

He hadn't been in touch with anyone from GameIT ever since he had joined Volcano. But Sweti would call him regularly. 'Porus,' she pleaded one day, 'you have to come to India for our marriage.'

'Swets,' Parush said calmly, 'you know how much I've been trying to keep away from the media. I'll come to your reception…'

A hundred eyes turned towards him the moment he walked through Bill's sprawling premise and appeared in front of the stage, wonderfully decorated with white and red flowers of various shapes and sizes. A few old employees of GameIT turned their faces from him, surely in disgust. Sweti and Arav got up from their thrones of one evening. Parush gestured to them to remain seated. He went up to them. Sweti held his hands and stared at him. 'My best wishes for both of you…' He didn't stay there long. Walking back, away from the stage, he shook hands with Bill, Sam, Kratu, his wife Afsar, Tista and a few others. The media had waited long enough for such a moment.

'Why the hell did they invite him here?' said an employee of GameIT to someone else, loud enough for him to hear.

As he walked away, towards the gate, not turning back even for once, he felt that Sweti and Arav were perhaps staring at him, as long as they could see him. Once inside his car, Parush rested his head on the steering and broke down. He cried aloud, banging his head on the steering. He suddenly wanted to see Bitasta. In all these years he hadn't attended any marriage. Seeing Sweti and Arav getting married, he had an intense feeling of incompleteness, a lonely void, a withered desolation, an inexpressible grief and an agonising longing for Bitasta. It was more than seven years since he had seen her last. In all these years he hadn't heard anything about her. In all these years he had cursed her, hated her, tried to throw *her* out of *his thoughts*, but still she remained somewhere in an inaccessible corner of his mind, like a lava hidden deep inside the crater of a dormant volcano. Suddenly, he felt as though the molten lava was crawling out of the crater, silently, stealthily.

It was the middle of December, just a few days from Bitasta's birthday. An excess of memories, thoughts and feelings suddenly wanted to burst out of his heart. He remembered Panchali, Bitasta's mother, the woman who had made him fall in love with Bitasta, perhaps out of his jealousy towards her, for possessing a mother he had always craved for. He remembered Panchali's diaries filled with poetry, which was an integral part of his lovemaking with Bitasta. Each and every day he had spent with Bitasta appeared like one of those colourful beads in a kaleidoscope, all of which collectively created enticing patterns. He wondered if Bitasta too had kept him alive within her. Where was she presently? How did she look? Had she got married by now?

A few days later he called up many florists in India and finally got one in Shillong to deliver a bouquet of rhododendron, camellia and rose, all white, to Bitasta's house in Calcutta on her twenty-eighth birthday. He took care to hide the identity of the sender, knowing very well that she would know it anyway. He had always known that those were her favourite flowers, but strangely, he couldn't remember why this was the first time ever he had given her a bouquet with them. He hoped that the moment she would see the bouquet, she would somehow find out his contact and immediately send him a mail, at the least. But the mail never came.

He would have slept on the bench. When the sun sparkled on the waters of the Bay, he woke up. He walked back to his house, got ready, and by eight he was in his office.

***

In February 2005, Volcano filed a complaint in the U.S. District Court arguing that both Patents – 446 and 112 – held by GameIT were invalid due to prior art and publicly disclosed technology.

In his official statement Rajesh said, 'GameIT's Patent 446 is invalid because it uses prior art – the book *From the Horse's Mouth*. Patent 112, jointly held by GameIT, Stanford and Berkeley, is also invalid because of publicly disclosed technology contained within – it uses the paper "*Mathematical Modelling of Astrology Based on Statistical Dependence*", published in July 1996 in *Mathematical Modelling and Numerical Analysis*, Volume 30, Issue 4. Moreover, Patent 112 is jointly owned by Berkeley and Stanford and hence licensed to Volcano as per the patent cross licensing agreement Volcano has signed with these universities in 2002. Our cross-complaint alleges that the Delaware lawsuit filed by GameIT is fraudulent and anti-competitive…'

Jeff, the VP Engineering, who had been with Volcano since the beginning, was not at all happy with the way things were moving. A man of few words, he had been opening his mouth too often lately. 'In 2004, our revenue grew from 50 million to 75 million – it's a

50% growth,' he said quite agitatedly to Rajesh in a staff meeting. 'But still we had a loss of 2 million. This could have been avoided.'

'What do you mean?' asked Rajesh.

'I don't find any reason why we had to indulge in this fight with GameIT. Whatever we may claim or whatever the technicalities may be, the fact is that we've used an invention which Parush made during his tenure in GameIT. I don't know why GameIT never raised any objection. We released our game *Changers* in January 2004. They knew very well that it was based on the work Parush did in GameIT, but still, they kept quiet for seven months till we instigated them by sending a legal notice in August. If we hadn't sent them the notice there wouldn't be any litigation and we would have enough money to invest on R&D, which is not seeing any growth now. And if this goes on for long we're going to lose out to all our competitors.'

Parush knew Rajesh was getting irritated. Even he was surprised that Jeff had brought up these points. 'We'll win Jeff,' Rajesh said sternly, 'and GameIT would be out of business.'

'And what are the chances for that? We've claimed that GameIT's Patent 446 is invalid because of a prior art. However, the same prior art is also applicable to our Patent 465. We're also saying that their Patent 112 is invalid because it has used a publicly disclosed technology – a paper, which was anyway written by the founders of GameIT. It's a big mess and I don't think it will be resolved soon. In the meantime we'll spend hefty amounts fighting the case, we'll have more losses, we'll further reduce our R&D spending and by the time we decide to go for an out-of-the-court settlement, our competitors would have overtaken us...'

'Isn't he talking too much now-a-days?' Piu asked Parush, after the staff meeting.

'Yes, he is. Be *nice* with him,' he chided, winking at her when he uttered the word 'nice'. He already knew what the subsequent events would be. Piu got up, winking back at him. 'You're such a horrible guy...'

Parush got a call from the CFO. 'Yes, you can come now,' he said over the phone. 'I'm free.'

It was not that he didn't know what the CFO would talk about. Still he listened to him patiently. 'The salary cost and the severance package is hurting us badly. We can't sustain like this.'

Parush kept quiet for some time. 'Didn't you listen to Rajesh today?' he said, closing his laptop and folding the coil of the adapter. 'We'll win the case...' He got up from his chair.

***

The trial began in San Francisco in July 2005 and that in Delaware a few months later, in October. And the very next month came a communication issued by the United States Patent and Trademark Office. It paved the way for a grand celebration by Rajesh – Volcano was literally absolved of the charges of infringing on one of the two patents currently under litigation with GameIT, because the patent itself was deemed invalid on a technical ground.

'Communication issued by PTO says that GameIT's Patent 112 was not filed within one year of the publication of the paper on a similar topic authored by its CEO Mr Kratu Sen and others, and hence can be claimed invalid based on the publication available in public domain,' Sweti read out from *San Jose Mercury News*. 'The existing patent laws require the inventor to file a patent application within one year of the publication, public use or marketing of his or her invention. The paper titled "*Mathematical Modelling of Astrology Based on Statistical Dependence*", authored by Kratu, Tista, Sam and Hubbard, was published in the *Mathematical Modelling and Numerical Analysis*, Volume 30, Issue 4, in July 1996 and the Patent 112, based on the same paper, was filed in August 1997, more than a year later...'

'Swets,' Arav interrupted, 'do you remember the first time we won the ILLU for RK Hall?'

Sweti was a little surprised at the abrupt reference to something that appeared irrelevant to the present context. 'Yes, I do. No one believed that it could be possible, but Porus made it happen, isn't it?'

'No, Porus didn't make it happen. Bitasta manipulated everything so meticulously that it appeared all natural. But, in reality, the whole thing was fixed from the very beginning.'

Sweti came and sat beside Arav, putting her arm over his shoulder. 'Swets, can you believe she was just a school kid then? I don't blame Porus. It's not easy to forget her...'

***

Parush and Piu travelled to Las Vegas on the same flight. 'Want to come to my room?' she asked him, taking the security card for the Royal Suite from the reception of Caesars Palace.

'Some other time Piu,' Parush said. 'Have to catch up with a few things.'

Piu pressed his hand and said, 'Sometimes catch up with me too...'

The next few things happened as planned. Keeping his stuff in the suite he came down to the lobby. Diana was waiting for him – he had hired her from Executive Playmates, one of the leading providers of escorts in Las Vegas. He went to the pool with her. On the way he left a message on Rajesh's voice mail informing him that he would be at the pool. Changing to swimming trunks he entered the pool with Diana. As expected, little more than an hour later, Rajesh appeared at the pool, tagging along with Piu. Parush waved at Rajesh. As they came closer he could see Piu, glaring at him. 'Have fun,' Rajesh said, 'we can talk tomorrow.' As they were leaving, Piu turned back. 'Catching up well, I see,' she said. Parush didn't say anything. He just smiled at her and kissed Diana.

The next day, at the grand party to celebrate the recent developments in the ongoing litigation, Rajesh announced his ambitious plans. Piu clung to Rajesh, often in a way which made even him a little uncomfortable, especially when Parush was around. 'What a slut,' commented a disgusted Jeff. Parush made sure that Piu got to know of Jeff's admiration for her. By the time they returned to the Bay Area, Jeff had been already fired. Eventually, Volcano didn't have anyone to drive its R&D.

***

'What the hell is this?' shouted Rajesh, throwing the paper towards Parush. 'I want to file a defamation case against Jeff.'

Parush looked at the news item – the same journalist, he recalled, whom he had met at Garry Danko many years back when he had asked some uncomfortable questions to Sam at a JavaOne conference.

Even if Volcano wins the litigation filed against them by GameIT – it's a remote possibility despite the tall claims and premature celebrations – the integrity of its executive team is questionable. Jeff, an ex-employee of Volcano, recently fired for raising uncomfortable questions, feels that Parush Sengupta, the present Chief Operating Officer, and Rajesh Malhotra, Founder and Chief Executive Officer, are solely responsible for the current state of affairs at Volcano, whose losses have grown considerably over the past few quarters, owing to several factors like exorbitant legal costs, unrealistic salaries and impractical severance packages doled out to retrenched employees…

***

In a few weeks, the law firm *Milberg Weiss Bershad & Schulman LLP* filed a class action suit against Volcano and its three top executives, including Parush, on behalf of the investors. The complaint alleged that Volcano had failed to disclose that the company faced "serious risk" of infringing on the intellectual property rights of GameIT. Volcano's stock plummeted as the analysts felt they might lose the litigation. The Board of Directors called for an emergency board meeting. 'Mr. Rajesh Malhotra,' said the Chairman of the Board, 'there's a feeling among the stockholders that you shouldn't have sent that notice to GameIT at all.'

'Why the hell are you all assuming that we've already lost the battle? The trials have just begun. Do you realise that if we win, GameIT will be a thing of the past?'

'We don't want to take any more chances. I'm very sorry to say that the board and the stockholders have lost confidence in your abilities to steer the company out of the current mess…'

'Are you firing me?' Rajesh interrupted.

The Chairman kept quiet, taking his stare off Rajesh. 'Am I being fired?' Rajesh raised his voice, his irritation visible in his face.

'I'm really sorry Rajesh,' the Chairman spoke again, 'the board wants you to step down.'

'You can't do that. I've put my blood and sweat into this company.'

'And the stockholders have put their money. We've analysed all the major decisions you've taken in the past one and a half years and we've found that you've overruled almost all other opinions.'

'What do you mean by that?'

The Chairman flipped through a few pages kept on the table in front on him. 'There's an e-mail sent to you by Parush on 23rd January 2003. It says, "*I can get started any time. Think about the legal implications once more. If you're confident of handling it, should there be any problem later, I've no issue.*" The same day you sent the reply, "*Leave the legal things to me. You go ahead*." This means that you were warned against the legal implications of using the invention Parush had made at GameIT.' He paused and passed the printouts of the two e-mails to Rajesh.

'Then, there's another e-mail sent by Parush to you on 15th August 2004. It says, "*There may be legal implications. It was my idea, no doubt, but their Patent 446 is based on the white-paper Kratu and I co-authored during my tenure at GameIT*." Your reply was, "*Leave it to me. Go ahead and sue them*." Here too, you were warned against the legal implications of sending the legal notice to GameIT. There are many such instances where you overruled every suggestion and single handedly took all decisions, which have finally led this company to its present state. Do you deny any of these?'

Rajesh banged on the table, got up abruptly, pushing the chair with force, and left the room.

'Mr Parush Sengupta,' the Chairman continued, 'the board wants to appoint you as the new CEO of Volcano. Do you have anything to say?'

'It would be my pleasure to take up the new role. I did put all efforts to apprise Rajesh of the pros and cons of each decision he has taken. It's not that he had my consent for everything…'

***

Parush was again back in the news. His reputation, tarnished a lot in the recent past, got a fillip. Within a month, he entered into a dialogue with GameIT and settled all pending litigation, paying them $12.5 million. He had the full support of the board. Two months later, GameIT expressed its desire to take-over Volcano. Parush called for a board meeting where most of the members approved of it. 'This is perhaps the best way to protect the interests of the stockholders,' said the Chairman of the board. 'The finances are not good. The morale of the people is low. It's not easy to turn it around. For its own interest, GameIT will pump in money, energy and positivity to revive Volcano, whose technology is still among the best in the mobile gaming industry…'

In June 2006, GameIT announced the take-over of Volcano, subject to approval by the Federal Trade Commission. 'The combined entity will have more than a 50% market share in mobile gaming…' Sam said in a press release.

***

By the time Parush came to Bill's house in Atherton everyone else had already arrived. He felt weird to enter his father-in-law's house after three and a half years. He had been here just for a while during the reception of Sweti and Arav's marriage. But then, he hadn't entered the house. Walking down the long driveway, he tried to think why exactly he had taken such a drastic step to kill a competitor. Was it just because he hated Rajesh? Or was it just another opportunity to torture himself? Did it hurt him more that he had used Bitasta as the inspiration to put himself through an unfathomable four-year ordeal which everyone had resisted vehemently? Had it been necessary to go to this extent to orchestrate this meticulously scripted decline of Volcano, like Bitasta had done many years ago for RK, his hall of residence in IIT KGP, to win ILLU? What if he had failed? Even then, he would have succeeded in killing himself once more. For close to four years he had led a lonely life, cut off from everyone at GameIT, spending sleepless nights, feeling helpless, desolate and despondent. He had pretended as though his main purpose in life was to kill GameIT, the very company he had died for, in so many ways, to give it life. Holding Ru in his arms, he would cry like a child every time she visited him.

It should have been a very happy moment for Bill, Sam, Kratu, Sweti and Arav. Parush would be back to GameIT very soon, but the ambience was that of anything but happiness. 'Hi guys,' Parush greeted everyone. He sensed an awkward uneasiness in everyone's face. 'Welcome back, my son,' Bill came forward and hugged him. 'I never wanted this, we never wanted this. You know it. Even without all this, we would still be strong, I would still be rich. For whom did you do all this?'

'Bill, haven't you realised by now that he does everything just for himself?' Sweti howled. Everyone, except perhaps Parush, was shocked at her sudden outburst. 'Swets,' Arav whispered to her, 'please, not now.'

'Arav, can you please keep your fucking mouth shut?' she shouted at her husband. 'Guys, someone has to speak out. Otherwise, this devil will one day kill all of us, like he has killed Bill's daughter, his own wife. He is just a sadist who takes pleasure in killing everyone who loves him. A decade ago a girl had dumped him and since then he has been using everyone as a bait to take revenge against, god knows, whom. We're all his bait, nothing more than that. Does he realise how we all survived these four years, dying every moment of guilt? He may think that he has played a game with Rajesh, for our sake, but he has actually played a game with all of us, to satisfy his hellish desires…'

***

'I knew you would get in touch with me,' Jeff said, sitting in front of Rajesh. Jeff was not surprised when Rajesh had called him this morning.

'Tell me everything you didn't mention in your mail.'

'Just take a closer look into the chronology of events. In December 2002, a few weeks after Parush had joined us,' he started speaking, referring to Volcano as "us", 'GameIT sent a letter to us enclosing his employment agreement with GameIT, asking us to confirm that we would not use any confidential GameIT information. They sent a laundry list of many things that we were not supposed to do. But strangely, there was no mention of the white-paper which later became the main bone of contention between us and them.'

'Even I was surprised. Around the same time Parush talked a lot about how Sam would always ignore his ideas.'

'Very shrewdly, Parush convinced you that using his invention, which Sam had anyway ignored, wouldn't call for GameIT's wrath. Then in May 2003, you announced a game that would revolutionise the world of gaming. "*You can now control the fate*", you said. Even an ass at GameIT would know it was the same thing as the white-paper. Still they didn't say anything. We launched *Changers* in January 2004 – a whole eight months after GameIT had known what we had been doing. Still they kept quiet.'

'Then in August 2004, when *Changers* was doing exceptionally well in the market, Parush told me that GameIT too had started working on a similar game. The way he talked, it meant that they were actually copying our game.'

'And did you ever find out how Parush could get to know so much internal information about GameIT? As far as I remember, there was no press release and Sam is always tight lipped, unlike you. Anyway, keep this aside. Then, Parush instigated you to send a legal notice to them. You acted as a puppet in Parush's hands. Soon, they sued us for violating the *Proprietary Information and Inventions Agreement* Parush had signed with them. But, they could have sued us way back in May 2003.'

'Why do you think they waited for one and half years?'

'Parush needed that much time to destroy a successful company. He brought in Piu…' Jeff paused to see Rajesh's reactions.

Rajesh kept stirring the scotch with a stirrer. 'He hired people at unheard of salaries and got key people fired, paying unheard of severance packages. Anyone who had some problem with Piu eventually got fired. By the time the trials began, a year later, we had already screwed up our finances. After paying off ridiculous salaries, hefty severance packages and extremely high legal bills, we were not left with anything to invest on R&D, something which had always been our key strength.'

Rajesh stopped stirring the scotch. 'Who was GameIT's law firm?'

Jeff smiled. 'A new firm, which would have cost them a tenth of what we paid to *Susman Godfrey L.L.P.* Rajesh, we had lost even before the game started…'

HOMECOMING

Waiting at the Frankfurt airport for the connecting flight to Bangalore, Parush's attention went to a lady, sitting a few rows ahead of him, tending to an infant. She had her back to him and hence he couldn't see her face. But even after so many years, he knew, he couldn't be wrong. As he walked up to her, she was still trying hard to put the baby to sleep in the stroller, uncomfortably removing her long cascading hair coming in between her and the baby. Parush stood dumbfounded, stunned, staring at her. She had put on some weight and her hair had grown longer. An open book lay on the seat beside her, turned upside down. The cover read *The One Percent Doctrine: Deep Inside America's Pursuit of Its Enemies Since 9/11*. When had she started reading these books? Parush wondered. That was when it occurred to him that a lot of time had elapsed. Close to ten years, he realised, since he might have last seen Raka. In all these years he had rarely thought of her, the girl he had always known would be by his side, come what may.

Since his breakup with Bitasta, Raka too had sunk into oblivion. Bitasta had alleged that he had been cheating on her with Raka. She had also claimed that Raka herself had told her about it. Later, he never felt like asking Raka why she had lied to Bitasta. Raka too, in all these years, had never reached out to him. Now, he felt awkward that in all these years, he had totally banished her from his thoughts, his life.

Raka lifted the baby from the stroller and sat straight. For a moment, she froze when she saw him, staring straight into her eyes. She got up and stood in front of him, face to face, with wonderment and jolt in her looks.

'How have you been Raka?' Parush broke the ice. She didn't answer. The baby started crying. She remained unperturbed by the wails, patting his back out of reflex. When the wails increased, Parush took the baby in his arms and rocked him gently, which had a miraculous effect – he stopped crying.

'Yours?' he asked the obvious question, as though there could be some remote possibility of her carrying someone else's child.

'Yes,' she said calmly and sat down, he too sitting beside her, holding the baby tenderly in his arms.

'When did you get married?'

She turned towards him. 'Not yet,' she said with an unusual composure. 'We've to get married soon…'

Parush maintained an eerie stoicism, not expressing anything, neither surprise nor shock. Raka smiled. 'Don't have anything to ask?'

'Tell me…' he said, looking at the patterns on the carpet, 'whatever you want to say.'

'After plus two,' she spoke like a soliloquy, 'I lost a year, not getting anywhere and not doing anything. That one year … perhaps the longest in my life … seemed like an endless solitude. Every day I waited for a call from you. I had this trust on you and … on myself too, that you would surely call me, if not to find out how I was, at least to give me a chance to speak. When Bitasta wanted to breakup with you, she wanted to use me as the bait that you were cheating on her with me. I knew for sure you wouldn't believe this crap... I knew for sure that things would be just fine. But…' she looked up and stared at Parush. The baby turned his head towards her and giggled. She took him from Parush's arms.

'In a few months, I got to know you had left for the US … and the rest … I know as much as anyone else knows … that you're the *Big Bong who has created a totally new universe of corporate values…*'

'That was how Aru covered me in CNN,' Parush laughed. 'You remember Aru?'

'Ya, I do. Where's she now?'

'She's in the US, doing quite well in CNN...'

'I'm doing a case study on you in the "*Intellectual Property Law and Society*" course I'm taking this session...' she interrupted.

'What do you do?'

'I've recently joined London School of Economics as a faculty in the Department of Law...'

'That's great... Congrats! Where did you study law?'

She laid the baby in the stroller and stroked him with her hands as Parush couldn't but stare at a new Raka who seemed like an older look alike of someone he had known more than a decade ago.

'That one year suddenly matured me. I transformed from a teenager, who always did everything her heart wanted to do, to an ambitious woman, who rarely listened to her heart. The next year, I managed to get into NLS in Bangalore. After graduating from there I joined LSE, completed my PhD last year and, a few months back, I joined them as a faculty...' The baby had fallen asleep. She took her hands off him and leaned back on the seat, closing her eyes. Parush felt awkward that this chance meeting with Raka was so different from what he would have imagined, had this possibility ever crossed his mind. Raka's behaviour lacked the usual warmth, frivolity and flirtatiousness he had got used to so much in the past. Had he also changed so much in all these years?

'Last year on that unfortunate morning of 7th July,' she continued, 'I had taken a train from Liverpool Street and in few minutes, there was a bomb-blast in my compartment. I survived with minor injuries. That evening I saw on TV that the cops had arrested a guy of Pakistani descent from Leeds. He was allegedly very close to the suicide bomber who had detonated the bomb in my compartment. I recognised the guy as the one who had been lately travelling quite often with me in the same train in the mornings. We had interacted a few times. I knew that he owned a chipper in Leeds and that he wrote poetry in Urdu in the night…'

Raka paused and looked at Parush. He had an inkling of what the story would turn out to be. Raka hadn't been the one that would love poetry. 'Don't say you would read poetry even while making out,' she had joked once when he had said he would have never fallen for her because she didn't love poetry. Love and poetry, Parush realised, had exited from his life along with Bitasta. But now, he felt jealous that poetry had entered Raka's life.

'I knew Massoud couldn't be a terrorist. I met him at the local prison where he was remanded into custody and took up his case. In a few months his wife gave birth to Armin and ran away with someone else, abandoning the baby and him…'

As Raka spoke Parush realised she hadn't changed much, perhaps. She could still fall in love with someone, selflessly, unexpectedly. He learned that she was going to Calcutta to meet her parents and discuss her marriage with Massoud, whenever he came out of prison. Parush looked at Armin, sleeping so peacefully in the stroller. He was no doubt in safe hands, Parush knew.

In those few hours at the airport it was only Raka who had talked. Parush just listened. When it was time to leave, Parush said, 'Raka, I've to leave … again… Please give me your number. This time, I'll be in touch.' He pulled out his phone, but Raka sat quiet. 'What?' he asked, 'Give me your number.'

Raka closed her eyes. 'Parush,' she said after a few moments, looking at him, 'would you misunderstand me if say something?'

'What?'

'There's no reason why I shouldn't be in touch with you. But then, why now, after all these years? I've moved on, Parush. My priorities in life have changed. I've new responsibilities. Now you're like a memento from the past, something that you neither throw off, nor flaunt. If my instinct tells me, I'll get in touch with you myself. And if again we bump into each other, by chance, I'll cherish each of those moments of togetherness, but…'

Parush got up, looked at Armin and then at Raka. 'Bhalo thakis,' he said, pulling out the handle of his bag. 'Wish you all the happiness in your life… Be happy … Be yourself… and…' he bowed to take her hands. He kissed the palms, touched her chin, put his hands on her head and walked away. Raka got up and called him. He didn't turn back. Raka ran up to him, pulled his hands and made him turn back. She hugged him tight and kissed him on his lips so abruptly that he couldn't react. 'Bye,' she said and walked away, not turning back. Parush stood still, seeing Raka picking her bag and pushing the stroller. Parush knew that she had really moved on. Perhaps, he thought, everyone else had moved on.

***

'When are you guys coming to Bangalore?' Parush asked Sweti, sitting in his sprawling new office in Bangalore on the Outer Ring Road, overlooking a vast green wasteland merging slowly into the Bellandur Lake. 'I'm missing you guys.'

'Since when have you become emotional? I thought emotions and sentiments are not your cup of tea.' Parush didn't say anything. 'What?' Sweti asked.

He shifted to something else. 'Do you think we'll get a clean chit from the FTC?'

'Your plan was so meticulous that it's really hard to prove that you played the game to kill competition. Still, it will take time to come clean. It's good that you moved to India so abruptly. Bill is handling the media which anyway can't do much as you're not here. A few are raising questions about business ethics and corporate culture…'

Parush stared at the open space in front of him. Yes, the decision to move to Bangalore had been drastic, but unavoidable. His presence in the Bay Area would have complicated things. Also, he suddenly felt too weary to face people and answer their tough questions. Escaping to Bangalore appeared to him as a momentary respite, a much-awaited refuge, a place to sleep peacefully after years of insomnia. The India Design Center for GameIT had already started a few months ago and all it needed was to make an office worthy of the stature of its COO working out of India.

'May I come in?' someone asked. Parush looked at the door of his office. Mitali Sharma was standing at the door, smiling. A PhD from Texas A&M, he had hired her in the US for the R&D team in IDC. Over the past few weeks, since she had joined IDC, she had reminded him more and more of Bitasta. Apart from their similar age, some aspects of her mannerisms resembled that of Bitasta's, especially the way she leaned her head while talking. In all these years he hadn't met anyone else of Bitasta's age, other than his sister and Aru. The chance meeting with Raka at the Frankfurt airport had made him restless. He suddenly realised that the world had changed a lot while he had declined to move on. Had Bitasta too changed so much, like Raka, like everyone else? Where was she? What was she doing? How could he get in touch with her? He had sent a gift to Bitasta two years ago, on her birthday. Since then, he had waited for a mail from her, but that mail never came. Mitali always reminded him that Bitasta too had grown up, that she was no longer the girl he had last seen.

'I've a request,' Parush said, as Mitali entered his office. 'My sister has been after me to create an account on Orkut. Can you help me?'

'Sister?' Mitali said with a naughty smile. 'Come on, guys like you go to Orkut to find their lost girlfriends.'

'Meets,' he felt embarrassed, 'what do you mean by guys like me?'

'Young and overtly successful, but lonely… I'll send you the request.' She left the room. Parush wondered if she had psychic powers to read people's minds.

He felt dizzy when he accepted Mitali's request and created his own account. He looked for his sister, then Arushi, and then many other people he knew, though that was not the first thing he had wanted to do. He wondered why he was hesitating so much to search for Bitasta. Was he trying to run away from facing the reality, that Bitasta was no longer the same girl and that she too had *moved on* in her life, unlike him? Finally, he typed 'Bitasta Roy' and waited for the results to appear in the screen of his laptop.

He was surprised that there were other Bitastas too in the world. The one he had been waiting for appeared in the third place. He identified her from the profile picture, where she looked very much like what he had seen her last. An old picture, he thought. He clicked on it. It took him to her profile page. She was in New York, working for Boston Consulting Group. Such a job really suited her, he thought. Where had she done her MBA from? He read a few scraps to learn more about her. But strangely, there was not much useful information, unlike his sister's, which even had the calories she had consumed for dinner the previous night and the number of the page of the book she had read before she slept. He waited a few minutes before finally writing on Bitasta's scrap board.

Hope you remember me. It was not hard to identify you from the old picture you've put. How are you? And how's Kakima? It's so long since I've seen her.

It was surely not the way he wanted to initiate a communication with her, after so long. But he hadn't ever thought of the right way to do so either. He felt awkward that he had to mine for words to talk to Bitasta. Was it that, he too had changed a lot?

His mailbox made a sound. There was a new mail. He opened it. It was from Meher, Bitasta's best friend at KGP. He read and re-read the few lines of the mail many times and felt numb. Meher would have seen Parush's scrap the moment it had appeared on Bitasta's page.

I don't think you know that Bitasta's mother expired last month. Looks like you guys are really out of touch…

Kakima was no more? Parush released himself completely in the chair and sat like a lump of flesh. *Kakima* – the woman who had, for a few years, filled the void his mother could never fill … the woman who had made him forget for a while that he was incomplete … the woman who had brought love and poetry in his life … the woman whose poems would arouse within him a fervent passion, a burning fire, an eruption of molten lava of love and desire – was dead?

'Where are we going for the offsite?' Mitali broke into his room suddenly and interrupted his thoughts. Suddenly he lost his temper.

'Offsite? That's all you have in your mind? Don't you guys have anything else to do at work?'

Mitali was shocked at the sudden outburst. She stared at him for a few seconds and then ran away, rubbing her eyes. Parush pulled his hair and breathed heavily. His eyes were burning. He felt thirsty. He drank a full bottle of cold water. He opened the small freezer kept in his office and pulled out the tray of ice. He went to his private toilet and put the ice on his head. The ice melted slowly and the cold water dripped down his shirt. Returning to his seat, he called Mitali. 'I'm really sorry. Would you please come to my office?' She didn't say anything. Few minutes later when she entered his office, he was sitting at the edge of his desk, his shirt wet, his eyes red, his hair messy. She came running towards him. 'What happened?' she asked, holding his arms. He pulled her close to him and broke down, embracing her tightly.

***

'I can't believe there's a totally different person behind the dreadful one that destroys everything which comes in his way,' Mitali said, staring at a different Parush she couldn't have thought of. Parush had brought her to his home in Palm Meadows, the elite ghetto of most of the expatriates in Bangalore.

Parush smiled. 'I just destroy myself…'

'Talk to her,' she said before getting into the cab. 'I should have guessed there's something, for sure, behind all the dreadful things you do in life… Isn't it enough? Just calm down…' He watched her waving at him from the cab.

It occurred to Parush that it had been the first time he had told his story to anyone. He felt exhausted. He lay on the sofa and slept immediately. When he woke up it was two in the night. There were many missed calls on his mobile. The first one had come at seven, a little after Mitali had left. It was from a US number. He looked at the number once more. It was a New York number. He again felt numb. He drank some water, washed his face and went to the terrace with the phone. After some time, he dialled the number. 'Hi,' he heard the familiar voice he could recognise even after nine years, 'kemon achho?' He couldn't say anything. How was he? That was perhaps the toughest question anyone could ask him. He again mined for words. 'How could you put your mobile number in your Orkut profile?' she asked. 'You're a famous person, do you forget that?'

'I'll take it out.'

'I've already done that.'

'How?'

'I knew you would be still stuck in the past. You still have "arcadia" as your password as you had nine years back. I've changed it to "big bong".' Parush felt comfortable. He started talking normally. He cried like a kid, he howled like an injured lion, he sighed, he whined and Bitasta listened quietly. When he calmed down she told what had exactly happened to her mother – a surgery done incorrectly twelve years ago had created some fatal complications in her abdomen. 'She didn't want to die… She wanted to live… By the way, it was she, who had received your bouquet. By then I had already joined BCG in New York. She had called me and said, "*California to New York via Shillong and Calcutta, what a waste…!*"'

'She knew I was in California?'

'She also knew about that Bong slut you all in your office slept with.'

'And you?'

She didn't answer immediately. 'I told you, you're a famous person. Everything you do is news...' she paused. 'Why didn't you send me a bouquet last year?'

Parush felt nice. 'I expected a mail from you…'

'When have you last seen your mother?' she asked abruptly.

'I haven't seen her in the last nine years.'

'It's strange that when Ma was dying, she wanted to see her,' she let out a heavy breath. 'I realised they had always been in touch. I had brought Ma to Delhi and she was recovering. One day your mother came to see her in the hospital. I was shocked to see Sairi Kakima. She looked dead. I had hated her all these years and still when I saw her, I felt sad. She sat on the bed for hours, holding Ma's hands. Ma died the same evening… Porus, Sairi Kakima is dying… Go and see her…'

Bitasta's words would soon prove to be so literal.

NOT A GAME

Kratu and Tista were visiting India with their families and they stopped over in Bangalore for a few days in December. Parush's large and lonely villa came to life for some time. Parush stared at Kratu's and Tista's kids, running around playfully in the unusually sparse house, excited that there was nothing their parents could ask them not to touch. They dashed against Parush, destabilising him for a moment, and ran around him in circles, trying to catch each other. Tista was watching him, and the kids. 'Come to the terrace,' she pulled him by his hand when the kids left him. Once on the terrace, she stood against the parapet and looked at him. 'What?' he asked.

'You were watching the kids.'

Parush didn't say anything. He knew what Tista would say. Suddenly he had been feeling isolated, rather quarantined in a claustrophobic dungeon. He realised that his circle had reduced just to the confines of this empty house. Everyone else had sprawling spaces in their respective lives and he was the only one left behind, suffocating in an airless loneliness. The kids reminded him how out of place he was presently. 'Don't you think you've made a big mistake?' Tista shook him up.

'Perhaps,' he conceded, perhaps for the first time. 'I've recently got in touch with Bitasta… Her mother has died few months back… She seems to be a completely different person… I seem to be the same…'

The revelation was a shock to Tista. 'You're in touch with her … after so long? Why screw up more when nothing in your life can be fucked any further?' She kept quiet for some time, closing her eyes, breathing heavily. 'So, now you know that even she's not waiting for you anymore. Now can you please come out of your fixation and start a new life, a life that you don't have to kill every moment?' She stopped abruptly. Parush turned behind and saw Afsar, Kratu's wife. She put her hand around his shoulders. 'A few years down the line,' she said, 'even we may not have any time for you. What will you do then? Come on, it's enough...'

***

That night when everyone else had slept, he called Bitasta. Most of the times she wouldn't take his calls and very rarely she would call him back. And whenever she would talk to him, she talked normally, as though nothing had happened between them, nothing, neither the good things, nor the bad. That would shatter him the most, that he had been relegated to a normal acquaintance. She would be always very courteous, apologising for not being able to take his calls, enquiring about his health, advising him to sleep properly, workout regularly, take meals on time, do medical checkup from time to time. 'Do you think I'll come clean? FTC is still investigating if we're wrongfully killing competition,' he would ask, and she would analyse the odds against him in explicit details. 'Our stocks are not doing that great. The buzz seems to be dying down...' he would say some other time. That night when he called, Bitasta took the call. 'I'm tired Bits. I can't take it anymore. I want to quit ...'

When the night was fading out, he was still talking to Bitasta. 'Don't give up like this Porus. First come clean and then leave like a winner. Don't escape like a thief...' she was explaining, when someone banged on his door. 'I'll be back,' he said to Bitasta and opened the door. It was Kratu. 'Your line is coming busy. Arushi's on the line...' he hesitated to speak. 'What?' Parush asked. 'Your mother is in hospital...'

Parush took the phone from Kratu's hand.

***

'When your father moved out I would meet her every day,' Ru said. Parush was waiting with her outside the ICU at the Woodlands Hospital. 'She was losing weight. I asked her to consult a doctor but she said it was fine. Most of the time, she had fever. If I knew these were all signs of cancer, I would surely have done something. When Bitasta's mother was in hospital, I took her to Delhi, to meet her. When Panchali died, she entered a shell, never to come out again. She had already taken voluntary retirement. She didn't have any reason to go out. Apart from me, no one ever saw her again. I had been to the US for a month. My maid would cook food for her every day, but your mother never talked to her. My maid told me that she would be always in her room, reading books or just sleeping. I returned yesterday. I was shocked to see her. She could barely stand. I took her immediately to Woodlands. She is in the final stages. Doctors indicated she won't survive unless there's a miracle. So, all these months, I've been tending to your dying mother, while neither her son nor her husband was around...'

'Have you talked to Baba?'

Ru stared at Parush. 'I've left that to you.'

Srinjay and Parushni, Parush's sister, arrived from the US in two days, during which Sairandhri had never been awake. Parush hadn't yet talked to his dying mother. Srinjay and Parush sat quietly outside the ICU, no one saying anything. Perhaps both were equally responsible for Sairandhri's present state. Perhaps both were thinking how their lives could have been different. Who was to be blamed? Sairandhri? Srinjay? Parush? Parushni? And who had suffered the most? Sairandhri? Srinjay? Parush? Parushni?

One day when the doctors allowed visitors to see Sairandhri in the ICU, Parush went first. He was seeing his mother after nine years. Her stunningly beautiful face had withered away. She was lying on her death bed, like a lifeless lump of flesh. She could barely look at her son. Parush went close to her and stared at her open eyes, not moving much. She tried to hold his hands. He took his hands close to hers. She touched his hands with her fingers, barely moving. She struggled to move her lips. In trembling vibrations, the jumbled words came out of her mouth, 'bhalo thakis…' Stay well, she tried to say a few more times before the doctors indicated him to leave.

Out of ICU, he hugged his sister for a long time, trying hard to control his tears. 'Have we been too harsh?' he asked, burying his face into her shoulders.

***

'You all take rest this morning,' Ru said a few days later. 'I'll go now. You can come in the evening.' She rushed out of their house in Rupsa. The three of them – Srinjay, Parush and Parushni – had been in this house together after so long. It occurred to Parush that they all had perhaps come together again for the same person for whom they had also got scattered – his mother.

In the hospital, Ru took Bitasta to the ICU. The doctors were surprised that Sairandhri's family hadn't come to see her on a day she was a little better. Bitasta sat on a stool, close to her face. She took her hands and stared at her. 'I've lived till this day because I had to tell you this…'

The doctors indicated Bitasta to leave many times, but Sairandhri hadn't yet completed speaking. When she did, she looked fresh, happy. And content.

Bitasta came out of the ICU and embraced Ru. She didn't break down. Neither did she say anything for a long time. 'Bye,' she said finally, before leaving, 'take care of him...' She didn't turn back. Ru watched her as long as she could see her, the long shadow of hers sweeping the floor. Not much later, Sairandhri breathed her last, before anyone from Rupsa could come.

***

Bitasta suddenly stopped taking Parush's calls. Neither would she ever call him back, nor would she respond to his mails. Parush would leave long voice messages and write long mails, sometimes pleading with her, sometimes fretting about her insensitivity, sometimes deploring her. But still there wouldn't be any reply. Gradually, Parush realised she might not ever respond. But he didn't stop writing to her. In fact, the mails grew longer and appeared more like diaries – as though, instead of writing in a notebook, he was writing in the form of emails to Bitasta.

'Last year 3D became a mass market. Gameloft made a killing with "*Paris Hilton's Diamond Quest*". Our 3D is still not the best in the class...'

'Apple is going to release iPhone this year. We've to capture their user-base...'

'I know writing to you is like talking to a dead wall. But I don't see it that way. It's like talking to myself. Today, no one has time to talk to me. In your words, "*they have all moved on*", while I'm still stuck. I invent and reinvent myself in these emails. I know they are going to a black hole, and perhaps that's why I feel so uninhibited to write whatever I can...'

Over the next few years, Parush wrote to her almost every day. Gradually, he became obsessed with it. If he would fail to write any day, he would get restless. 'Oh Bits,' he wrote one day, 'I'm so tense. I'm taking a big chance. I feel over the next few years the Chinese and Taiwanese phones would have the majority market share in

India. While none of our competitors are taking them seriously, I feel that monopolising them would make a killing for us very soon. If my estimates are correct, half of India would be soon playing our games, while our competitors would be stuck with the elite brands and their miniscule niche market...'

'I've asked Mitali to take a transfer and move to the US,' he wrote another day. 'These people are crazy here. There have been rumours about something hanky-panky going on between me and her. She is such a sweet girl and I like talking to her. She's the only one I talk to now-a-days. But if it's hurting her reputation I can't sit quiet. She will leave next month...'

One day he came to know that Bitasta had called off her marriage at the last moment. 'Why are you doing this?' he wrote. 'Why are you hurting yourself, like I do? You had told me that many years back, knowing I would be married soon was the last nail in your coffin. Perhaps that was my intention too. But you don't have to do anything like that. I'm already dead. You don't have to kill me again and again. If you don't want, just don't get married...'

And then, when she finally got married, Parush didn't sleep the whole night, while the ceremony commenced half the world away in New York in a chapel. Parush ran around his empty house, his eyes burning, his body sweating, his hands trembling. He looked for the puff, but he couldn't find it. He called his neighbour early in the morning. They took him to hospital. 'He should keep a nebulizer at home,' the doctor at the Manipal Hospital told his neighbour.

***

Half way round the world, Bitasta was looking for her phone. Rajiv Malhotra, a colleague at BCG whom she had never liked, handed over a phone to her. 'Is it yours? It was lying on the grass.'

She thanked him and took her phone back. She had been absent-minded all day. When the crowd had thinned and she finally got some respite, she had opened the mail in her phone and read it again and again. 'Remember what happened, that fateful day when I came out of your house, after our very last meeting, knowing I would never see you again! It happened today too! I couldn't breathe for some time. The only thought that came to my mind was whether I would be able to see you again…' Someone had called her, and the phone had slipped out of her hand.

Presently Bitasta opened the mail again, read it and kept it in a folder named "Prembajar".

***

'Read the few mails I've forwarded and come to my place, ASAP,' Rajiv, Bitasta's colleague at BCG, left a voice message on his brother's phone and rushed back home. His brother, Rajesh Malhotra, the founder of Volcano who was unceremoniously kicked out of the company he had founded, read the mails and smiled.

***

'No Sam, this is no game,' Parush said. 'I don't have anything to deny. I'm resigning. Take legal action against me.' He pressed the "End" button on the phone.

Parush looked at the TV and saw Rajesh Malhotra talking to the media. 'For years he has been sending insider information about GameIT to this lady. There are thousand plus mails with so much information that I wonder what could have been the purpose. What's the new game Parush has been playing for the past four years? And who's this lady whose official ID he has been sending all these mails to and who has preserved each mail in a folder? The system admin of BCG has recovered all the mails. I really feel sorry for GameIT…'

Parush's phone rang. 'Aru, tell me,' he received the call.

'I'll be in India in a few days. Take a new SIM card and just leave Bangalore for now. It's a big mess. 1132 mails in total. Out of that 739 mails talk only about stuff which can be considered "insider information". And I wonder why she had to keep all those mails. You are crazy. But she's no lesser…'

Parush felt good that Bitasta had preserved each of his mails. He wondered why she had never replied.

He took the earliest flight to Calcutta. Ru received him at the airport. She drove for many hours and when she finally stopped, it was early morning. He came out of the car and stretched his limbs. 'I've recently bought a house in the Sagar Islands, very close to the mouth of the Ganges,' Ru said. 'There's no Internet. Even the mobile signal is weak. Stay here for some time. Aru will come in a few days. There's no place better than this. As long as you're here, rejuvenate yourself. The days ahead may not be fun for you…'

DACTYLIC HEXAMETER

Parush had walked a little away from the upturned boat on which we had been sitting the whole night. The night was ending. A diffused glow trickled through the thick blanket of mist, which had enwrapped the riverbed. Both of us had acclimatised to the biting cold of the night. Still, the chilling wind flapping over the trees and our faces made me shiver. He turned back. 'That's my story…' he said. He came and sat beside me. Seeing me shivering in the cold, he pulled me closer and wrapped his shawl around both of us.

'In the past few months, you didn't try to get in touch with Bitasta?' I asked.

'Yes Saoli, I did try. More so because I wanted to know what my mother had told her before dying. I was not aware that she had come to meet her in the hospital, till Ru told me recently.'

'Really? You didn't know?'

'No, I didn't know. Ma had asked Ru to call Bitasta. Ru didn't say anything about it to me. Neither did she ask Bitasta about what she had told her. It happens to be the last thing Ma spoke before her death. I always wondered why Bits suddenly stopped talking to me immediately after Ma's death.'

'So you've renewed your hatred for your mother after hearing this?'

'I no longer have any hatred for anyone…'

'Has it ever occurred to you that there's something more than what you can understand? I mean, isn't it really tough to believe that your mother wanted to meet Bitasta before her death, just to tell her that she shouldn't be in touch with you? Now you know that your mother was always in touch with Bitasta's mother. If she really hated Bitasta or her family why would she do that?'

'I really don't know. I have no clue why she did everything possible to break our relationship.'

'I'll tell you why. Let's go back.' I removed the shawl and got up.

Parush stared at me in surprise. 'You know why?' he asked in disbelief.

'Yes. I knew it even before I heard your story. Now I'm more convinced… Let's go.' I walked towards the car.

***

Ravishing looks, and the raven hair locks, she is ravenous Rikshi,
Artemis nymph, the prime mistress of wild, bare Arcadia pristine,
Silence embodied in Panchal, the mountains primeval seductive,
Yoked and entwined with Callisto, Kalyani so green and enticing,
Krishna as though, is revealed as the girls five united in fervor,
Purged by the bards, to ensconce the forbidden yen with fib so ersatz.

From the raw wilderness recondite Artemis sculpted her craving –
Knotty Parush flowed with her Kalyani's allure and all kallos.

Zeus when smote lovelorn Callisto, her yearning for Artemis forth came –
Surged it out from her vitasti, as Arca the damsel of Rikshi.

'You want to say this cryptic poem written by Kakima says it all?'

'Yes, that's correct. Let me now explain. Rikshi and Kalyani are the Sanskrit words nearest to the Greek Artemis and Callisto. The first two lines are quite straight forward: *Ravishing looks, and the raven hair locks, she is ravenous Rikshi, Artemis nymph, the prime mistress of wild, bare Arcadia pristine.* "Mistress of wild" is a common epithet for Artemis in Greek mythology. She is said to be the huntress goddess. Arcadia is a mythical place of virgin beauty and "bare Arcadia pristine", now I know for sure, refers to the ravishing and scintillating beauty that exudes from the quietness and barrenness in the personality of Rikshi, the *desi* Artemis…'

Parush looked absent-minded. He looked out of the window. 'Are you listening?' I asked.

'It's so much like my mother – barren but beautiful. I always felt she was like a wonderful portrait, always silent and expressionless, barren, from within. Ru would tell me she was like the extremely beautiful but barren landscape of Ladakh. Rikshi is my mother?'

I stared at him. 'Yes, Rikshi is your mother. Let's go to the next two lines: *Silence embodied in Panchal, the mountains primeval seductive, Yoked and entwined with Callisto, Kalyani so green and enticing…*'

He got up from the chair. He looked restless. He held the grills of the window tightly and leaned his head back. I embraced him from behind and whispered into his ears, 'She had written it with the hope that someday someone would read it … and know the secret, which she and your mother died with…' I pulled him by his hand. 'Come…'

'Their art teacher at Shantiniketan would say, "You're like the two sides of the beautiful Pir Panjal,"' he said, stretching himself on the sofa, his eyes shut, his hands crossed behind his head. '"Panchali," he would say, "you're the Kashmir Valley, expressive – green, full of blue placid lakes, and Sairandhri, you're the Lahaul and Spiti Valleys, silent and quiet – miles and miles of barrenness…" Is Panchal the Pir Panjal Mountains?'

'Yes, Pir is Mountain and Panjal comes from Panchal…'

'*Yoked and entwined with Callisto, Kalyani so green and enticing,*' he uttered the line a few times. 'Ma would often call Kakima by the name Kalyani… *Kakima* is Callisto…' He opened his eyes. 'Now I know why she loved that character so much…'

He looked at me and then snatched the piece of paper where I had written down the poem.

'*Yoked and entwined with Callisto, Kalyani so green and enticing, Krishna as though, is revealed as the girls five united in fervor, Purged by the bards, to ensconce the forbidden yen with fib so ersatz.*' He started breathing heavily. I brought him the puff. He released the healing gas into his mouth and tried to take a few long breaths. '*Purged by the bards, to ensconce the forbidden yen with fib so ersatz,*' he repeated the line. 'What exactly does this line mean?'

I was wondering what exactly to say. 'Parush, reality is often more stunning than myth and fantasy. Now that you're at the threshold of a reality, let's not be prejudiced or judgmental.' I paused to check his reaction. He was sombre and calm. Perhaps he too had an inkling of what it would turn out to be. 'Do you remember the title of the paper Bitasta's mother had written about Draupadi?'

'Yes, I do. "*Draupadi Syndrome: Camouflaging Lesbianism Through Obscurities*". Kakima believed that Draupadi may be five girls united in love and the lesbian aspect has been camouflaged by bringing in male partners. The lesbian aspect of Artemis and Callisto too, she believed, has been camouflaged through several obscurities. She felt this was how the classical poets would throw in subtle clues for the intelligent readers to peel off the layers of obscurities and discover the true identities of the lesbian characters...'

'It may be a coincidence,' I interrupted, 'that your mother's name was Sairandhri and Bitasta's Panchali – both, along with Krishna, are various names of Draupadi. In reality too, they were like the five girls of Draupadi, like Artemis and Callisto, like the two sides of the Pir Panjal Mountains, "*yoked and entwined*", "*united in fervor*". Parush, they were two people in love... And, like Artemis and Callisto, like the five girls of Draupadi, who were

"*Purged by the bards, to ensconce the forbidden yen with fib so ersatz*", sanitised and protected by the poets to hide the forbidden love with stories of lies, they too have protected their forbidden relationship through deceit that they were not lesbians, that they too had male partners…'

'All those poems in Kakima's diaries were for my mother…' he muttered. 'And Bitasta and I used them…' He closed his eyes, not completing the sentence. I understood how awkward he was feeling. Those poems would arouse in him the same passion, the same yearnings, for Bitasta, as they would do in her mother, for his mother. When Srinjay, his father, would make love to Sairandhri, perhaps it would be still Panchali's thoughts, her fantasies, her allure, her *kallos*, which would bring the frenzy, the spasm, the moment of ecstasy within her. That was how one day that moment of procreation would have arrived, when Parush was born, out of Sairandhri's love and craving for Panchali.

'*Zeus when smote lovelorn Callisto, her yearning for Artemis forth came – Surged it out from her vitasti, as Arca the damsel of Rikshi,*' Parush read the lines, slowly. 'Now I know why Kakima had given Bits the nickname Arca – *Arca, the damsel of Rikshi…*'

'Sage Kashyap, after whom Kashmir is named, worshipped Lord Shiva and induced his wife to purify the country with her waters. Lord Shiva struck the Panchala Mountain with His trident and made an opening measuring one vitasti, the distance between wrist and the tip of the fingers. The eponymous river Vitasta flowed out of this opening which is metaphorically the yoni, the vagina of the Panchala Mountain, the Pir Panjal range in the Kashmir. That's the myth around the origin of Vitasta, the present-day Jhelum River.'

'And so nicely Kakima has morphed this myth with the birth of Arca…'

'Interestingly, though Callisto and Artemis both are shown to have male partners, Callisto's son is called Arkas, which is related to the name Artemis. Both Arkas and Artemis come from the Greek word arktos, which means bear. As Panchali points out in the paper, this is a subtle hint that Arkas is also the child of Artemis...'

'And Arca is also the child of Rikshi, my mother...' Parush interrupted me.

***

That night, Parush took me to Chhedi's. We sat beside the railway track, on the rounded pebbles, taking big bites of *tinku*, their signature egg-burger and a very nostalgic thing for most KGPians who are fanatically passionate about this ramshackle shack adjoining the railway track just outside the IIT campus.

'Kakima believed that when it comes to love, the gender of the person or the social relation is so irrelevant that at the end you may land up loving a guy, or a cousin, or a friend's wife, or a sister-in-law ...' he said, sipping tea from a small earthen pot. 'Lots of poems in her diaries were purely guys' stuff, fantasising about naked female bodies and bare breasts. My sister had once pointed out that many of the female poets, like Browning, Rossetti and Emily Dickinson, whose poems Ma often recited, had strong lesbian tones. The most explicit one must be Rossetti's *Goblin Market* about two sisters Laura and Lizzie, whose relationship has strains of lesbianism. Strange that even Bits failed to get a whiff of it...'

He started playing with the pebbles, plucking blades of grass and placing them on the track till a train came and blew them off. The track was so close to us that I got frightened when the train passed by. He pulled me closer and shut my ears with his hands.

'If the belief is that love is not bound by gender or relation,' I resumed the conversation, 'a person propagating this ideology would also naturally not view incest with the same suspicion as anyone else. But then, why do you think Sairi objected to your relation? Just because, she saw Bitasta as her own child? But, on the other hand Panchali encouraged the relationship… it is all quite quizzical.'

'Saoli,' Parush interrupted me, 'I don't know. I really don't know Saoli. We never understood Ma…'

We didn't speak for some time. Many trains passed by and I felt I was not getting as much scared, when the trains passed, as I had been the first time.

'Can you think of sex just as an emotional and mental affair, totally dissociated from the body?' I asked him, when no train passed by for a long time.

'Now I can…' he said, placing blades of grass again on the track. 'Most of the times a guy's orgasm doesn't need a female body. It's just about the thoughts and fantasies. What's strange is that Ma really believed Bits was her child, the child of her love…' He paused for a while when another train passed by, blowing the blades in the wind. Plucking more blades, he said in a choked voice, 'I always thought… Ma was like a stone… with no feelings… no love… no passion… But…' he broke down, embracing me, drowning his head into my hair. 'But, her love was so intense, so passionate … but we never came to know… I hated her all my life… Oh my God, she was so deeply in love…' he couldn't complete, as sobs shook him. I rubbed his back, gently, comfortingly..

Sometime later, while he was driving back to Prembajar, he asked, 'Why do you think Ma had wanted to see Bits before she died?'

'She would have told her everything… She thought you wouldn't understand. And … how could she die without seeing her child, the memento of Panchali's love for her?'

He sighed. I couldn't resist asking him something that had been haunting me ever since I had heard everything about him and Bitasta. 'Parush,' I said, 'would you mind if I said something?'

'Please go ahead…'

'Bitasta, I understand, is a strong-willed woman. Would she resist from following her heart just because of pressure from another person? Breaking up with you, I understand, might have been under pressure, as she was only nineteen then, though that too is not that young an age. But her severing all ties with you again, just because your mother had said something from her death bed, is really surprising.'

'Why do you say so?'

'Come on, it doesn't suit her otherwise strong personality.'

'I never tried to analyse... possibly because I never questioned her judgement… but if we ever meet again, I may ask her…'

We had reached Prembajar.

***

Next morning Parush looked fresh and happy. By the time I woke up, he had already got ready and prepared the breakfast. 'Where are you going?' I asked.

'I'll go to Calcutta first, then to the US. They want to arrest me. I'm ready for everything. After all, what's there to fear? I love Bitasta, and everything I did is out of my love for her… I've learned the meaning of love from my mother – the true and fearless meaning of love. Everyone hated her. But still she lived. My condition is much better…'

***

A few hours later, when Parush had got inside the car, ready to press the gas pedal, he waved at me. 'I've got to say something…' I asked him to wait. He switched off the ignition. 'Parush, I too have to finally accept this to someone else. Now I know for sure, I too love a woman... I don't love men. Even after the failed relationships and the broken marriage, I declined to realise the truth. Panchali and Sairandhri have given me the courage to realise it, to accept it, to be what I am... Thanks to Panchali for the dactylic hexameter and *the heroic ode to her life...*'

'All the best,' Parush replied and looked at my blank face. 'Do you want to say something more?'

'Umm,' I fumbled.

'Anything wrong, Saoli?' Parush enquired.

I looked into his eyes. 'Parush,' I said politely, 'I love your sister, Parushni.'

Parush's eyes sparkled. He patted my hair and said, 'I know Pushi will be happy with you.'

'Thanks,' I replied. 'We were scared. But later, Panchali and Sairandhri just showed us the way.'

Parush nodded his head. 'I'm sure they did. I hope to see you soon... Take care.' He smiled and started the ignition.

EPILOGUE

I wondered how the name 'Prembajar' would have come into existence. Literally, it means 'Love Market' which sounds quite gross, the term 'bajar' being the epithet of not-so-good things in Bangla. A *bajari meye,* a market girl, means a prostitute. The association of love with market surely can't be respectable. I'm sure none of these implications comes to anyone's mind in Prembajar. Most likely, the name was coined after some Prem who would have started a market at this place. I wondered why suddenly now the questions about its origin had come to my mind.

In those few days, Parush had become a part of my daily routine. Once he was gone, and I was again alone in the house, all sorts of weird thoughts jammed my mind. No doubt, I thought, this house in Prembajar had played such a crucial role in the lives of a few people, associated with each other through unusual relationships. The reason why Sairandhri could never think of Bitasta as her son's partner could be laughed at by many. I had apprehensions that even Parush would find it tough to believe. Perhaps, one needs to feel like Panchali, that when it comes to love, the gender or the social relation is so irrelevant that at the end you may land up loving anyone, if you're true to yourself.

***

I looked at my phone. The clear glass reflected my face. I saw my own eyes, full of words. I picked up the phone. Going through the dialled numbers, I stopped at a certain name. Fiddling with it for a few moments, I left it on the table and opening my laptop,

I logged onto my email. My eyes were fixed at the screen as I started typing…

Dear Parushni,

I thought of calling you but my voice trembled.

After my return to Prembajar, what all happened, you will be surprised to hear. My discovery of Bitasta's mother's diary got me interested in your brother and you helped us meet. Your brother confided the story of his life: his growing up with you, his love affair with Bitasta, the break-up, the marriage, the GameIT episode and finally the death of your mother. But the reason I am writing to you is more than the fact that I know about your brother and your family.

I could decode Panchali's diary and Parush's narration affirmed my hypothesis. Parushni, this is hard to believe but yes, the incidents that have occurred in your life, in your brother's life, in Bitasta's life, prove the verity of the love that existed between Sairandhri and Panchali. It is heart-wrenching to see such love not finding its place in our society, such a pure feeling being relegated to the pages of a diary, closeted, discarded. It was an unusual, or rather unconventional bond of love they cherished forever, and they died loving each other, not allowing anyone a chance to know anything of it.

Remember Tagore's Shesher Kabita, Parushni? The bond between Amit and Labanya was preserved in separation, the last poem singing the elegy. Don't you think that there is too much tragedy around us to live with? Why, Parushni, should we accept the norms of a society and live our lives in tears like another Sairandhri or another Bitasta? Can love never have any fulfilment? Is there no hope left in this world? Can love not stride through the turbulent waves of societal norms, and win for once? Can it not lead the way for others to follow? And can it not dedicate the victory to all those lovers who have died in ignorance?

Parushni, I sense the feelings that connect us. And all that I heard and felt in these last few days gave me the strength to write this to you.

Since ancient times, poetry has connected lovers, poetry has delivered the hidden and forbidden feelings, and I too, like Amit and Labanya, like Sairandhri and Panchali, have taken refuge in poetry. Unable to create that perfect verse, here I am, expressing my feelings for you, through the verses of one of my favourite poets.

The fountains mingle with the river,
And the rivers with the ocean;
The winds of heaven mix forever
With a sweet emotion;
Nothing in the world is single;
All things by a law divine
In another's being mingle–
Why not I with thine?

Parushni, don't you agree, love is as obscure as its struggles, only visible to the ones who face it, only readable to the ones who wish to read it?

Don't you believe too, love takes us back in time, a leap, and then to the future, weaving feelings, transcending moments, like Spenser did?

Just the other day I read, once again, the obscure sonnets of Spenser:

So I alone now left disconsolate,
Mourn to myself the absence of my love:
And wandring here and there all desolate…

Why should every life be disconsolate, desolate, like a shattered sonnet, like the broken amoretti?

With love,
Saoli.

I instantly hit 'Send.'

What's in a name? There must be something in the name Prembajar, the place of love – **LOVE**, in any form – I thought.

AFTERWORD

The inspiration to write The Broken Amoretti was doubtless the wonderful memories of those four years I've spent at the serene and sprawling campus of the Indian Institute of Technology, Kharagpur, more popularly known as the IIT KGP. That was the place where, apart from acquiring an engineering degree, which has been more of a passport to the newer and unknown lands of earning a decent livelihood, I acquired something totally orthogonal and unassuming – the *kick* of creativity. Whether it was writing or music, I not only developed a zest for both, but got enough opportunities to pursue them with full sincerity.

The IIT life, and of course the place called Prembajar, which adjoins the campus at one end, left so much a mark in my mind that I couldn't have not written about it, especially when I decided to take up writing in a serious way. The Broken Amoretti is not an autobiography or even a story inspired by real incidents. Nevertheless, many characters and incidents would have camouflaged into the narration so well that I myself wouldn't be able to sieve through the layers of obscurities and identify the real ones.

Sudipto Das

ACKNOWLEDGEMENTS

SUDIPTO DAS

Creation seldom develops in isolation. Inspiration, support, help, partnership and assistance, all play unique roles, often in unnoticed and unprecedented ways, in shaping up the final version of a creation. Here too, from the beginning, there have been contributions from various fronts in many a way, only a part of which I might even recall, as the rest might have played the role subtly, influencing my subconscious mind - it's my ignorance and lack of wisdom that I can't recollect everything.

There's one chapter on ILLU, a very special and unique cultural heritage of IIT KGP. I relied heavily on the book *Illuminati*, by Devendra Purbiya, a fellow KGPian turned full time photographer, for many facts and titbits about ILLU.

Anirban Mukherjee, my KGP batch-mate and an all-weather living encyclopaedia of things which even Google doesn't know, supplied me with forgotten anecdotes from our KGP days, something which no one else would have remembered after twenty years.

Arup Bhattacharya, my partner in many a crime at KGP, Aniruddha Bagchi, my class mate at high school, Sumana Basu, my niece, Sharmistha Ghosh, my sister-in-law, have read all my manuscripts, in various stages, ever since I started writing seriously. Their inputs and suggestions helped me immensely in maturing The Broken Amoretti. Given the complexities in human relationships dealt with in the novel, I and my co-author Aparajita Dutta couldn't have come up with the final version of it without the multiple levels of reviews and discussions with them.

The novel wouldn't have been possible without the innumerable academic papers, articles and news items in print and online media and books I've referred to. Had it not been for the unfathomable amount of resource and energy spent by Google (https://books.google.com) in painstakingly scanning more than 25 million books (out of perhaps the 130 million distinct titles in the world) and making them readily available at the ease of a click, I would have never dared to be an author. Without Google, it would have been practically impossible for me to put my hands on original Sanskrit works of Kalidasa and an unending list of books, without which I wouldn't have managed to get even a fraction of the material I've used so liberally all throughout.

Equally significant are the repositories of https://archive.org, The Digital South Asia Library program of the University of Chicago and the Center for Research Libraries (http://dsal.uchicago.edu), https://www.scribd.com, to mention a few.

Arundhati Chaudhury, a co-musician at our band Kohal, and a professional psychologist, helped me with the psychological analysis and background needed to realistically develop many of the characters in the novel.

Bitasta's poems used in the novel are original compositions by Arundhati Chaudhury and Sanchita Chatterjee.

Aparajita Dutta, my co-author, brought in a totally different dimension to the novel. Her background in comparative literature came in handy in dealing with ancient literature and mythologies which play a big role in the novel.

I'm thankful to Kavita Bhanot and Urmila Dasgupta for their diligent critique, reviews and editing.

I'm also grateful to Jug Suraiya, a senior columnist with *The Times of India* and one of the most revered journalists of our country, for his encouragement.

Thanks also to Pooja Prabhan (*Deccan Chronicle*), Sravasti Dutta (*The Hindu*), Shevlin Sebastian (*The New Indian Express*), Sooraj Rajmohan (*The Hindu*), Chandreyee Ghose (*The Telegraph*) and Ayesha Tabassum for their kind support.

***

APARAJITA DUTTA

My writing begins with two loved ones without whom anything I write would fall incomplete. My grandfather, Late Sushil Mukhopadhyay (founding member and first president of Book Sellers' and Publishers' Guild, Kolkata) and my jyatha, Late Souren Dutta (writer and translator) have been my inspiration and my guiding lights.

I am extremely grateful to my co-author Sudipto Das who believed in my writing skills and gave me the opportunity to work with him on such a sensitive topic. This journey with him has been a wonderful one and filled with some crucial lessons of life.

I would love to express my gratitude towards my mother, Mrs. Kalpana Dutta and Mummum, Mrs. Rita Dutta who made me the woman I am now. My big brother, Atri Dutta, has been the pillar of my life. Thank you, Dada, for helping me pursue my dreams. I would like to express my gratefulness to my father Arun Kumar Datta for keeping me on the track by his strict discipline and retaining my focus. When I was working on this novel, my little one came in my life giving me a new identity. Dear Baakyo, the acknowledgement is incomplete without you. I wouldn't have come all this way without the constant support of my best-friend and better-half Sayak Ray Chowdhury. Thank you, Sayak.

I am grateful to my sisters, Lipilekha Mukherjee, Atreyee Chakraborty and Ankita Roy Chowdhury for their endless love and the way they have always cheered for me. Amprapali

Chatterjee, Sumana Banerjee, Bhaswati Ghosh, Rinita Mazumdar, Indrani Ganguly, Paulami Dutta Gupta, Rhiti Chatterjee Bose, Rubina Ramesh, Nikita Parik, Amrita Roy Chowdhury, Paramita Mukherjee, Kathakoli Seth, Chhanda Banerjee, Koyeli Mukherjee, Chandana Mukherjee are some of the strong, talented, independent women who have been with me through thick and thin, motivating me to write and explore myself. This world needs women like you. Thank you so much for teaching me various shades of womanhood.

My kid brother Sobhan Pramanik deserves the credits for helping me polish my writing and sharing my dreams. I would also like to thank Kapil Mukherjee, Kanad Mukherjee, Samudra Mukherjee, Kaniska Mukherjee and Anirban Nanda for helping me write the book.

Last but not the least, I am indebted to my pet birds, Lemon and Puchun, and every one of my imaginary land, Crystallasia.

Reviews for other books by Sudipto Das

The Aryabhata Clan

'A very readable sequel to The Ekkos Clan. Sudipto Das is a gifted storyteller'—*Jug Suraiya*

'An ambitious piece of fiction…—*The Times of India*

'Intelligent narration and mindful suspense'—*Deccan Chronicle*

'Attitude of genuine scientific curiosity'—*Asian Age*

'A woman Indiana Jones or a Bond'—*The Hindu*

'Sends chills down your spine'—*New Indian Express*

'Extravagant plots'—*The Hans India*

'Taut in building the story and the selection of its characters' —*Bartaman*

'Roller coaster ride to Sri Lanka, Bangladesh, Pakistan' —*Business Standard*

The Ekkos Clan—Flipkart best seller

'A promising debut in the growing realm of modern Indian fiction' —*Jug Suraiya, The Times of India*

'An Indian thriller inspired by Dan Brown & Harrison Ford! Fast-paced thriller, replete with murder and miraculous escapes' —*The Telegraph*

'If you are a history buff and a thriller aficionado, then [it] might just be the book for you'—*The Hindu*

'A tale of the Indian civilization and culture…takes you on a roller coaster ride'—*The New Indian Express*

'An interesting read for an afternoon. One feisty woman's partition story'—*Bangalore Mirror*

'Should be read for its sheer aspiration and the intelligent handling of historical material'—*The Sunday Guardian*